"*The Lost Rainforest* feels unlike anything I've read. Eliot Schrefer has mined the richness and depths of his setting to find a deeper magic, immersing us in a world that is at once complex, dangerous, beautiful, and ultimately demanding of our protection. Meticulously researched and superbly written, this novel is a thrilling start to an exceptional new series."

—SOMAN CHAINANI, *New York Times* bestselling author of the School for Good and Evil series

"*Mez's Magic* is packed with as many jokes as fast-paced fight scenes. And Schrefer has created a stock of memorable characters—including Gogi, a monkey with self-esteem issues; Rumi, a delightfully urbane tree frog; and a manic, pixie-dream bat named Lima."

—*NEW YORK TIMES BOOK REVIEW*

"While the story is pure fast-paced fantasy, the underlying issues are real. Ignorance among the species, racism, and intolerance of differences are rampant. An author's note highlights the beauty and importance of the rainforest. Magic with depth in this new series stunner."

—*KIRKUS REVIEWS* (starred review)

"Just right for middle grade readers who want an engrossing fantasy adventure."

"With a memorable, quick-bantering cast, this kick-off to the Lost Rainforest series, a playful departure from Schrefer's ape novels, brings fresh perspective to the magical animal subgenre. And, despite the fantasy setup, readers will come away learning quite a bit about this ecosystem and its inhabitants."

THE
LOST
RAINFOREST

GOGI'S GAMBIT

Books by Eliot Schrefer

THE LOST RAINFOREST TRILOGY

MEZ'S MAGIC
GOGI'S GAMBIT
RUMI'S RIDDLE

THE
LOST
RAINFOREST
GOGI'S GAMBIT

ELIOT SCHREFER

KATHERINE TEGEN BOOKS
An Imprint of HarperCollins Publishers

Katherine Tegen Books is an imprint of HarperCollins Publishers.

The Lost Rainforest: Gogi's Gambit
Text copyright © 2019 by HarperCollins Publishers
Illustrations copyright © 2019 by Emilia Dziubak

Library of Congress Cataloging-in-Publication Data

Names: Schrefer, Eliot, author.
Title: Gogi's gambit / Eliot Schrefer.
Description: First edition. | New York, NY : Katherine Tegen Books, an
  imprint of HarperCollinsPublishers, [2019] | Series: The lost rainforest ;
  [2] | Summary: "Gogi and the other shadowwalkers race to save their
  magical rainforest home before the Ant Queen makes it her own"—
  Provided by publisher.
Identifiers: LCCN 2018013965 | ISBN 978-0-06-249115-2
Subjects: | CYAC: Monkeys—Fiction. | Rain forest animals—Fiction. |
  Rain forests—Fiction. | Magic—Fiction. | Fantasy.
Classification: LCC PZ7.S37845 Gog 2019 | DDC [Fic]—dc23 LC record
  available at https://lccn.loc.gov/2018013965

Typography by Carla Weise
19 20 21 22 23   PC/BRR   10 9 8 7 6 5 4 3 2 1
❖
First Edition

For those who fight for the Earth's real—and really magical—rainforests

Excerpt from

THE SONG OF THE FIVE

Verse Two

(Translated from the original
Ant by Rumi Mosquitoswallow)

Their enemies vanquished, the shadowwalkers returned to their homes for a well-deserved rest

["In one year we will return," they said
. . . though they couldn't know that not all of them would.]
Lima the Healer,
Mez the Unseen,
Rumi the Windbringer,
Gogi, Monkey of Fire
(and their untested fifth)
. . . went their separate ways.

. . . but the eternal powers of Caldera do not need a year to rest.

After centuries of sleep, the Ant Queen
was again freed to make the rainforest
what it was destined to be.

[The Five did not understand our queen.
They did not understand how peaceful oblivion can be.]

And little did the Five know that our queen was not the only ancient force . . .

awakened by the eclipse.

CREAKING STICK, SNAPPING branch—an intruder is approaching.

From her spot high in a fig tree, Sorella goes still, sniffing the air. The hairs along the back of her neck rise.

If a predator has spotted her, the best plan for the uakari monkey is to stay as motionless as possible. Eagles and ocelots respond to movement.

When a few long moments go by with no more sound, Sorella returns to foraging. She's soon got a nut between her hands and is working her teeth into its hard casing. Uakari are the only monkeys around with the strength to break into this kind of nut, but that doesn't mean it's exactly easy. She loses herself in gnawing and piercing.

Another crack. But it's not from the nut.

Sorella whirls, drops her nut, and races farther up the tree, primed to attack or flee. Leaves, branches, and even an unfortunate praying mantis rain down on the clearing below as she squawks and demonstrates. Teeth bared, she howls in the direction of the intruder—until she sees who it is.

It's a sloth.

Sorella has been snuck up on by a sloth! So embarrassing. Her bald red face turns even redder as she leaps to the ground, shakes out her stinging ankles, and races back up the tree, teeth bared at Banu where he holds on to a branch of the next fig tree over. "What do you think you're doing? You don't sneak up on someone like that!"

The sloth yawns, staring at her blankly from his branch. A wasp picks its way across the hair of his eyebrows. "I'm sorry," Banu says, in the slow and deliberate manner of all sloths. It makes them sound either incredibly wise or incredibly stupid, depending on who's doing the listening. "I've never managed . . . to sneak up on anyone in my life. . . . I'm not sure a sloth *can* sneak up on anyone . . . and certainly not someone so alert and powerful . . . as a young uakari like yourself."

Sorella sniffs and allows her shoulders to relax. "I

suppose you're right. You didn't sneak up on me. That would be impossible."

Banu nods, satisfied with himself.

Sorella starts poking through the underbrush, lifting leaves and sniffing underneath. "You did make me drop a nice fat nut, though. I was just about to get it open."

"Sorry about that," Banu says, nodding. "Try . . . between . . . the fronds of . . . the scrubby palm."

By the time Banu's finished speaking, Sorella has already searched the palm twice and emerged victorious, the nut held high in her palm. She peers up at Banu and squints her hard, dark eyes. "So, what's a nice sloth boy like you doing deep in uakari territory?"

He blinks at her. "I'm on my way to the ruins! . . . Remember, after we defeated Auriel, and the Ant Queen escaped . . . we all promised we'd spread the word back home . . . then reconvene at the fallen ziggurat . . . to discuss what we'd discovered. What . . . did you fall out of a tree and hit your head . . . or something?" He grins. Slowly.

"Of course I remember all that," Sorella grumbles. "But the moon has three cycles to go before a year has gone by."

Banu holds up a clawed arm in mock surrender. The move takes a few seconds. "When you move at the pace I do . . . you have to get started early for any trip. Took me six moon cycles to get home. . . . I had to turn right back around . . . to get back in time."

"That's too bad," Sorella says.

Banu shrugs. "It's the life of a sloth . . . not bad or good. . . . Do you want to travel . . . with me?"

Sorella shakes her head. "No offense, but I'd drive myself crazy having to go at your speed."

"Is Gogi . . . around?" Banu asks.

"The capuchins are in the north, not west like us uakari."

Banu nods. "Too bad . . . I like that . . . friendly little monkey."

"His magical streams of fire are pretty useful too," Sorella says.

"I discovered . . . my power," Banu says. "Water. I . . . can move water."

"Sounds very, um, slow," Sorella says.

"Well, I shouldn't . . . dillydally anymore. Do you have any more . . . of those tasty nuts around here . . . that I could take on the road?"

"You get started, and I'll bring them to you," Sorella says dryly. "I think I'll be able to catch up."

By the time Banu reaches the edge of the clearing, Sorella has cracked open four nuts. She lays the meaty white bits into one of his claws. "When you have a sloth metabolism," he says gratefully, "this much food . . . will last many days. . . . Thank you, Sorella."

She watches the sloth leave. Sorella was the most brutish and aggressive of the shadowwalking animals, but after she nearly died in the final assault at the ziggurat, she's come to see there's a time and place for being competitive, and there's no way to go back and show kindness to those who are now dead and gone. Who knew? Even a uakari can show some heart . . . at least every once in a while.

Sorella feels a prickle under the fur of her knee and reaches down to scratch it. *Crack* and *squish*. It was a soldier ant, but she's gotten to it before it could sink its mandibles into her. Luckily, she has plenty of thick, wiry fur.

She forages through the greenery, enjoying the whistling sound her breath makes through her sharp teeth. The light shifts, going from blinding white to a more orangey tone as the afternoon wanes on. The ants become more and more of a nuisance, streaming over the spongy orange piles of dead leaves. Sorella switches to the canopy, but then she finds columns of ants streaming up there, too. She tries not to let it worry her—maybe there was a heavy rain somewhere nearby and the ants are fleeing it.

She hears another cracking sound, and again goes perfectly still.

Maybe it's Banu, returned for another nut?

The tree trunks around her start to shimmer, but Sorella, her eyes trained in the direction of the noise, can't spare even a moment to investigate.

The fronds of a giant fern begin to tremble and then part. Whatever it is, is *big*.

Sorella sees the antennae first, then the smooth plane of a head and two giant mandibles, each big enough to spear a uakari.

It's the Ant Queen.

As big as the largest buffalo, she's made of shining, invulnerable plates, interlocking in sharp and narrow joints, the many surfaces reflecting the ruddy late-afternoon light. The queen's purple-black surface is unmarred except for stiff yellow hairs sprouting along the broad plates.

Sorella shrinks back against the tree trunk, making herself as motionless as possible while the Ant Queen comes closer and closer. Once she emerges from the scrubby palm, the insect's many legs are as noiseless as a panther's, the only sound the sighing of wet leaves being tamped under the monster's weight.

Sorella forgets her desire to stay hidden away and shrieks out an emergency call, to warn the rest of the uakari troop that an enemy is near. There's no specific call for a centuries-old ant ruler, so she uses the warning for eagles and ocelots—she just makes it *very* loud. She hopes that some of her family will hear her.

In the clearing down below, the Ant Queen flicks her antennae, maybe in irritation, maybe from some other, unknowable ant emotion. Then she tilts her head until she's looking right up at Sorella in her tree. The uakari gasps. She's forgotten how horrible it is to look at the Ant Queen: there's infinite depth in the queen's shiny black eyes, but no feeling there. "Before you call out any more hysterical warnings, maybe you should hear what I have to tell," the Ant Queen says. She has a low, resonant voice, harmonic, sounding neither male nor female, but something older than both.

Sorella climbs farther up her tree, hands and feet flailing so she can feel for obstacles, not daring to take her eyes off the emotionless jewels of the queen's eyes. The Ant Queen's voice is hypnotic and strangely calming. It's as if nothing in the current moment could matter as much as the long history the queen has witnessed, or her centuries of imprisonment at the hands of the rainforest animals.

Sorella feels her short tail press against a branch and instinctively brings her legs up onto it, climbing farther out into the forest canopy, craning her neck to look down at the Ant Queen, teeth bared. The enemy is far below now, and well out of reach.

Her fur feels bumpy and crackly. Sorella is confused, until she realizes she's crawling with ants. So that's what the shimmering was. Ants are all through the clearing now, in concentrations Sorella has never seen before, swarming over their queen and across the jungle floor— and up into the trees.

"I will give you a choice," the Ant Queen says. "It is not complicated. One option will result in your continuing to live, and the other will result in your death. I hope you will listen carefully."

I would rather die than help you, Sorella thinks. There's no question about that. The shadowwalkers saw the carvings the two-legs made ages ago on the stones of the ziggurat at the center of Caldera, depicting the queen and her minions overrunning the rainforest, slaughtering the animals they came across, multiplying as they consumed everything in their path.

"I must go and build my horde," the Ant Queen says in her harmonic and otherworldly voice, "so our numbers will be great enough for absolute conquest. We need sustenance for our army, but ants have always been good at procuring food—we have mulched the trees and foliage as we fanned across Caldera, creating fungus farms that we tend and harvest. These farms are self-sufficient and, unfortunately for you, this means we have little need for other animals. Almost all of you will have no role to play in the Age of Ants."

Sorella climbs higher and higher in the tree until she's at a dizzying height, crushing as many ants as she can beneath her fingers as she goes. "Why are you telling me this?" she yells down to the queen.

"You haven't heard all I have to say. *Almost* all animals will die. You, however, could survive. If you agree to my demands," the Ant Queen continues. "I will be . . . occupied for some time. I need animals to work for me while I am away. They can place logs across streams so the army can pass across. Flying creatures can carry new seed colonies of ants to the distant regions of the land. I will not need many to help me, but I will need some. And those who are so honored will be rewarded . . . with their lives."

"Never," Sorella says. "We will stop you!"

The Ant Queen makes a sort of grating sound that Sorella comes to realize is a horrifying chuckle. "Forgive me, but I don't see how that is possible."

While Sorella stares down at the Ant Queen, she scratches through her fur. More and more ants cover her, working their way to her skin. She rubs her back and limbs against tree bark, hoping to crush as many of the ants as she can. They're everywhere she looks, shimmering throughout the clearing.

"You would not be the first to join me," the Ant

Queen calls up to her. "Animals you know have come to my side, friends of yours. I still have room for more allies. This is your last chance, Sorella of the uakari. Side with me, or perish."

Sorella's bald face, already a bright red, turns even more livid. She bares her teeth. Then she lifts her mouth to the sky and lets out the most piercing shriek she can. It's not a louder version of the ocelots-or-eagles call this time. It's the most serious alert a uakari can make in the rainforest—it's the warning of a flash flood, the warning that the homeland must immediately be abandoned. If the other uakari hear her call, it might be enough to save some of her troop, even if there is no hope for Sorella herself.

"I will never abandon the uakari and the shadow-walkers," Sorella says proudly, fixing the Ant Queen far below with a furious glare. "And you *will* be stopped. Someday you will remember my words and realize that Sorella the Uakari was right."

The Ant Queen opens and closes her sharp mandibles, clacking over the drone of the late-afternoon cicadas and the rustling chatter of thousands of ants. The queen's body pulses and bulges, like it's infested with worms. "I was afraid that would be your answer. I will never understand why any creature would choose death when it could choose life."

At least Banu is already well on his way, Sorella thinks, blood quickening through her veins as she prepares for the fight.

The Ant Queen waves her antennae, tapping them together once. The clearing stops shimmering as all the ants go still.

Sorella detects a tang in the air, and she realizes the queen has released a pheromone, a chemical signal to her minions. She whirls around, desperately brushing as many ants as she can off her body. But there are so many.

The last wisp of pheromone enters the porous armor of the ants, and they receive the signal as one. And as one, every ant on Sorella pierces her skin with its stinger and releases its venom.

No, she thinks. *I had so much more to do.*

The poison of a thousand ants courses through her bloodstream. It paralyzes her arms and legs, her lungs and her heart. She tumbles from the branch, plummeting through the air, dead before she even hits the ground.

WHAT A BEAUTIFUL day it is!

Gogi the Twelfth stretches out in the sunshine, so that the length of his belly is exposed to its warmth. There's a whole day ahead of foraging and grooming, all part of the agreeable life of being in the best capuchin troop in Caldera. He's made it up to number twelve in the rankings! Eleven is so near, he can almost taste it. What a great year it's been!

Outlined by the sun, combing one another among the broad leaves of a fig tree, are Gogi's foraging companions for the day: Lansi and Pansi (ranked fifteenth and sixteenth), Urtinde (seventh), and Urtinde's baby (not yet ranked). Of course, a number seven like Urtinde gets the bulk of the grooming attention from the others, but every once in a while Gogi gets some love too, and the feeling of nimble monkey fingers picking parasites out of his sun-warmed fur while he dozes is almost too much joy to take. A year ago, after his mom died, he'd dropped to a seventeenth—which meant he was never groomed by anyone, was always the groomer. Not anymore! He cracks his knuckles and smiles up into the sky.

"Morning, Gogi!" calls a bright voice. Gogi's best troopmate, Alzo, leaps from one treetop to the next, showering the rest of the foraging group with leaves and bugs. While he waves back at Alzo, Gogi plucks a katydid from his arm fur and absently bites its head off. Capuchins usually stick to fruits and nuts, but sometimes it's nice to have something crunchy between your teeth.

While the others grumble at the interruption, Alzo bounds down to sit next to Gogi and groom him. Alzo is younger than Gogi, but is already number eight. Even though Gogi traveled far from the homeland, saved the world from a treacherous magical boa constrictor, and has the power to shoot fire out of his palms, Alzo is ranked higher because he's funny and has such good hair. The world just isn't fair sometimes.

Hard to get mad at Alzo, though—not when he's an eight willing to groom a twelve. Not when he flashes that goofy smile. "I'm going to go check the nutty palm to see if it's ripe yet. Want to come?" Alzo asks.

Gogi checked the nutty palm the day before and knows for a fact that it won't be ripe for days, but an outing with Alzo is not to be passed up. He nods.

The two young males head off, pelting each other with pebbles and sticks, tickling and giggling and guffawing all the way to the nutty palm. Sure enough, the nuts are green and shiny, like they were yesterday. "Not ready yet," Gogi says.

"That's too bad," Alzo says, running his tongue over his lips. "They would taste so good!"

Gogi imagines it: the tart skin breaking, the juicy orange goo inside, the crunchy seeds rolling under his molars, some getting trapped between his teeth so he can enjoy them one by one all the rest of the day. He wipes a line of drool from his chin. "Maybe it wouldn't be so bad, if we just ate one or . . . I mean, if we . . ."

"I totally agree!" Alzo says. He bounds up the side of the tree and shakes a branch. The nuts don't fall on their own—another sign they're picking them too early—so Alzo gets a stem under his teeth and begins to gnaw. "Just . . . one more . . . second . . . could you help?"

Gogi knows Ravanna the First would be furious if he discovered them eating unripe nuts, but who's a twelve to refuse anything to an eight? Gogi bounds up the tree to join Alzo. With Gogi pulling and Alzo chewing at the wood, they're able to rip down a full branch. Alzo hauls it higher and higher up, until they're out of view of any other capuchins that might wander by.

They look nervously around before biting into the fruit. The hard flesh hurts Gogi's gums, and tastes bitter. "I think we picked them too early," he says sadly.

"Yeah," Alzo says, his face wrinkled. "Monkey-brain problems. Mom always said it would take a few years to grow out of it. Guess I still have a ways to go."

The troop spends the year traveling the jungles of the north, moving to a tree once its fruit is ripe, then moving on to the next after the first is emptied. Pick a tree too early, and the fruit is bitter and toxic. But it's so hard to resist! Gogi's monkey brain provides him with dozens of excuses (Birds will get to the fruit first! The tree might fall in the meantime! What if beetles infest the tree before they can eat?) in order to eat fruit that doesn't taste very good and would be much sweeter in a few days anyway.

It's one of the reasons he and Alzo are always getting into trouble—they bring out the worst monkey brain in each other.

"We should have a code word for when one of us is getting monkey brain," Gogi says, letting the inedible fruit drop from his fingers, wasted. He starts climbing higher in the tree, to make sure no one better ranked catches him eating the palm nuts too early. "Like we could shout out 'monkey brain'!"

"That's a very clever code word," Alzo says dryly as he follows Gogi up the branches.

"Okay, maybe we could come up with something—wait, what is that?" Gogi says, sitting up straight and pointing.

Alzo huddles next to Gogi and begins grooming him for comfort. "What are we seeing?" he asks, voice trembling.

Trying to get out of sight means they've gone higher up the tree than any of the capuchins normally would. That means they get a view of the next valley over, the marmosets' territory. Capuchins aren't particularly fond of marmosets, but that doesn't mean they would ever wish anything like *this* on them.

The trees are all knocked down. It's not from a typhoon or anything—the capuchins would have heard that. The trees have been leveled. Where once was leafy green is now the slick brown of upturned earth, speckled with white and the mossy greens of fungus. It's all shining, as if it's wet—or swarming with insects.

"What happened to the forest?" Alzo asks.

Gogi is already scampering down the trunk. "We have to warn the others. Hurry, Alzo!"

Ravanna the First is not pleased. "What do you mean, you were up at the top of the nutty palm? It's not ripe yet!" He leans forward, teeth bared, as he takes Gogi and Alzo in shrewdly. "I can smell unripe fruit on you. Naughty monkeys!"

"The palm nuts aren't what matters!" Gogi protests, then shrinks back before Ravanna's enraged expression. "I mean, don't get me wrong, they *matter*, of course, but not as much as what's happened to the marmosets. You have to come see! Their land has all been mowed down, we think by ants! All the marmosets are gone!"

"You may have risen from seventeen," Ravanna says, "but that doesn't mean you may speak out of turn, Gogi the Twelfth."

"Especially not to a number one," Alzo adds.

"Alzo!" Gogi mutters. "Have my back here!"

"If this is about your new Ant Queen–alert system," Ravanna says, "I'm frankly getting tired of hearing about it. The Ant Queen is a myth. She doesn't exist."

"She's not a myth!" Gogi says indignantly. "I met

her! And her minions are about to invade our home-land."

"Yes, she is a myth," Ravanna says. "And don't start in on how you and some creepy nightwalkers brought down the 'ziggurat.' I won't tolerate being lied to."

"Nightwalkers eat monkey babies, everyone knows that," Lansi and Pansi add in unison.

"They do *not*," Gogi says. Even in the current crisis, his thoughts go to the friends he made a year ago, the fellow shadowwalkers born during the eclipse, who as a result developed magical powers and the ability to walk both by day and by night. After facing the evil of the Ant Queen and Auriel, the treacherous boa constrictor, Gogi returned home with a mission: he'd get the nearby animals unified, daywalker and nightwalker alike, to defend their land against the unleashed menace of the Ant Queen. That way, the moment she finally showed herself, the shadowwalkers could unite to defend Caldera from her.

It's been a little harder than he predicted. Daywalkers really hate nightwalkers. And maybe Gogi *did* get a little distracted over the last year, by new friends and so many good fruits to eat. But he's back on track now!

At the thought of the ants milling on the next rise, Gogi forces his worry down so he can present a calm face to Ravanna. He knows from a lifetime of being low-ranked that there's no surer way of losing Ravanna's attention than seeming more upset than he is. It's taken Gogi forever to become a twelve (bliss!), and it would only take one quick moment for him to drop back down to seventeen (or worse!). "Please consider coming with me up to the top of the nutty palm, Ravanna the First," Gogi says evenly, "so that I can show you something that might pique your interest."

Ravanna, nose in the air, considers Gogi's request. He nods. "I will allow it."

The troop follows as Gogi and Alzo lead Ravanna along the jungle floor until they're all climbing the nutty palm. Ravanna goes serious once he's at the top and can see the devastation the next hillside over. "I see why you would be concerned, Gogi the Twelfth."

Gogi smiles. Alzo grooms him, sharing in the good feeling.

Ravanna continues. "But there is no need to worry. Ants have destroyed that stretch of forest, it is true. But no ant would dare do the same to capuchin monkey territory. Not with Ravanna the First in charge."

Gogi watches, mouth agape, as the rest of the capuchins—even Alzo—screech and scream their agreement.

"Forgive me, Ravanna," Gogi says, "but—"

"Enough, Gogi. We are well familiar with your weird nightwalker sympathies and your alarmist theories," Ravanna says, yawning. It makes him look bored, but it's actually a way of showing his teeth as a warning. "Despite any 'ziggurat carvings' you might have seen, no animal could walk on two legs. And ants do not go about conquering the rainforest. I've never seen that happen, and I've been around much longer than you have."

"Forgive me for speaking up yet again, Ravanna the First, but the ants have never had a *queen* before, so how can we know—"

"Enough!" Ravanna says, his yawns turning to full threats, teeth gnashing.

Alzo tugs at Gogi's tail. "Come on, Gogi-Goge, listen to Ravanna the First. Let's get going."

Gogi wants to keep pressing his case, but a lifetime of instincts brings him cringing submissively and racing down the trunk, obeying Ravanna at any cost. That's just what a capuchin does when a number one tells him what to do; there's no changing it. Once Gogi's at the bottom and cowering off to one side, Ravanna bounds by with the rest of the capuchins.

Like that, Gogi's hopes of warning his troop are gone. He almost sends a flare of fire off into the sky, to get Ravanna's attention back, but using his magic would be taken as a challenge for dominance, and that's a fight Gogi would lose.

Number eight and number twelve are alone again. Alzo gives Gogi a sympathy groom. "Don't worry, buddy," he says, picking out a tick and eating it. "You did your best."

"Clearly I didn't!" Gogi says. "What is Ravanna going to do when the ants come to destroy our home like they did the marmosets'? Bare his teeth and throw poop at them?"

"Yeah!" Alzo says. "That'll show 'em!"

"No," Gogi says, wagging his head. "We're talking about ants. That will *not* 'show 'em.'"

"Well, what are you going to do?" Alzo asks.

"What can I do? I'll continue as planned, head back to the ziggurat ruins and check in with my friends. Maybe they've had more luck than I have."

Alzo lets out a low whistle. "If you're not here to keep up your position, you might drop back in rank while you're gone. What if when you come back you're a lowly seventeen again? I'm not sure we could hang out anymore."

"Alzo!"

"Gogi, that was a joke!" Alzo says, shrugging.

"Seriously, even for a capuchin, you're a little too ranking-obsessed. I barely even think about the fact that I'm an eight."

"It's *because* you're an eight that you're able to do that," Gogi says. "I can't afford not to worry about it. Anyway, if those ants decide to cross the river and invade this part of the rainforest, I might come back as Gogi the *First*."

Alzo cocks his head. "I don't get it."

"'First' because it will be a capuchin troop of *one*," Gogi explains, with a hollow laugh.

Alzo lets out an even lower whistle. "Wow. I get what you're saying now. That's dark. Back to what I was trying to say. Don't confuse rankings with actual relationships, okay?"

"Fine," Gogi says. "Alzo, come with me to the ruins. I'll introduce you to my friends. We'll work together to stop the Ant Queen—and save our troop too, since Ravanna's so intent on ignoring the danger."

"No way," Alzo says. "We wouldn't be here for when the nutty palm ripens! How could we pass that up?"

Gogi shakes his head. "I hear you, Alzo. But can't you see that the Ant Queen is a bigger concern?"

"Nope. Can't, really."

Gogi shakes his head. "Capuchins."

"I'm kidding, Gogi," Alzo says. "I'm not that shallow.

But I don't think I could spend time with nightwalkers like you do. They're spooky."

Gogi sighs. "At least help me with packing?"

"'Packing'?" Alzo asks. "What's that?"

"You've never packed a bag before?"

"What's a bag?"

"You really need to get out more," Gogi says.

As their final good-bye, Gogi and Alzo spend a warm afternoon prodding each other's closed eyes with their fingers. It feels good, trusting someone else's fingernails near your eyeballs. Gogi would find it hard to explain to his shadowwalker friends. Sometimes it's just a monkey thing.

Alzo watches Gogi prepare his traveling sack. It's made of woven fibers, two cords tied so the pouch can go across one shoulder and drape along his chest, tight so it won't snag on any branches as he scampers along unfamiliar treetops. When Gogi first headed to the ziggurat after Auriel called him there, well over a year ago, it was the only possession he brought with him.

"That used to belong to your mother, right?" Alzo asks.

Gogi nods, not saying anything so he won't have to hear his own choked-up voice. His mother went out to forage one day soon after Gogi was weaned, and never returned. It was probably a harpy eagle that got her. Having no mother in the troop is what started Gogi out in life with so low a ranking. If he climbs closer to number one, though, he'll have done his mother's memory proud.

Inside his mother's pouch he places dried berries, the sharpened twig he uses to pick seeds out from between his teeth before bedtime (oral hygiene—very important), twelve small pebbles, and a pat of damp moss, useful for putting out any fires he inadvertently makes with his magic.

It has been so long since he's made any fire! In a monkey troop, unless you are on top, or have a plan to quickly come out on top, it's best not to draw any attention. So, for his own safety under Ravanna the First's rule, Gogi has only used his fire powers when he was sure he was totally alone. But soon he'll be able to use them again!

"What's up with the pebbles?" Alzo asks.

"Oh, those," Gogi says. "It's a little silly, I guess. After my mother . . . after she died, I scrabbled together seventeen pebbles, and I've tossed one away each time I rose in rank. I guess I sort of imagine that she knows, and she'll be proud of me?"

"I bet she'd be proud of you anyway," Alzo says quietly.

"That's nice of you, Alzo," Gogi replies. "Good-bye, friend. I'll miss you!"

"You too, Gogi-Goge. Ooh, look, mushy bananas!" Alzo scampers off.

Shaking his head, Gogi tiptoes along the treetops, away from the ant devastation and toward the ruins of the ziggurat. Dread pools in his stomach at the thought of leaving his troop. It's just not something monkeys are supposed to do. And though he saw only ant hordes ravaging the marmoset land and not the queen herself, he can't get the thought out of his mind that some evil plot is definitely afoot.

Before he's realized it, he's slowed down to a crawl. If he lets himself get this worried and depressed, how will he help his friends once he meets up with them? Luckily, he knows just the thing to make himself feel better. Gogi sits with his back against an ironwood tree and holds his cupped hands out. He concentrates.

In between his palms appears a small flicker of flame. *Yep, still got it!*

Gogi allows the fire to grow. He means for it to

increase in height, just an inch or two, but some of the flame licks sideways instead, singeing his hair. Gogi howls, dropping his hands. The flame is extinguished right as it reaches the ground. That could have been a disaster! Apparently, not using his ability for a while makes it go rusty. At least there's plenty of time to practice.

Heartened, Gogi holds tight to his mother's pouch, and the twelve pebbles inside it, and hurries along on his way.

◇

Gogi thought he'd made good mental notes of what he passed when he traveled from the ruined ziggurat back to his homeland a year ago, but now it's so hard to remember. Is he supposed to ford the tan-colored river above or below the falls? Is he supposed to follow the tops of the kapok trees, or hop along the trunk of the fallen wimba? Both routes end up in the same place, but it turns out one way involves falling into a bed of nettles, and the other does not. Ouch.

Eventually, though, he makes it to Agony Canyon, the last obstacle before the ziggurat. This was the place he first met Mez the panther, Rumi the tree frog, and Lima the bat. He'd be seeing them all soon! Gogi starts whistling.

As he crosses the vine bridge, he causes smoke to

rise from his skin. It's something he's been experimenting with along the journey—providing enough flame magic to get a good smoke up, but not enough to burn his hair. He coughs as the wet-smelling smoke wafts over his nose. It's acrid and unpleasant, but there are no whiffs of burning monkey. Success!

Gogi takes a deep breath. He's leaving the normal rainforest now, and entering the place where the shadowwalkers met their biggest enemies.

No point delaying, not when his friends are waiting for him! Gogi starts across the vine bridge, confident that the smoke surrounding him will keep any wasps at bay. It works. The few wasps that emerge from under the vine bridge are sluggish and aimless, batting harmlessly against Gogi's side. Excellent.

All this smoke makes it harder to see the actual bridge, though. Lucky that capuchin monkeys have prehensile tails! Gogi curls his tail tighter and tighter around the vines of the bridge, letting his smoke float off as he scampers over the raging river. Once he's on the other side, Gogi rushes toward the ziggurat ruins.

It's only a little farther until he's there at the spot where the shadowwalkers disbanded a year before. The tall trees around him sway, and mists roll out of the nearby jungle. But there is no sign of his friends. *"Mez, Rumi, Lima!"* he sings softly. *"Mez, Rumi, Lima!"*

"Gogi!"

He goes stock-still. "Yes?"

"You're here! You're finally here!"

"Rumi? Is that you?"

A bright yellow blip skips into view, bouncing along the jungle floor until it's leaping up to land on Gogi's outstretched hand. "Hi, Gogi!" Rumi says.

Gogi cheers and gives the brainy little tree frog an affectionate tap on the head. "So good to see you, friend! Can you believe it's been a year?"

"I have so much to share with you," Rumi says. "So many fascinating discoveries! There was more knowledge locked away in the ziggurat's carvings than we ever knew, and after the structure fell apart, the interior carvings became visible. Come along, let's go to the ruins. I bet you can't wait to hear about everything I found."

"Give me a moment to put my bag down and have a snack first," Gogi says. Rumi would be giving him plenty of in-depth lessons on Caldera history sooner or later, there was no doubting that. But as a low-ranked capuchin, Gogi has gotten plenty of ribbing from the other monkeys, and he isn't looking forward to feeling dumb in a whole new place. "Has anyone else arrived yet? It's nearly the rainy season, so this should be the time."

"Not yet," Rumi says. "You're the first one. Which

means we can do a one-on-one seminar! Come on, to the ruins!"

"I don't know, Rumi," Gogi says, even as he follows the tree frog, who's bouncing along the jungle floor. "I'm just a monkey. It might not be the best use of your time to tell everything to me, because I won't have that much to add. Maybe it's best to wait until Mez gets here. A panther has a better chance of understanding than I do. And Lima . . ." Gogi pauses. Lima the bat has many wonderful qualities, is full of courage and cheer, but . . . "And Lima will be here soon too," he finishes.

"Okay, we can wait, that's fine, all you had to do is ask. Look, I set us up a cozy little home," Rumi prattles on. "Turn left up there, then go straight. There it is!"

Gogi rubs his hands together. It's been a long journey, and a nice snug rest sounds perfect.

Whistling, he follows along after Rumi, then startles when he realizes the frog has stopped.

"Ta-da!" Rumi says.

Gogi swivels. They're in the middle of a swampy patch of mud, a few pathetic-looking ferns sticking up out of frothy black muck. "This is the 'cozy little home'?" Gogi says, keeping his tone as even as he can manage.

"Yes, isn't it wonderful? There's mud to keep cool in, lots of bugs to eat, some slime to run your fingers through whenever you feel the urge."

"Wow, thanks, Rumi," Gogi manages to say. "This all looks, um, super."

"So, what do you know about ellipses?" Rumi asks, plopping his little yellow body down into the mud and peering up at Gogi with his wide, inky eyes.

"Don't you mean eclipses?"

"No. I definitely mean ellipses."

Gogi scratches his butt. "Oh, in that case, I have to tell you, my knowledge of . . . what did you call them? Ellipses. It's, um, I guess you could call it basic?"

"Don't worry, I'll explain it all to you in detail, starting from the very foundations of mathematics!"

"Oh great! That's just wonderful," Gogi says, suddenly feeling frantic. He climbs onto a narrow log so his feet don't get dirtied by the gray swamp water. He looks around, whistling tunelessly, trying to keep an impressed expression on his face. A movement startles him, and he sees the red tail feathers of a bird as it flees from a ficus tree overhanging the clearing.

"Do you want a snack or anything?" Rumi prattles on. "I'm being so rude, launching right into my discoveries when you must want something to eat first. I think I hid some fish eggs around here somewhere. The good kind, too, not the inferior eggs I serve to other guests."

"Other guests? You have friends around here?"

Rumi doesn't respond, instead whistling away as

he rummages under a banana leaf. Gogi wonders if a frog would find something rude about his question. He always tries to be hyperaware of the differences among his friends. "Anyway," Gogi continues, "fish eggs. Wow. That would be awesome. But I brought some dried fruit, and I think I'm in the mood to eat some of that." Gogi pulls a wrinkled guava from his woven satchel and chews it showily, as if to explain how very much capuchin monkeys enjoy wrinkled guava, and that's the only reason he's not eating Rumi's fish eggs.

"I'll explain as we go, come on," Rumi says, bounding out of the "cozy little home," chattering all the way. "A circle is the set of all points a fixed distance to a given point, but an ellipse is the set of all points the sum of whose distances to two given points is constant."

"Hmm?" Gogi says, scratching his navel.

"I know what you're thinking: Doesn't that just make an ellipse basically an eccentric circle?"

"Uh-huh."

"An oval, Gogi. An ellipse is an *oval*."

"So, Rumi, as I was saying, explaining all this to me might not be the best use of your time," Gogi says, his head already spinning.

"No, no, it doesn't get too much more complicated than this."

"Goody."

"So anyway, the eclipse that made us all shadow-walkers was formed by the moon passing in front of the sun, combining the magic of night and the magic of day. Everyone knows that. But because the moon is in an elliptical orbit, I was able to use the two-legs' charts to locate where we are in their calendar."

"Wait. It was an ellipse eclipse?" Gogi asks, chewing on a bit of lichen he found in his belly button.

"Yes! That's it! And their approximation function is carved into one of the stones, so I'm able to use it—after teaching myself analytical geometry, of course—to predict the next *lunar* eclipse. That's when the Earth passes between the sun and moon."

Gogi's ears perk. "That sounds useful. When is that?"

"You won't have to ask me," Rumi says proudly. "Just look. You can do the calculations yourself!"

There in front of them is a broad block of stone, etched throughout in carvings that are themselves covered in moss and muck. There are still symbols on it to be made out, though: little handprints are visible in the moss where Rumi has painstakingly removed sections of the debris. It must have taken the frog days and days to clear it all.

Gogi can't make any sense of what he's seeing. There are arrows circling spheres and ovals, crosses and dashes.

Rumi follows Gogi's focus and points to the symbols. "Numbers—those are called 'numbers,'" he says gently.

"I suppose this isn't just a guide to when each fruit nearby is in season?" Gogi asks.

"Nope," Rumi says, shaking his head. "It's a calculation of when the next eclipse will happen, provided that the trajectory of the celestial bodies is precise and predictable. Of course, we have no reason to believe otherwise."

"So—when will it happen again?" Gogi asks, tilting his head and smacking one ear, as if to pour out the nonsense clogging his brain.

"Eight-hundred-eleven-point-seven days after the first time."

Gogi stares at him blankly.

"In other words, when the Veil drops twenty-three nights from now," Rumi says proudly.

"Oh! That's not very far away," Gogi says.

"No, it isn't."

"And it will come with another burst of magical energy?"

"That's right, potentially just as strong as the one

that gave us our magical powers," Rumi replies.

"So . . . what does that all mean?"

Before Rumi can answer, there's a screech from the surrounding trees, and a burst of motion. At the sight of shaking branches, Gogi ducks for cover, monkey reflexes ready to dodge an ocelot or an eagle or a python. When he peers out from the security of a stand of ferns, though, he sees that Rumi didn't scatter. He's looking into the treetops, where Gogi glimpsed the red bird flying away.

"What was that noise?" Gogi asks.

Rumi, a faraway look on his face, snaps his attention back to Gogi. "Nothing."

"Riiiiight," Gogi says.

A calculation passes behind Rumi's eyes. "It was a parrot, I think. Parrots aren't generally risks to tree frogs. That's why I didn't run for cover like you did."

Gogi nods, eyes not leaving Rumi. "Sure. Makes sense."

An awkward silence falls. Awkward silences aren't all that uncommon around Rumi, but this one is especially dense. Gogi knows his friend is hiding something from him, but he figures Rumi will fill him in once he's ready.

"So!" Gogi finally says, poking his way out of the fern and looking around, running his hands up and down his arms, even though there's no chill in the air. He steps back to take in the pile of rubble that is all that remains of the Ziggurat of the Sun and Moon. At their highest, the ruins crest the tops of the surrounding trees. Monkey wisdom would say to move as high as possible, to get a good vantage point. Gogi climbs up the stones, looking back toward Rumi. "Come on! Let's see if we can spot Mez and Lima!"

Rumi leaps, but even with his powerful back legs, he's too tiny to clear the first stone, and he tumbles back to the ground. "Excuse me, do you mind giving me a hand?" he calls up to Gogi.

"Sorry, buddy," Gogi says, making his way back down and holding out an open palm. "I've been around nothing but other monkeys for too long."

Rumi hops onto Gogi's hand and then makes his way to his preferred position on top of Gogi's head, holding on to his eyebrows, one tuft in each hand. "Okay, ready!"

Gogi starts clambering up, enjoying the feel of moving upward to where things are safer, using all five limbs (capuchins call their grippy tail a limb, causing a bit of controversy in the monkey world, since it makes the howlers feel insecure about their limp tails). He's up to the top of the ruins in no time.

It's only been a year, but the rainforest has been

merciless in taking back the land. Where once was the stone-gray ziggurat, an otherworldly reminder of the bizarre two-leg civilization that used to inhabit Caldera, now are mostly shades of green and brown. Vines are swarming the surfaces, already working their way into cracks in the stone so that water can get in, and fungus and roots. In another year's time, there might be no more sign of the ziggurat at all.

By then, the lunar eclipse—and whatever changes it will bring—will be long past.

4

Twenty-Three Nights Until the Eclipse

THE SUN DESCENDS and rain begins to fall while Gogi and Rumi hunker down on top of the rubble. It's a misty, light rain, not enough to penetrate Gogi's thick fur and soak his skin—but still, no monkey likes getting wet. He brushes water from his eyebrows whenever the droplets of rain get dense enough to drip in front of his eyes.

Rumi, on the other hand, is in amphibian bliss. He lies out in a puddle that's formed in the depression of one of the carvings, arms thrust over the side, eyes closed as he smiles up at the rain clouds. "They'll be here soon, I'm sure," he says. "It's hard to coordinate a journey from far off in the rainforest. I've waited a whole year for this day; we can give them some extra time."

Gogi lets himself gingerly sit on the edge of a rock. His butt is instantly wet. He sighs as he swings his legs over the edge, giving in to the fact that he's going to wind up soaked. He kicks his heels at the stones. "Sure, of course we'll wait, but I really miss them, I don't know how much—oh wait, oh no, oh no!"

The vine bridge, just barely in view, has started shaking. If it weren't a full moon, he wouldn't have been able to make out any movement at all. "Is that the Ant Queen, coming to hunt us down?" Gogi cries, leaping to all fours.

"Of course it's not," Rumi says. "Unless she's figured out how to morph into two cats and a bat."

"Oh," Gogi says, sitting back down. "I guess I'm a little jumpy these days."

There, just in view, cautiously picking their way off the vine bridge, are Mez and Chumba, with Lima swooping over them, back and forth, making a torrent of conversation that Gogi can't hear from his distance. "They're here!" the capuchin says, bounding to his feet and waving his hands to draw their attention. "Rumi, you're right, they're really here!"

As Gogi yells, the panthers pause, then look up to the top of the ruins. While the panthers leap about gleefully,

Lima leaves them, zooming through the air toward Gogi and Rumi, gesticulating wildly with her wings once she gets within shouting distance. She needs those wings for flying, of course, so waving them around makes her bob every which way in the air. "Gogi, Rumi, oh holy bat fingernails, you're okay!"

Lima soars right into Gogi, her wings wrapping around his rib cage. She's so light that the impact barely budges him, but for her sake he pretends to fall backward, splashing into a puddle on the stone. "Lima, hey there! You've gotten so fierce!"

Rumi bounces all over them, here, there, and everywhere. Frog kisses. Not the worst.

By the time the three have finished greeting one another, the two panthers have arrived. Mez and Chumba scramble up the stone, claws digging into rock, until they're beside the others. Chumba's missing one of her front paws, but you'd never know it—she easily keeps pace with her sister. They nuzzle in close as greeting. Never have cold, wet panther noses felt so good.

"So, how are you guys?" Gogi asks.

Mez and Chumba look at each other and then press in close. "We're okay," Mez answers. "The panthers are okay. Aunt Usha is home with the triplets, training them to hunt. They're nearly as big as we were last year—"

"—until we got bigger," Chumba adds proudly.

Gogi cocks his head. Maybe the sisters have put a *little* weight on, but they'll always be small for panthers. They look practically like ocelots, to tell the truth, but Gogi would never say that out loud—cats are ridiculously competitive. "You two have gotten so impressive!" he says.

"Aunt Usha almost didn't let us go," Chumba says. "She wanted us to stay near to give the cubs extra protection. Very unlike Usha to ask for help."

"Well, she wanted *you* to stay around," Mez says. "You're second-in-command now, with Mist missing. She was perfectly willing to let me go."

"In any case," Chumba says shyly, "the rainforest around the den is tense. We haven't seen the ant armies in our territory, but we have seen the refugees—capybaras passing through where there never were capybaras, even an arrau turtle. All with stories of devastation."

"I saw the queen's ants on the attack, not far from my home," Gogi says. "They've uprooted all the vegetation, cleared out the animals. The marmosets that used to live there are just . . . gone. It's only ants."

"Yuck," Lima says.

"My homeland is next," Gogi says. "I tried my best to get the capuchins mobilized, but they're not very willing to hear much of anything from a number twelve."

"I'm sorry, Gogi," Mez says. "We'll try to stop the

Ant Queen before the ants overrun your home."

"Wait, *twelve*?" Lima asks, holding out a wing for a high five. Or a high wing. "Gogi, that's five ranks better than last year!"

Gogi gives her wing a light tap, so he doesn't bowl her over. "I know! Thanks!"

"How about you, Lima?" Rumi asks as he rubs rainwater into his arms. It reminds Gogi of a capuchin saying: *Happy as a tree frog in a rainstorm.* "How are the bats in the colony doing?"

Lima looks to Mez and Chumba and then back at Rumi. "I didn't actually go back. I stayed with the panthers."

Mez smiles. "It was great having her with us."

"I guess I'm sort of a panther now!" Lima says, baring her slender teeth. "Bat colonies are different from the families you monkeys and panthers have. We don't get all snuggy and cozy. If I'd gone back to the bat cave, I'd have been waiting by myself all day for night to fall so we could go feed. Spending the year as an honorary panther was *much* more fun."

"Usha agreed to that?" Gogi asks. It's hard to picture Mez's severe aunt letting a chatty bat come live with her family of sleek hunters.

"We had the whole journey home to warm her up to the idea," Chumba says. "She seemed a little shell-shocked by the disappearance of Mist, truth be told. We probably could have gotten her to say yes to just about anything."

"I was very useful," Lima sniffs. "Every panther family should have a resident bat. Like, tell these guys how many mosquito bites you got all year."

"Only one, and that was while Lima was asleep," Mez says.

"See? Call me Lima, Slayer of Mosquitoes!"

"Careful," Rumi says. "My last name is Mosquito-swallow, after all. People might think we're from the same family."

"No, they won't. Because you're a *frog*," Lima says.

Rumi sighs. "That was me joking. I'll study up on how senses of humor work one of these days."

"I thought it was a very funny joke," Gogi says, patting Rumi on the head. Then he yanks his hand back. "Oh wait—were you upset enough to . . . ?"

Rumi smiles. "No, no poison came out. You can tell by the sheen. I'll warn you guys if that ever happens."

Mez blinks up toward the sky. "So, have you two been hanging out in the rain this whole time? Boo. Let's go get somewhere cozy. That makeshift den Usha put us and the triplets in is still around here someplace. Chumba's got the better nose—she can pick up the scent, even a year later."

Chumba nods and starts slinking down the ruin stones.

"Wait, stop," Rumi calls after her. "I already made us a camp!"

"You know how panthers are about getting their way," Gogi whispers diplomatically to Rumi. "Let them bring us to the old den for now, and you can show them the camp you chose later."

Rumi sighs as he leaps up onto Gogi's forehead. "Yes, I suppose that will be fine."

Gogi falls in beside Mez and they pick their way down the slick stones of the ruin. "So, really no sign of Mist?"

Mez shakes her head, her eyes on the surrounding trees. "Not all year. Right around here is the last place we saw him."

"So strange," Gogi says, his own eyes scanning the forest line for any hint of Mist's white fur, "for your cousin to leave his whole family. I mean, we capuchins will get in a big fight and not groom for days, poop in one another's nests, that sort of thing—but leaving the only family you've ever known forever? It's surprising."

"Believe me, I've been thinking about that all year," Mez says. "But Mist was so proud of his favored position as Usha's son, and his famous white fur, and then when Chumba and I took the lead in stopping Auriel, and he was accidentally attacked—"

"—I saw the damage," Gogi says, shuddering, remembering the young panther's face, half intact and half full of scars and twisted sinew.

"He fell hard on his pride," Mez says, shrugging, "and I guess it was too much to recover from." They've reached the bottom of the ruins. Mez looks out at the greenery as she elegantly picks her way over a thicket of vines, a wistful expression on her face. "I hope he's okay, wherever he is."

"Panthers are meant to be solitary hunters after a certain age, right?" Gogi says. "I guess you could say he sort of jumped right into adulthood."

Relief softens Mez's face. "That's a nice way to think about it. Maybe he's fine."

"Just telling it like I see it," Gogi adds.

"We're here!" Chumba says as she parts a patch of reddish fronds and heads in. It looks like any other stand of ferns to Gogi, but he knows he should leave the den-finding to the panthers. If he had his way, they'd all be nesting up in the trees.

The nondescript patch of ferns hides a passageway, and at the end of the passageway is a den, tight and cozy, a little stuffy for Gogi's tastes but completely dry. "Thanks, Chumba," Gogi says as he clambers in. Since he's the last to enter, he draws the fronds closed over the entrance so they're hidden from view, then draws his knees to his chest and settles in.

". . . feeling we're overly day-biased last time we were together," Rumi is saying. "I mean, look at us, we are all eclipse-born, so obviously we can be awake day and night if we want to, but we keep doing stuff during the day! And if we do the numbers, we have Mez and Chumba, nightwalkers. Lima, nightwalker."

"I prefer the term night*flyer*," she says.

"—and me, nightwalker," Rumi finishes. "Gogi's the only daywalker here."

Gogi looks around, astonished. "I'm useless at night, guys. We're better off during the day unless you want me bumping into things."

"I'm not a shadowwalker like you guys," Chumba says. "I couldn't daywalk even if I wanted to."

"I might have a solution," Rumi says, gesticulating wildly. "Gogi, how subtle can you make your fire?"

"Subtle? Fire's never exactly subtle."

"What I wonder is if you might be able to make a ring of fire around you, so that you could see better at night."

"That sounds, um, deadly."

"The most subtle, soft fire. Not enough to burn anything. Like concentrated sunlight. After all, light is just fire that's far from home."

"I'm not sure what that last part even means, but I'm up for trying your idea," Gogi says. "It could work. As long as it doesn't work by, you know, searing everyone I love to death."

Mez gives Gogi a nuzzle. "We'll travel whenever's best for everyone in the group. Including our resident daywalker. But we should look into that night-light idea."

"Can I ask a question? Okay, good, here it is," Lima says. "What are we traveling toward? Or traveling from? Hypothetically?"

They all look at one another, waiting for someone to speak. "That's a good question," Chumba finally says.

They are all quiet, except for licking sounds as Mez and Chumba work to get the moisture out of their fur. Gogi's never understood how a cat can lick itself dry, but apparently it works. Suddenly Chumba looks up, eyes alert.

"What is it?" Gogi asks.

Chumba smiles. "Anyone want to play a game?"

"No," Mez says patiently. "We still have important things to discuss."

"That's too bad," Lima says mournfully. "I'd have played with you. You know how good I was getting at whisker taunt. And I don't even *have* whiskers."

"Proud of you," Gogi says.

"Um, guys, Mez is right. We really do have more important matters to discuss," Rumi says. "For starters, where is Banu the sloth? Or Calisto the trogon? Or Sorella the uakari?"

"Maybe they're . . . late?" Lima says quietly.

"It could be as simple as that," Rumi says, nodding gravely. "But I think we might be wise to assume the worst—that we have all survived the year to make it here only because the Ant Queen hasn't yet reached our homelands. Now, let's think: What do we all have in common, that we made it here and they did not?"

"We're all *really* good-looking," Lima offers.

"Think of it: Usha's territory, the capuchin palm forest, the ruins . . . We all spent the past year in the west half of Caldera!" Rumi says.

"Question. What does 'west' mean?" Lima asks.

"Shh, let him finish," Gogi says, tucking the bat in close. "But yeah, what's 'west' mean, Rumi?"

The tree frog shakes his head sadly. "I see that I have to start further back than I thought." They all huddle close as he picks up a dried seedpod and starts scratching with it in the dirt. "Based on my studies of the two-leg carvings, this is a rough map of Caldera. The ruins we're in are near the center; and here's where you're from, panthers; and here's roughly where your cave is, Lima; and, Gogi, this is where the capuchin forest is, in the northern hemisphere."

"I just thought of something. If this is Caldera, what's outside it?" Mez asks.

Gogi blinks. He's never considered that there could be an outside to Caldera.

"I have no idea," Rumi says. "I don't know if anyone alive in Caldera knows. If the two-legs had that knowledge, it went with them."

"Okay, then, what's at the *edge* of Caldera?" Mez asks.

Rumi shrugs. "Believe me, I'd love to know. But there's nothing in the ziggurat carvings to tell us."

"Tell them about all that ellipse-eclipse stuff you figured out, Rumi!" Gogi says.

"I will, I will. But first things first—since we're the only shadowwalkers to make it back here, I think we can assume that the rumors are true, that the Ant Queen's armies are moving in from the east."

"I saw them in the distance," Gogi says. "If I'm not totally turned around, the marmoset lands might have been toward that 'east' place you're talking about." He scratches his head. He might know exactly where each tree in his homeland is, and precisely when they fruit, but this larger-scale mapping makes his monkey brain hurt.

Mez's ears, which had perked up at the mention of

the coming eclipse, lower flat against her head. "That's a pretty grim conclusion, that the other shadowwalkers have already succumbed to the ants. Let's hope there's some other explanation."

"I'm pretty sure I'm right," Rumi says.

"Well, you can't be *sure* you're right," Gogi gently corrects.

"No, I'm almost completely certain," Rumi says. His eyes flick upward, past where the foliage of the den's roof locks in.

"Is there something you're not telling us?" Gogi asks.

"Of course not," Rumi says.

But Gogi saw the moment of calculation pass over his friend's face. Gogi might not be the smartest member of the group, but no one beats a capuchin for emotional awareness. There's no doubting it anymore: Rumi has a secret.

5

"RUMI, IS EVERYTHING okay?" Gogi asks. "It just seems like maybe, maybe, you're not being totally—"

"Everything's fine, of course everything's fine, why wouldn't everything be fine?" Rumi sputters.

"I don't know, friend, it's just that it seems like there's something off," Gogi says as gently as possible.

"Something's off with Rumi? What do you mean?" Mez asks, sniffing the ground around the little tree frog.

"He *looks* okay," Lima says. "Well, sort of okay. Or maybe not okay at all."

Actually, Rumi looks miserable. He's hunched down

low, membranes over his eyes and chin pressed into his clasped fingers.

"*Are* you okay, Rumi?" Lima asks.

He lets out a long and low croak and pulls the membranes back from over his inky eyes. "Well, the truth is that I guess I have something to tell you all. I just need you to promise not to flip out when I do. Promise you'll hear me out."

Lima springs into the air, does a somersault, and lands back down. She bows. "There. I've already flipped out. Nothing to worry about now."

"Rumi, what's going on?" Mez growls.

"There's someone that I think you guys should meet. It turns out we misunderstood him a year ago, and I've come to get to know him over this past year. . . . I should start at the beginning," Rumi says.

"Or maybe you could stop delaying and spit it out," Mez says, her voice still a growl. "That would also be a good idea."

Gogi would trust Mez with his life, but having a panther growling so nearby still sets his heart racing. He tries to make his hand stop trembling as he places it on Rumi's back, before hastily removing it when he remembers that the frog exudes poison under pressure. "I'm sure there's a reasonable explanation for all of this," Gogi says.

"So, you remem-ember how Auriel seemed like a friendly little boa constrictor at first?" Rumi stammers. "Be-before he turned out to be horribly evil?"

"Yes," Chumba says dryly, "it's hard to forget that."

"I never trusted him from the start," Lima says. "I always knew something was off about that snake."

"That is so not true!" Mez says. "I was there, remember? You were all 'ooh, your scales are so pretty, I wonder if they taste good, I'll go anywhere you say.'"

"I was not!" Lima squeaks.

"Come on, let's give Rumi a chance to tell us what he has to tell us," Gogi says. "Go ahead, Rumi. We're listening."

"Well, just like we misunderstood Auriel, I think we also misunderstood this other . . . creature."

Gogi shoots Mez a look that says, *Are you thinking what I'm thinking?* She seems confused more than anything; then her eyes widen and she narrows her eyes at Rumi, ears flat against her head and teeth exposed. *Mist.*

Lima's the one to speak first, though. "Are you friends with the *Ant Queen*?!"

"No, no, nothing like that," Rumi says, staring into his hands. "After you all left I was very lonely. I was researching the carvings all day, figuring out what I could about the two-legs and what they knew, when I started to feel this . . . presence. Not like the howler monkeys that were hunting us last year, but something . . . observing me. It felt like I was in the company of a friend, even though I didn't even know who it was. Does that make any sense?"

Gogi nods. "Kind of."

"It could easily have been something tricking you," Mez says, her growl going ever lower. Gogi jumps, despite himself.

"Yes, of course. But I don't think it was," Rumi says, "and I'll tell you why. Eventually I made a plan. For many nights I'd been doing the rounds of the carvings, walking through them in the same order. Deliberately. I wanted to lull whoever was following me, you see, into thinking they would always know my next steps. But finally I whirled around instead of going forward like I normally would do, and I—I caught him!"

"Caught *who*?" Rumi's friends say in unison.

"Oh," Rumi says, blinking in surprise. "Have I not said yet? I'm sorry. It's—wait, what was that?"

Gogi groans. But Rumi was right to go silent—there was a strange noise outside. A creaking sound has turned into a crash, then voices.

"Does anyone know what that was?" Chumba whispers.

"No," Rumi whispers back. "After the ziggurat fell, the animals that were hunting us dispersed. I've been basically by myself since then."

"So, who's out there?"

They all stare up at the interlocking fronds of the den, dust swirling down in the close air.

"Let's go investigate, guys," Gogi says. He marshals his courage, springs to his feet, and promptly bangs his head on an overhanging root. "Ow!"

Low and silent, Mez takes over the lead, followed soon after by Chumba. Gogi takes up the rear, after Rumi, who's still quivering. "Hey, it's okay, Rumi, we'll get all this sorted out," Gogi says.

Lima whistles to herself as she picks her way through the greenery. "I'm hoping it's Banu. I just adore that sloth. So handsome."

Gogi follows the bright yellow blur of Rumi's back as he hops along, all of them tracking the scent of Mez's pantherfear. Once they're out in the moonlit rainforest, the group goes still.

The distant voice is back, but then it cuts off again before Gogi can make out any words. Gogi looks to Rumi to see if he recognizes it, but the tree frog seems perplexed. His eyes reflect the moon.

Mez disappears. She was close to gone before, with

her dark calico fur, but now she's truly invisible. It's the magical power that the eclipse gave her, back when she was born.

"Wow!" Gogi says. "You've gotten even better at that invisibility thing."

"I'll go investigate," says the open space where Mez just was. "Then I'll report back on what I've found."

"No way," Gogi says flatly. "If you run into trouble, you'll need my fire."

"And my teeth," Chumba growls.

"And my wind," Rumi says.

"And my healing!" Lima squeaks. They all turn to stare at her. "What, come on, it's useful too! It just happens to be useful *after* the fight."

"Okay, we'll go together," Mez says, still invisible. "But let me at least go a few paces ahead, so I can warn you all of any danger."

Gogi nods. They hold still. "Wait, did she already start?"

"Yep," Chumba says. "I can track her by scent alone now. We've been practicing this trick during our year off. Follow me!"

"Look at those two noble sisters, spending their year off working hard on their saving-the-world skills," Gogi says, suddenly self-conscious about his own year spent eating palm nuts and fretting over his rank.

"Before we go," Rumi says, puffing as he hauls a small rock through the mud, "would you help me make an arrow of rocks? I want to let the other shadowwalkers know where we've headed as they arrive."

"Sure, buddy," Gogi says. He joins Rumi in hurriedly placing a half-dozen rocks in an arrow shape, glad that he's able to locate enough that he doesn't have to give up any of his precious twelve pebbles.

They hurry to catch up to the panther sisters. Mez leads them on a wide circuit of the ruins. Or at least Gogi assumes it's still Mez leading them, as he can see only Chumba, and that just barely. As the sole daywalker in the group, he'd better get working quickly on Rumi's ring-of-light idea. He probably already has minor brain damage from all the times he's conked his head on various rocks and low-hanging branches during their adventures.

Although he knows it might reveal them in the nighttime, he allows himself to create a small flame in his palm—just a lick, really!—in order to prevent himself from tripping over a rock and making a ruckus and exposing them all.

On the far side of the ruins, Gogi begins to hear a muffled roaring, what at first he takes to be a river. But making mental maps of things he's seen is a monkey's strong suit, and Gogi is sure that there was no river in this direction before. And rivers don't generally appear out of nowhere.

The air in front of Gogi shimmers, making him leap in fright. Then it resolves into the shape of a familiar panther. Mez's face is grim. "We're going to the next rise over. You all have to see this for yourselves." Her eyes widen in alarm as she sees Gogi's fire. "Gogi. Put that out! The moonlight will have to be enough. Do you want to let the enemy know exactly where to find us?"

"Let *what* enemy know?" Gogi grumbles beneath his breath.

Lima streaks into the sky so she can see what Mez is talking about. "Wow!" she calls from above, chirping in surprise. Then she lands and claps her wing over her mouth. "Sorry!"

Mez leads Chumba, Rumi, and Gogi along a dark alley through the greenery until they're on a small rocky rise, looking out over a misty valley.

At first Gogi thinks he's seeing a muddy pool at the far end, but then he realizes that the area is swarming with ants. The roaring sound he heard before? Ants. That many ants. He shudders.

It looks like a flash flood, like a foaming crest of invading water. Up to a point there is unmarred green, trees and bushes in perfect health. Then there's a line, after which the green is gone. Simply gone. "Just like the marmoset forest," Gogi whispers.

Lima lands lightly beside Gogi. "It's terrible. The ants are destroying everything."

She's right. The line of ants appears motionless, but that's only because it's creeping forward at such a slow pace. Gogi squints. At the front, where there are no more trees to block the moon's light, he can see the ants using their millions of sharp little mandibles to slice through grass and fern and tree, the leaves disintegrating and becoming sprays of green morsels, rippling back over the horde. In front of the ants is the rainforest, unbroken and seemingly eternal. Behind them is a swarming mass of brown, broken earth and glinting ant bodies.

"Look. A hoatzin. And a fer-de-lance," Chumba says under her breath.

Heart dropping, Gogi peers far back into the mass of ants. The first thing he sees is the fer-de-lance, a pit viper swarming through. The ants let it pass unfettered, parting for the snake wherever it moves. Farther along, Gogi sees a hoatzin, a magnificent bird with clawed legs and a ridge of orange plumes running along the back of its head. The hoatzin, too, has a wide-open space around it, as the ants circle. Before Gogi's eyes, the hoatzin kneels in the soil and lowers its beak to the ground. The ants swarm onto it, soon covering the bird in moonlit browns and purples. Once it's covered, the hoatzin takes off, soaring to the top of a nearby palm. Then the ants pour off its feathers and into the tree's fronds, where they start right in on sawing away, bringing leaves and chunks of bark raining down to the horde below.

"The hoatzin—it's *helping* the ant army," Gogi says.

"And now the fer-de-lance is too," Rumi says. "Look!"

The snake has made its way to a brook, where the ants are milling, the unfortunate ones at the edge pushed in by the pressing swarm and swept off by the current. Once the fer-de-lance reaches the edge, it threads into the water, slowly making its way until its head reaches the far bank. There it loops its neck around an overhanging root and pulls its body tight so it's strung across the water.

"It's made itself into a bridge!" Lima says.

"Shh," Mez warns as the hoatzin goes alert, peering toward them and tasting the air.

The ants begin to surge across the fer-de-lance, the viper wincing as more and more of the horde climbs onto its back to reach the far bank.

"Fascinating," Rumi says. "It appears that the Ant Queen is not without allies. That she has collaborators among the animals of Caldera."

"Why would any animal *help* her?" Lima asks, wrapping her wings around her.

"I'm sure there are many potential reasons," Rumi says, his tone vague. "Helping the Ant Queen could have been the best of some terrible options."

"What is that supposed to mean?" Mez whispers. "I *know* you're not saying there's any possible excuse for helping the Ant Queen destroy the rainforest."

"No," Rumi says hastily. "I'm not trying to say that. It's just that we don't know what this hoatzin and fer-de-lance have been through to bring them to this point, that's all."

Once the ants have reached the far side of the fer-de-lance, they set to work sawing into the roots of a tree that overhangs the brook. Eventually, with a groan, the tree tumbles across the water. More of the ants begin to cross, and the fer-de-lance finally releases, slinking back through the brook and curling up to rest on the bank.

"Snakes are cold-blooded like I am," Rumi says. "It probably caught a chill from the water."

The hoatzin flaps down from the top of the palm to join the fer-de-lance. They enter into conversation, too far away for Gogi to make anything out. Both of them hang their heads low, moving listlessly, in postures of defeat. "We need to find out what they're saying," Gogi says, "and we need to find out why they're willing to betray all of us, what the Ant Queen might have offered them. It could be our best chance of figuring out what we can do to stop all this."

"On it," Mez says. She turns invisible, the air shimmering for a moment until even that glistening effect fades. Gogi can make out only the faintest signs of her stealing away toward their enemies, a leaf curling over here, a frog going silent there. Even though he knows Mez is in motion, he can still barely sense her.

"Now we have to wait for her to report back?" Lima says. "That's too frustrating for words."

"Say, Lima," Rumi says. "You're a bat, and it's night. You could fly over there without it looking too suspicious."

Gogi shakes his head. "Stay here, Lima. We only need one of us to eavesdrop, and I'd prefer the rest of us stay together, for safety's sake. We don't want to risk your getting noticed. You may be a bat, but you're not invisible like Mez."

"I agree," Chumba says. "You stay here."

"Okay, fine," Lima huffs, lowering her head to her folded wings. "You don't have to be so bossy about it."

"I'd play whisker taunt with you if we could," Chumba whispers.

"Thanks, Chum."

The friends watch the hoatzin and fer-de-lance continue their whispered conversation.

"I really wish that had been Banu or Sorella out there instead," Lima says, "and not some traitorous poisonous snake and a jungle chicken and—oh, wait, who's that?"

Gogi leans forward, squinting. More creatures *have* joined them, four strange beings that look like they're made of glittery mud. They almost look like branches that have come alive, standing vertically up from the ground, only they're slowly moving forward. "What in the world are those?" Gogi asks.

"Most strange," Rumi says. "Is it really possible that the ants are coming together to form larger creatures?"

"No," Chumba says, her hackles standing straight up. "It's *Mez*."

"What do you mean, those little brown monsters are Mez—oh!" Gogi sees it now. Mez is still invisible. But the ants have begun to swarm her, like they would anything they came across. And the ants are *not* invisible. Those are Mez's legs.

"She probably has no idea that this is happening," Gogi says, dashing to his feet. More and more of the ants are swarming up. He can make out Mez's underside now, and the broad outlines of her flank.

"If I'm not mistaken, those are army ants," Rumi warns. "They swarm without stinging, until one of them sends the signal, and then they all sting at once. The combined poison is enough to bring down a buffalo."

"We have to warn her!" Chumba says, getting to her paws and starting forward.

"On my way," Lima says, and zooms into the air.

Gogi watches, breathless, as Lima soars into the twilight sky, outlined for a moment against the moon before she floats down toward Mez and the hoatzin and fer-de-lance some forty monkeylengths away. She slows and flutters down from the sky. It's hard for Gogi to see well in the looming night, but it's almost as if, as if—

"She's not going to land *on* Mez, is she?" Gogi asks, hand over his mouth.

"Oh no," Chumba moans. "That's a terrible idea, Lima."

Lima was never the greatest strategist of the group. She lands right on Mez's invisible shoulder—or what would have been an invisible shoulder if it didn't suddenly have a bat sitting on it.

If the bat perched in the middle of thin air wasn't enough to warn the enemies, then Lima's words definitely are. Gogi can just make them out. "Mez, watch out, you have ants on you!"

"Oh, Lima," Rumi says, shaking his head.

"It's like they always say: Never send a bat to do a panther's work," Chumba mutters as she stalks forward, smoothly falling into a sprint as she races toward Mez.

"Do they *really* always say that?" Gogi grumbles under his breath as he scampers up the nearest tree, running along the tops of branches so he can get a vantage point high above the inevitable fight. He always feels better when he's up in the canopy. Rumi comes along for the ride, clutching one of Gogi's ears.

Ant-covered Mez springs into motion, spreading out wide on all fours and shaking mightily from side to side. Plenty of ants remain to cover her, but Gogi hopes that she's gotten rid of enough of them that if they all bite at once, it will no longer be fatal.

The hoatzin and fer-de-lance, though, have gotten over their surprise. Lima may have called it a "jungle chicken," but Gogi has heard stories of hoatzin fighting off monitor lizards, and now he can see why: the hoatzin goes after Mez with its slashing beak, harassing the snarling cat, piercing the ground where her tail had just been, Mez dodging just in time to avoid the razor beak cutting through the air.

Mez has clearly decided that invisibility is no use anymore when she's covered with ants, or maybe she can't keep up her concentration under the onslaught. Either way, she's gone fully visible, giving the hoatzin back as hard as it's giving to her, teeth snapping and claws outstretched as she wheels and strikes.

Meanwhile, the fer-de-lance has worked its way

around to Mez's tail. The snake is thin as a vine and very agile, its bladed head threading easily through the uneven terrain. It will be on Mez's unprotected backside in a moment.

All the while the ants throng around them, climbing back up Mez as quickly as she can throw them off.

"All right, Mez," Gogi says under his breath. "I'm coming." He's still far away, but he doesn't have time to get any closer before the fer-de-lance will be in attack position. He raises his hands. Shaking. He takes a deep breath to still them. Then Gogi creates a red flame in one palm and an orange one in the other. There's a familiar surge along his spine, like there's pepper juice flowing through his vertebrae. Slowing exhaling, he grows each flame into a tendril, then braids the tendrils, easing them forward. As if using a lasso, he flings the fire out toward Mez and the fer-de-lance. "Come on, come on," he urges, sweat dripping into his eyes. He's just not great at maintaining focus like this.

"Gogi, wait!" Rumi cries.

Gogi looks up, his flame wavering along with his concentration. He sees the problem: Lima is harassing the fer-de-lance. Her little fingers and toes can't do much damage, but by arrowing at its eyes she's managed to slow its progress. Unfortunately, she's also gotten herself in the way of Gogi's attack. He lets the flame drop. "Come on, Lima, come on, take off again," Gogi whispers.

"My turn!" Rumi says, hopping off Gogi's shoulder and into the fray.

Chumba arrives. The young panther makes it to the fight just as the hoatzin is bearing down on Mez, hooked beak glinting. Focused on its quarry, the hoatzin is totally unprepared for an attack coming from its flank, and it goes down in a cloud of feathers as Chumba digs her claws in, using her momentum to roll with the bird. They're soon covered in ants, and now the insects must be biting freely; Chumba makes yips and yells of pain as she comes to a stop beside the now-motionless hoatzin. It's been knocked out by the attack.

Mez, also shrieking and crying as the ants sting, bounds over to Chumba. Gogi knows from experience that each of the ants has a small amount of toxin, and with each dose the level of poison in the victim's bloodstream increases—no animal can survive too much of it. They're running out of time.

The sinewy fer-de-lance keeps an easy pace behind Mez, dodging Lima's harrying attacks as it maintains striking distance from the panther. Its poison would be instantaneous—one envenomated bite would be the end of Mez. "Lima, out of the way! I need to use my fire!" Gogi yells across the distance.

Lima is too focused on her harrying strikes to hear.

Rumi bounces into view. The tree frog ricochets through the midst of the ant horde, a bright yellow speck within their shining red mass. The eclipse magic gave Rumi power over the wind, and he uses it now to send out a powerful stream of air, right at Lima. She shoots straight into the sky, whirling in surprise and then delight, little bat wings flung out wide.

Now Gogi can attack. He readies his braid of flame, keeping his focus on the distant fer-de-lance instead of his fire, so he doesn't get dazzled by his own magic. Then he extends the line of flame, smoking the air, the searing braided rope gaining speed as it whips toward the viper. The snake rears back, mouth open wide, fangs extended, while Mez, totally vulnerable to its deadly strike, helps her sister to her feet.

A roar starts up between Gogi's ears. It's hard to keep his accuracy up over this distance, and the fire is smoking the air over the fer-de-lance's head. Pointless. Tongue between his gritted teeth, Gogi adjusts his wrists so his hands point the flame lower, lower—there!

He traces a line down the snake's head, until the fire is aimed right into its open mouth. The snake looks up in surprise, smoke clouding its features, and then drops to the ground, still.

Bitter figs! Gogi thinks. *I've killed it.* He's never killed anything before. Well, except for a bunch of bugs and a worm, but those were mostly accidents. His concentration lapses, and the fire drops.

Mez whirls, clearly scenting the burning snake, then sees its lifeless body. She looks up and around before she spots Gogi. Then she yelps and starts digging through her fur, trying to bite the ants away. More and more of them are swarming. They're all over Mez and Chumba, and even the bright yellow speck of Rumi has ants crawling over it.

Gogi shakes the sight of the lifeless viper from his mind as he bounds down the tree, plummeting sheer drops before catching onto a branch with a foot or his tail to swing around, controlling his descent so he lands beside his friends. Immediately he sends smoke up through his fur. Made groggy by the fumes, the ants around him quiet and go motionless.

Still, there are plenty more arriving, and Gogi can't smoke them all. "Come to my side!" he cries. "We have to get out of here!"

Mez and Chumba limp to him, while Gogi wades them through the sea of smoking ants, toward Rumi. Gogi's own smoke makes him choke and gag, makes his eyes water. He can only hope he's kept his bearings, that he's leading them out of the army of ants and not deeper into it.

He sees a bright yellow shape in front of him, and plucks Rumi up from the swarm. "Are you okay, friend?" he asks.

"Best as I can be under these conditions," Rumi says, voice trembling and eyes streaming tears. He holds tight to Gogi's elbow fur. "Ouch. This smoke is so painful on amphibian skin."

Gogi turns his lope into a sprint. "Sorry about the smoke. We'll get you out of here as soon as we can."

He hears Lima's voice, high above: "Straight ahead, but curve left a little, Gogi!"

Panting heavily, he continues across the ant horde, his scurrying feet and hands crunching insects with every heavy step. The ants start to thin. "Just a little more," Lima calls, "then a stream cuts through. That should slow the ants for a while."

Before he realizes it, Gogi is knee-deep in water. Rumi bounds off him and into the stream, making gurgling sighs of relief as he washes the smoke residue off.

"You there, Mez and Chumba?" Gogi calls as he sloshes forward.

"Right with you," Mez says.

"Ouch, those ant bites *hurt*!" Chumba says.

Gogi pauses at the far bank and turns around. The line of ants has stopped at the bank. Maybe they're waiting for further direction—direction that won't be coming, of course, now that the companions have defeated the fer-de-lance and hoatzin. They're safe. For now.

Gogi ducks under the water, running his hands over his fur to get any remaining ants off. Mez and Chumba do the same, dragging themselves out at the far bank and shaking the water free. "I'm going to have some really spectacular ant welts," Mez says. "But with a little of Lima's help, I'm going to be okay. Thanks to you guys."

"Sorry I was getting in the way there," Lima says. "I didn't realize you could do that pretty flame-rope thing. That was amazing! I just wish you'd warned me first."

"You weren't getting in the way," Gogi says. "You kept Mez alive, going after the viper like that. But yes, we should definitely work on battle strategies ahead of time."

"I think the hoatzin survived," Chumba says. "I saw it staggering away while we were fleeing."

"I can't look," Gogi says, covering his eyes with a furry hand. "Is the fer-de-lance . . . ?"

"Dead as a rock," Lima says.

Gogi shudders. "That's a first for me."

"It had to be done," Chumba says quietly. "You'll get used to it."

They huddle at the bank, looking out at the milling ant army on the other side while they catch their breath.

"I don't know if you were close enough to see, but both the hoatzin and the fer-de-lance had a ring of ants around their head. Like a circlet. All the ants were connected, one to the next, and they walked—into their ears and out," Mez says.

"I thought that's what I saw," Rumi says. "Like the ants were walking into their brains."

Mez shudders.

"Whatever the reason, it's terrible what they're doing to Caldera," Chumba says. "It will take years for the forest to grow back."

"*If* it grows back," Gogi adds glumly.

"And assuming we can find a way to get rid of the ants at all," Mez adds.

"Not to rush us," Rumi says, "but the ants will eventually find a spot where they can cross the river to our side, even without those traitors helping them."

They steal through the jungle, going far enough that the ants are out of view, and they're all hidden from sight. Something about the leafy spot is familiar to Gogi, but he can't quite remember why.

"We need to get going," Rumi continues. "But where?"

"Did you get any more information from your eavesdropping?" Gogi asks Mez.

She pants for a moment, still catching her breath, then nods. "I was. It's clear that those two were working as henchmen for the Ant Queen. They didn't seem at all happy about working for her, but apparently she's been allowing some animals to serve her in return for their survival, to assist the ant hordes as they make their way across Caldera."

Lima shakes her head. "Despicable."

It doesn't seem as clear to Gogi. If the alternative is being stung to death by ants, or seeing their family die, he can see why animals would go along with the Ant Queen. "So the ants are just headed across Caldera, from east to west, destroying everything in their path?" he prompts Mez.

"You don't have to make it sound *so* bleak," Mez says dryly. "But yes."

"And if they've made it here, they've already overrun half of Caldera. It's hopeless," Rumi says.

"Not exactly," Mez says. "Here's the one useful thing I found out. They kept saying that they were at the 'target location.' They're on a special mission."

"A special mission?" Rumi asks, still looking dejected

but with a new gleam of curiosity to his eyes. "What's their special mission?"

Mez's ears droop. She looks from one of her friends to the next, obviously reluctant to say what she's about to say.

"What is it, Mez?" Gogi says gently. "We can take it."

"Okay, here goes, then. They're here to destroy the eclipse-born. To destroy us."

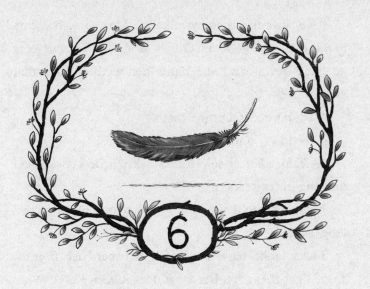

Twenty-Two Nights Until the Eclipse

LIMA GULPS. "THEY'RE going after . . . us, particularly? Like, not just because we happen to be in the way, but because we're their target?"

Mez nods.

"Oh," Lima says, bat nose wriggling. "That's not good."

"Definitely not good," Chumba adds.

"I think it gets even worse," Gogi says, fingers tapping on his lips. "How could they know we were going to be here? I mean, it's not like all the animals across Caldera knew that we were meeting up here."

"No, just the shadowwalkers," Mez says, her ears perking as she ponders Gogi's words. Then her ears go back down, and she bares her teeth. "Does that mean . . . ?"

"It can't be," Chumba gasps.

"Afraid so," Gogi adds.

"Afraid *what* is so?" Lima asks, little clawed feet dancing in frustration.

"Someone told the traitors what our plans were," Gogi says.

Lima looks back and forth between her friends. "Yes. I got that part. But what does it *mean*?"

"It means that one of the shadowwalkers has turned to the Ant Queen's side," Mez says.

"Oh," Lima says. Her face crumples. Then it fills with fire. "How *could* they? I'll show them! If I get my wings around them, just wait to see what I do. Why, I'll—"

"Okay, okay," Mez says. "Let's keep thinking about what to do *next*. The Ant Queen knows about our plan to meet up, but that doesn't mean she knows anything more than that."

"That's because *we* don't know any more than that," Chumba grumbles.

"Yeah, hard to think of that as a positive," Gogi adds.

"Let's keep looking forward, that's all I'm trying to say," Mez says. "At least we know that none of *us* gave away our plan to the Ant Queen, right?"

"Right," Mez says.

"Right," Chumba says at the same time as Lima. They look at each other, eyes wide in excitement. "Jinx!"

"And I didn't," Gogi says. He waits for Rumi to add his voice, but Rumi is staring off into the treetops. He hasn't been listening.

"Rumi?" Gogi asks.

"Oh, sorry!" Rumi says, snapping to attention. "No, of course I didn't turn against my fellow shadowwalkers. Why are you even implying such a thing?"

"We weren't," Mez says quietly.

"No one else got all defensive about it," Lima points out.

"I'm not, it's just that I—I'm a little distracted—" Rumi's gaze flicks to the canopy again.

"Rumi, is this at all related to the 'misunderstood' friend you were talking about earlier?" Gogi asks. "I'm sure this all has a reasonable explanation. Why don't you try telling us?" Gogi sits as low as possible, even if it means making his haunches dirty, so Rumi doesn't think he's staring down at him. It's got to be hard for the little frog, everyone literally talking down to him all the time.

"Oh my," Rumi says, his yellow fingers dancing nervously. "Maybe I can tell you about the magical lens first? Trigonometry is considerably simpler than matters of the heart."

Mez forces her lips back down, obviously trying to make Rumi less nervous than he is. She's not quite pulling it off. Mez is all inadvertently exposed teeth, making the most menacing smile Gogi's ever seen. "Why don't we go to that camp Rumi set up for us and talk about it there, where no enemies might overhear?" Mez asks. "I think you said it was somewhere around here, right, Rumi?"

Rumi perks up. "The camp? Why, we're in it!"

"*This* is the camp?" Chumba asks, lifting a paw from a puddle. A string of green muck dangles from it.

"I thought it was perfect for all of us," Rumi says. "But I'm realizing it's maybe more amphibian-perfect than mammal-perfect."

"I think it's just fine here," Lima offers, smacking mosquitoes between her teeth.

"So, about the 'lens'—" Rumi starts.

"Rumi," Mez growls, "if you don't tell us about this mysterious friend of yours right now, I'm going to get angry."

"I'd say *more* angry would be more accurate," Lima corrects, swallowing hard.

"Let Rumi tell us what he has to tell us in the order he wants to," Gogi says. "I'm sure we'll see the reason for all this very soon, right?"

The frog nods, takes up a twig, and begins to sketch in the mud. Gogi tries to figure out the lines, but can't make sense of them yet. "I learned from the carvings that, long ago, the two-legs developed a magical lens to harness the power of sunlight and moonlight."

"The removable carvings of the sun and moon that we found in the ziggurat!" Gogi says.

Rumi continues to scratch in the ground. "Right, just like those."

"We thought they were destroyed when the ziggurat collapsed," Mez says. "Did they survive after all?"

Rumi shakes his head. "There's no sign of them, I'm afraid. No, the lens is a similar magic, but in its purest, most powerful form. It appears the two-legs were able to melt sand and turn it clear through their magic, and install this clear stone in a frame. It seems to concentrate light."

"That's some cool magic," Lima says.

"Totally!" agrees Chumba.

"Yes!" Rumi says, face lighting up. "The carvings give some indication of the lens's massive power. Here's what they said." He puffs himself up and takes on an oratorical tone. "'Pour night into sun, and take away life. Pour sun into night, and create it.'"

"Ooh," Lima says. "That's got a good ring to it!"

"This lens was kept hidden away at the edge of Caldera," Rumi says. "When the Ant Queen attacked, ages ago, it appears to have caught the two-legs by surprise, and they were trapped at the Ziggurat of the Sun and Moon without the lens. So they improvised the carvings, which is why they were able to imprison the Ant Queen, but not destroy her. The lens would have gone all the way. It seems to redistribute all the magic contained in the eclipses, for good or for evil."

"We need that lens," Mez says.

"And by the time the lunar eclipse comes around," Gogi adds.

"Twenty-three nights away," Rumi says. "Well, twenty-two now, I guess."

"So, where is the lens?" Lima asks excitedly, hovering in the air so she can get a better view of whatever Rumi's scratching in the mud. "Is that a map?"

"This?" Rumi asks in surprise, dropping the stick. "No, I'm just doodling because I'm nervous."

"What have you found out about the lens's location?" Gogi asks.

Rumi shrugs. "Not very much, sadly. I assume that Caldera has very many edges. It was impossible to ascertain a more precise direction."

"The lens could be behind enemy lines," Chumba says.

Mez nods. "Or even in the Ant Queen's possession already."

"Do we just pick a direction and start going?" Lima proposes. "Like, find any edge and cross our wings that there's a lens there?"

"I hope it doesn't come to that," Gogi says.

Mez's nose twitches. "Hold," she says quietly. "Something is near."

"Is it that nasty hoatzin?" Lima chirps.

"Shh!" Mez says, slinking her body low to the ground.

Gogi peers around, looking to see what's caught Mez's attention. She's got a panther's senses, and she can pick up on minute signals that breeze right by a capuchin like him. What he has that Mez doesn't, though, is a constant sense of where his friends are and what they're feeling—and Rumi is pressing himself into the mud, as if to hide away, even as he focuses his attention on the treetops. "Rumi, Rumi, what's going on?" Gogi whispers.

But Rumi doesn't answer. All he does is say "Oh no, oh no, " over and over as he hides under the mud. Then, even more quietly, his words gurgling up: "He's here."

"*Who's* here?" Gogi asks, voice rising despite Mez's caution that they should all be quiet.

Then, with a crashing sound from above, he has his answer.

7

CRASHING BRANCHES ARE never good. Crashing branches mean monkeys falling or snakes attacking or any number of terrible things. The ruckus from above sends Gogi scurrying into the bushes, Mez and Chumba tailing right after, Rumi burrowing deeper into the mud as Lima flees to a distant tree.

The branches stop shaking. Cautiously, quietly as he can, Gogi presses down two spiny branches so that he can peer out.

There, standing insolently in the center of the clearing, is a bird. A scarlet macaw, one whose imperious expression Gogi knows all too well.

Sky.

The parrot struts through the clearing in his ungainly way, shifting from claw to claw and using his beak to lift himself up the side of a fallen log so he can approach Rumi.

Teeth bared, Gogi charges out of the bush. Once he gets his hands on that macaw, he'll, he'll . . . well, he'll figure it out once he gets there.

Sky flinches when he sees Gogi charging and then raises his wings, exposing the most vulnerable parts of him. He speaks slowly. "Please. I only want to talk. Rumi promised you would hear me out!"

Rumi promised what now?! Gogi glares in the direction of his friend, who has buried himself so far in the mud that only his two big black eyes are visible.

A branch creaks, probably from Mez or Chumba stalking forward, somewhere out of sight.

"Don't attack!" Sky says. "I know you think I was on Auriel's side, but I was betrayed as much as you were!"

"Someone told the Ant Queen about our plan to meet here," Lima squeaks from within the canopy. "And it was clearly you, traitor bird."

"I don't know what you're talking about," Sky says. "Really I don't."

Suddenly Chumba appears a few feet away, stalking silently out of the brush, body low and tail straight back, ears pressed against her head so they won't get snagged by a beak or a talon when she strikes.

"Rumi, tell them!" Sky caws shrilly. "You promised they wouldn't attack!"

"I didn't get a chance to tell them much yet," Rumi gurgles from his hiding place in the mud. "I'm sorry!"

"Tell us *what*?" Gogi says. He holds his hands out, licks of flame dancing over his fingers. He doesn't imagine the fight will be too difficult, if that's what it comes to. A macaw may have a sharp beak, but it's not made for out-and-out combat. And Sky's eclipse magic—divination—won't do him a lot of good in combat.

"Tell them to stop," Sky caws even more shrilly. "Rumi!"

"Stop it, guys," Rumi gurgles as he pulls himself out of the mud. "For my sake. I gave my word."

Chumba continues to stalk forward. Gogi is sure Mez is beside her, though he can't see the invisible panther. Sky was second-in-command to Auriel, the boa who nearly constricted Mez to death. The macaw should expect no forgiveness from the panther sisters. It will be up to Gogi to stop the bloodshed. "Hold!" he says. "Mez and Chumba, stop!"

Chumba goes motionless, ears cocked. She turns to the empty space next to her and holds up a paw.

The empty space growls. "You're lucky I've got a softie for a sister, bird."

Sky tilts his head. "Thank you."

Rumi wriggles all the way out of the mud, rubbing his hands over his yellow-spotted body to clear it. He concentrates his gaze on Gogi, probably expecting the capuchin to have the most sympathy. Gogi doesn't know what to think. Sky supported Auriel until the end, even warning the enemy that the panthers were about to attack him. The companions assumed that Sky perished during the fall of the ziggurat—but apparently he didn't.

Rumi hops over to Sky and stands up on his back legs, arms outstretched, as if to stop anyone from attacking the scarlet macaw. It looks silly, but Gogi's touched that Rumi is willing to put his life on the line to defend Sky. "When Sky announced himself, I was as suspicious as you all are right now," Rumi says, "but then he convinced me. He was as surprised by it as we were."

Sky cocks his head even further, so it's almost sideways. "In macaw families, only the first two chicks to hatch are fed. The rest of the hatchlings are there as insurance, and are left to die after they are born. I was the third to hatch in my clutch. If Auriel hadn't rescued me, I'd have perished. I owed him my life. That's no exaggeration."

"Okay," Lima says, "but didn't it make you question

him a little after he opened the ziggurat and sucked everyone inside, kicking and screaming?"

Sky nods. "Of course it did. But you all took an instant dislike to me, and shut me out entirely. I don't know if you realized how hard it was for the rest of the shadowwalkers to get the attention of your tight little group. Auriel was the only one who showed any sign of caring about me. I wanted to be the same to him. Staying loyal to him as long as I did was a mistake, I know that now, but I hope you can understand why."

"I actually believe you. But none of this means that you're coming with us," Mez growls. She shimmers into view, in full attack position, crouched just one body length away from Sky. "We'll have enough to deal with fighting the Ant Queen, without having to keep one eye on a treacherous squawkface the whole time."

Mez takes a step forward, and Sky startles. He flaps into the air and then forces himself to land again, holding his trembling wings out in a surrender pose. As much as Sky's playing at coolness, he's terrified. "You've gotten very good at your invisibility, Mez. Remember how I helped you discover your power?"

"Only so Auriel could choose who to constrict next," Mez growls.

"I didn't know that was what he was doing with the

information," Sky says. "You'll just have to trust me on that."

"Trust you? No chance," Mez says.

Giving up on Mez, Sky focuses one glittering eye on her sister. "Chumba, it is nice to meet you. I helped Mez see a vision of home. It's through that vision that you discovered where your sister was, and came to rescue her."

Chumba nods, gaze darting to Mez. It's true that Sky's vision allowed Chumba to track her sister down, but Chumba's not going to let Sky pit them against each other.

Gogi rubs his palms together. "So, Sky, I think that Mez is right, that we shouldn't—"

"Gogi!" Lima shrieks.

"What? What?" Gogi shrieks, whirling around to inspect his tail. It's always wrapping itself around things and getting him in trouble. Once he even discovered he was tickling a large caiman, quite accidentally.

"Your fire!"

Gogi looks down to see he has flames sprouting from each palm. He extinguishes them. "Yipes, sorry! I've been working on my impulse control, I promise. But then . . . sometimes I forget."

"You were saying?" Sky prompts, cocking his head in the other direction, looking at Gogi curiously.

"Yes, um, right. I was saying that . . . Oh, now I

remember. I was saying that . . . no, that can't be it."

"How Mez was right that . . . ," Chumba prompts.

"Oh yeah! Mez is right that you shouldn't travel with us. I'm sorry, but no. No way."

"Who said that I wanted to travel with you?" Sky replies haughtily. "Maybe you should be the ones asking *me* to come along with *you*."

"That's rich," Lima says.

"You guys should know that Sky—"

"—has information that would be useful to you," Sky says, cutting Rumi off.

"You see, this is the thing that made it hard to be friends with you," Lima says, flitting down so she's right in front of Sky. "It's not that we were excluding you, it's that you do this I-have-to-control-all-information-all-the-time routine."

Sky sighs. Well, he makes a sort of wheezy caw that Gogi assumes is a sigh. "Here's what I know. I grew up far from here, in a copse of the tallest ironwood trees in all of Caldera. There the macaws come in huge numbers to eat salt from the clay lick, before going back to their home territories. Macaws are very chatty—"

"Except for you, you're not chatty," Lima corrects.

"Yes, except for me," Sky says, cocking his head at the little bat. There's a twinkle in his eyes. It's the first time Gogi has seen Sky show something like warmth toward any animal. The macaw continues. "I know a lot about many parts of Caldera as a result of the macaws' many conversations happening all around me. That could be the wellspring of my magical power to divine. I often think our powers are related to our innermost hearts." He cuts an eye to Mez, whose invisibility, they all know, reflects how she felt in her home family—her cousin Mist got all of Aunt Usha's attention.

Gogi looks down at his hands, which just a moment ago were filled with accidental fire. *This* represents him? How does that work out?

"One of the conversations I heard was among the green parakeets of the north. They talked about an animal that lives near them, an animal older than any other in Caldera. She lives in a sluggish river, where she's been alive so long that—now it starts to sort of be rumor—she was around when the Ant Queen first attacked the two-legs. She might have witnessed their extinction. There's a chance she knows where they kept the lens. If anyone would, it would be her. The boto."

"What's a boto?" Lima asks.

"There's a 'chance'?" Mez asks at the same time, kneading her claws into the mud.

"Jinx!" Lima exclaims. But Mez is definitely not playing.

"Yes," Sky says. "Only a chance. But what else do

we have to go on? Believe me, Mez, I understand why you wouldn't like me. *I* don't like me. I've long ago given up any desire to be something as simple as 'liked.' But the boto is an important source of wisdom. And a little dose of wisdom seems to be exactly what this ragtag group needs."

"There was no need to add 'ragtag' there!" Lima squeaks. "That's just rude!"

"So there we have it," Sky says, shrugging his wings. "Leave me here alone, if you don't want me with you. Or take my life if you like. I'm already living on borrowed time; I knew it would come due eventually. Maybe that time is now."

"Now, now, no need to go there," Gogi says.

"We're not going to kill you," Mez grumbles. "Even if we might want to."

"'Pour night into sun, and take away life,'" Gogi recites, trying to remember what Rumi told him about the two-legs' carvings. "That could be our hope of stopping the Ant Queen. We need the lens to do that, and the boto might know where the lens is. It's not much to go on, but at least it's something. But before we go dashing off to this 'boto' lady, Sky, I've got a question. Were you there a year ago, when we discussed reconvening at the ruins?"

"He wasn't there!" Lima chirps. "Remember? It

was just me and you and Mez and Chumba and Rumi and Banu the sloth and Calisto the trogon—oh! Do you mean Sky might have been snooping?"

"Sky was—" Rumi starts.

"—I can speak for myself, thank you," Sky says. "I was not there. I did not hear your plan. Rumi let me know about it, once he knew he could trust me. But that was the first I heard of it."

Rumi stares furiously at the ground.

"Okay, then," Gogi says. He's not sure if he believes Sky, but he doesn't know how to get to the truth right now. He'll have to talk to Rumi alone sometime soon. "Sky, do you think you could just tell us where this 'boto' is?"

Sky shakes his head. "The location of her watery lair defies explanation, I'm afraid. I'd be relying half on instinct to get there. Magnetic navigation lines in the atmosphere and such. Bird stuff."

"Ooh!" Rumi says, perking up for the first time in this whole conversation. "That sounds very interesting!"

"Somehow I figured as much," Gogi says. He looks around at his friends, gauging their reactions to this latest development. Mez is usually the one to make decisions, but the weirdness of the situation seems to have scrambled her—she's looking at *Gogi* to decide. He appears to be in charge of matters of the heart. Maybe this level of responsibility is what comes along with being a twelfth. He combs his hair down flat on top of his head and tries to strike a heroic pose. "Okay, then. We're all off to the boto's lair. Sky, tell us how we start."

Thirteen Nights Until the Eclipse

"I'D NEVER HAVE predicted something like this could happen!" Gogi says, looking out in astonishment.

A series of boulders emerges from the forest floor, and they've made for a river of land that's exposed to direct sun. No tree cover! The companions take advantage of the odd formation to spend a long break lying out on the warmed stone, relishing the rare treat of open light. Well, they all do except Lima, who gets anxious in full sun. And Chumba, who's asleep, since she can't shadowwalk like the others.

It's been a long journey, from the dark and muggy

region surrounding the ruins out through the mangrove swamps, then past the mosquito-clogged low country (well, a little less mosquito-clogged, now that Rumi and Lima have come through and eaten a few hundred of the little bloodsuckers), then up along the salty river until it widened into salt flats and now this canyon of sunlight. Those trees lucky enough to have sprouted along the salt flats' edges are able to catch much more sunlight than their neighbors, and have grown to towering heights, sending dappled light along the ground. It's all quite lovely.

For all his talk of feeling left out, Sky seems not to want anything to do with the others. He surges forward, soaring over the terrain, disappearing for a long time before he appears again at the top of a tree, staring down at them with an imperious eye before heading off.

"I guess he's leading us the right way?" Gogi grumbles.

"I wish we didn't have to trust that bird," Mez says. "We got tricked by Auriel before, and Sky was right by his side. It could be happening all over again."

"I had many long conversations with Sky during the past year," Rumi says from his perch on top of Mez's head. "I'm not sure why he's refusing to travel alongside us now. I guess crowds make him anxious? Or he's worried that we'll snub him again?"

"It's hard to think of us as a crowd," Mez says, peering up at the trees dwarfing them on either side. They seem like a very small traveling party indeed.

"Sky's a prickly one, that's for sure," Rumi says. "But I know for a fact that he's furious about what Auriel did to us, and that carries over to the Ant Queen."

"Or he's very good at pretending," Mez says.

"We'll keep alert," Gogi says. "But it's not like we have a lot of other options. Following Sky is the best we've got."

"Enough resting!" comes a harsh caw from the top of the tallest tree ahead. "I have glimpsed the boto. She has just woken up and will be preparing to hunt. If we don't want to lose her, we need to get to her lair soon."

"Got it, Sky!" Gogi calls up, waving, but Sky is already gone. "As soon as the Veil falls and Chumba wakes, we'll get going!" he finishes to himself.

Once Chumba is yawning and smacking her jaws, they prepare for the next stretch of their journey. "You ready to try our trick?" Rumi asks Gogi.

"Yes," Gogi says. "Though I want to officially announce that potentially setting fire to all of you guys freaks me out."

"Very understandable," Lima says. "It freaks me out too."

"Remember, the smallest tingle of fire you can

manage," Rumi says. "Think light more than heat."

"Basically, you want me to have more self-control than I've ever had. This is the worst test of monkey brain ever," Gogi grumbles to himself. Then, clasping his hands tightly over his chest, he closes his eyes. *Subtle, subtle, not too much, not too much, you can do this, Gogi.*

He imagines little grooming fingers on his eyes, Alzo's fingers tenderly brushing his eyelids. Then he warms those fingers up and spreads them out, farther and farther.

When he opens his eyes, the night is illuminated. Just a little. It's like everything is under a ruddy moon, the edges sharpened and warmed.

"Everything looks so pretty!" Rumi says, clapping suction-cupped fingers.

"It's pretty good, if I might say so myself!" Gogi says, pivoting and looking at the red-rimmed world around him. "Just enough light to take the edge off the darkness."

"Don't get excited and incinerate us all, okay?" Lima asks.

"Yep. On it. It's not tiring at all. I think after a while I'll be able to do this without even thinking about it."

"That's sort of what I'm worried about," Lima says, swooping out of the shadows to perch on Mez's shoulder. "Anyway, what even *is* a boto?"

"Maybe it's something tasty," Mez says, licking her chops as she starts out.

"Mez," Gogi warns, "I know it's been a while since you got to hunt, but the boto has been alive for hundreds of years, and is here to *inform us*, not to *be food*. Don't kill the oldest creature in Caldera. That would be really bad."

"Calm down, calm down, I'm not going to eat our potential savior."

"If the boto has a friend, though . . . ," Chumba says. The panther sisters descend into a fit of giggles.

Gogi shakes his head. Carnivores are weird.

Sky doesn't come back into view, but he keeps cawing from somewhere up ahead, leading them onward.

"Am I wrong for wanting just a few more specifics from him?" Lima asks.

"I know, I know," Gogi says. "But once we meet the boto, we'll have a lot more information. We'll have more than just Sky's word to go on."

Outlined by Gogi's light, the rocky canyon broadens, until it joins a stream and becomes a slushy field, coated with furry algae and pond stink. Rumi and Lima are delighted, rolling in the goo and frolicking about. Gogi, Mez, and Chumba are less thrilled, delicately picking their way along the edge. "It's a little drier over here," Mez calls. Gogi and Chumba come over, only to get mired again as soon as they've gone a few paces.

"How much farther is the boto lair?" Gogi calls into the trees ahead.

"Faster!" is Sky's reply.

"He's just so charming," Gogi says under his breath.

The river of grass broadens, and there's the muted sound of falling water ahead. "Not another waterfall," Mez says. "Remember our last time with one of those, Rumi and Lima? Let's hope it goes better this time."

"You mean let's hope that owls don't attack us and we don't wind up falling a few thousand feet?" Rumi says. "Sounds good!"

One more rotten fallen tree, one more mucky pond, and then the waterfall comes into view. It's a modest one, not more than ten feet or so high, ending in a misty lagoon. The slow river splits around the waterfall's base, becoming a basin of murk, rimmed by Gogi's curtain of light.

From behind the brown mist of the waterfall comes a stranger's voice. "Sky, they have arrived?"

"Wait, Sky's already started talking to it?" Mez growls, pulling up short.

A red flap, and then Sky appears—from behind them. Like he's been spying on them for a while. "Calm, calm. I introduced myself to the boto just a short time ago. I wanted to make sure that she did not go off

hunting for fish before we had a chance to speak to her."

"Yes," comes the voice from behind the curtain of brown mist. "I do not wish to tarry too long answering silly questions from youngsters."

"Will you reveal yourself to us?" Sky asks in the direction of the boto's voice.

"Of course I will. One thing you learn at my age is not to stand on formalities."

Gogi watches the curtain of mist, waiting for it to part. But it just continues to fall. Cicadas drone loudly in the clearing, and he starts feeling a little light-headed. Chumba and Mez are panting, and Lima's wings are droopy. They haven't seen water clean enough to drink in some time.

"Where *is* this dodo?" Chumba asks out of the side of her mouth.

"*Boto*," Mez corrects under her breath.

"I used to be known as a river dolphin," the voice comes again. "Though the two-legged creatures that once called me that are long dead."

"Oh!" Lima says in surprise. "There you are!"

With a gurgling sound, the muck before them shifts and the boto—at least that's what Gogi assumes he's seeing—appears, half in and half out of the water. She's a strange-looking fish, about the size of Mez and Chumba, with broad flippers, a bulbous sort of head, a long snout like an anteater's, and no gills that Gogi can see. She's got a hole on the top of her head! Strangest of all is that where her body isn't covered in gooey mud, it's pink.

"Oh my gosh, you're so ugly-cute. I want to take you home and keep you!" Lima squeals.

The boto was about to say something else, but she closes her long-toothed mouth.

"Please forgive us," Sky says, bowing and laying his wings across the ground deferentially. "We mean no offense."

"I've never been called 'ugly-cute' before," the boto says. "Not in all my thousand-odd years." She pauses, taking in the sight of the shadowwalkers, then sinks a little in the mud. Gogi worries that she's going to leave, but then she speaks again: "I think I kind of like it."

"I'm surprised no one's ever called you that before!" Lima says, hopping to a large branch sticking out of the swamp in front of the boto. "I think you're adorable. I'm a bat that flies during the day. Have you ever seen one of those before? It's pretty cool too, don't you think?"

"You've really been alive for a thousand years?" Gogi asks the boto. He counts on his fingers. "Even putting all our ages together, I don't think it makes a thousand."

"It makes more like ten," Rumi says patiently.

"Oh yes," says the boto. "I've been alive at least that

long. Though to be honest I've lost track of the years."

"You are said to be the oldest animal in all of Caldera," Sky says, getting up onto his claws and turning to one side so that he can look at the boto better. Predators like Mez and Lima have eyes that look forward, the better to train on their prey, while herbivores like Sky have eyes on either side of their head, the better to see a wide area around them. Sky's are unusually extreme. Gogi realizes it's part of what makes having a conversation with him hard—it always seems he's looking at you sideways.

"We are hoping that you might help us, great boto," Sky continues. "A horrific menace plagues the rainforest."

The boto ignores him and keeps her focus on Lima. "You're right, little bat. I've never seen one of your kind up and about during the day."

"Oh yes, I'm a bat, for sure. And I get some funny looks for dayflying, let me tell you. But I can be up during the day because we're shadowwalkers, all of us, well, except Chumba, but she's great anyway, you should really get to know her. Shadowwalking means we were born during the solar eclipse, and now Rumi, that tree frog over there, has discovered that there's going to be a *lunar* eclipse in thirteen days. An ellipse eclipse. The next time the moon is full—you can look up in the sky whenever you want to keep track. We're hoping to use the magical energies of the lunar eclipse to put a stop to the Ant Queen once and for all. She's an ancient evil that seems pretty much invulnerable—maybe you've heard of her?"

The boto nods, a slight smile on her face. "Yes, I've heard of the Ant Queen."

"So apparently there's this lens?" Lima prattles on, gesticulating wildly with her wings. "That the two-legs developed to harness the magical power of the eclipse? And it's missing? Hey, why does your head have that huge bump on it? And why do you have a hole on your back? Does it hurt? Why are you pink? I've never seen a pink animal before that hadn't just been born."

"Lima, shh," Gogi says, with an embarrassed smile toward the boto. "One question at a time."

The boto looks up, making herself appear slightly cross-eyed. "This bump? It's for my sonar. Just like your echolocation, little bat."

"Oh wow, you can echolocate too! Cool!"

"But as a river dolphin, you must send out a quieter sound than Lima does, because otherwise you'd get too much information back to process," Rumi says. "The water is so clogged with debris that you probably get enough from just a few feet's worth of data."

"Who said that?" asks the boto, head swiveling.

Rumi waves a yellow hand.

"You're quite right, little tree frog," the boto says. "That's quite a mind, for such a small brain."

"Um, thanks, I guess?" Rumi says.

"So, this lens—" Gogi starts to say.

"—and the pinkness? Why are you pink?" Lima interrupts.

"We don't start out pink," the boto says, "but as the days go by, we bump into many things, and the abrasions cause our skin to turn pink. I am very old, so I am very pink."

"Your honorable boto-ness," Sky says, "forgive my being insistent, but it is very important that we obtain this lens before it is too late."

"And what about you?" the boto asks Lima. "What color are you? I see mostly shapes, not too much color."

"Black's my color!" Lima says. "I never really thought about why. I guess it's good for me to match the night sky, since night is when I hunt. That way it's hard for the bugs to see me."

The boto nods her bulbous head. "That's a very likely explanation, in my considerable experience."

"The lens, please—" Mez tries.

"In due time," the boto says, lifting one of her broad fins. "I am not here simply to dole out information to any ignorant young animal who wanders by, you know.

A dayflying bat is something I've never seen, and having lived as long as I have, things I've never seen are in rare supply."

"My sister is a panther who can walk during the day," Chumba offers, flicking her tail toward Mez.

But the boto isn't interested in the panthers. She keeps her attention on Lima. "Tell me, little bat, what do you plan to do with this lens?"

Lima suddenly looks nervous. "I'm not sure *I* am going to do anything with it. I'll leave that to the others. But we've got this plan, that the lens will help stop . . . the . . . We told you this, right? That at the eclipse, that . . . um, help me out, guys, I'm losing track of the details of all this."

"I understand your intentions," the boto says. "But they are riskier than you may know. The lens is the most powerful magical item in the history of our rainforest. It has tremendous destructive power . . . and the power to do tremendous good, too. But the two-legs, as you call them—I know them by their forgotten old name, which is a story for another time—hid it away, knowing its potential to do much evil in the wrong hands. They secreted it so far away, and placed so many safeguards on it, that it was ultimately their doom. Once they needed the lens, they simply couldn't get to it in time."

"Is it too hard to reach even now?" Gogi asks. "The

queen is making her way across Caldera. We might already be too late to stop her."

"Little monkey, who tried to protect me from the bat's many questions, I can see you are the beating heart of your group. Do not worry."

Gogi breathes a sigh of relief.

"If you are meant to die now, there is nothing you can do about it."

"Oh."

"After the two-legs locked her away for centuries, the Ant Queen certainly harbors a hatred of all vertebrates, and if she wants to return the rainforest to a time when there are again only ants and other insects, then there is no stopping her. But yes," the boto says, groaning as she shifts position in the water. "The lens can be reached, though the way is perilous. It is far from here, at the northern edge of Caldera."

"We all grew up thinking that Caldera didn't have an edge," Gogi says.

"Of course it has an edge," says the boto. "Otherwise it wouldn't need to be called Caldera. You only have a name, monkey, because there are other monkeys to talk to you. I don't have a name, because I am the last of my kind. Caldera is called Caldera only because there is something outside it that needs to call it Caldera."

Gogi scratches his head while Rumi nods sagely.

"I've often thought just this," the frog says. "I thought I was the only one!"

"The last time any animal came to me searching for the lens was hundreds of years ago, and she never returned," the boto continues. "The lens is secreted away very high up on the northern cliffs and guarded by a series of riddles. Perhaps it has other sorts of guardians as well. I don't know, because I have never been there. As you can imagine, it is difficult for a dolphin to climb a cliff face."

Gogi chuckles politely. "That was a good joke, boto."

"So only one among us who can fly should make the journey," Sky proposes, preening his chest feathers before looking up.

"Yes, I would agree," the boto says.

"Or one of us who would be good at riddles," Mez says, casting a sideways look at Rumi.

"Also that," the boto says, turning to swim away. "Yes. Good luck!"

"Before you go," Lima asks, "only if you wouldn't mind—do you have anything else to share that might help us? Anything at all?"

"Why, yes," the boto says. "What a smart question, little bat. I believe I do have something to share, for a nice bat like you. I will tell you three things: One, I like to eat just about any kind of fish there is in the whole rainforest. Two, my kind came from a large ocean, eons ago, and were trapped here in the jungle when the land shifted to close us in. Three, there is one other thing you might consider in your quest. You have heard of the Dismal Bog?"

Lima shakes her head. "I'm afraid not."

"Well, there's no reason you should go there. It is the dankest, dreariest, quietest part of all the rainforest. That bog is the only place where there are no ants at all. I haven't seen a single one in all the years I have swum by it."

"Not a single one?" Lima squeaks.

"Not one."

"That's strange," Lima says. "Do you have any idea why?"

"I'm afraid not. But it seems to me that it would be worth investigating."

"I have had visions of the Dismal Bog," Sky says. "Any animal who enters that swamp goes mad. They face their greatest fear, and no one can survive that. No one has ever returned from there. It is a fool's mission."

"Then maybe we should send *you*," Mez says.

Gogi's hands go over his mouth. "Mez!" he gasps.

Sky's feathers ruffle; then he cocks his head to one side, beak open as he rasps. He's laughing, Gogi realizes. "That was actually pretty funny," he clucks.

"What about lyre sap?" Chumba asks.

They turn to look at the young calico panther. Well, the boto doesn't. She just closes her eyes and listens.

"I've been thinking," Chumba goes on. "We give lyre sap to panthers who are raving from fever. It cools the mind and makes them calm again. Remember, back when you were a sick cub, Mez? Maybe lyre sap could help protect us from the bog's effects."

"I know nothing of this lyre sap," the boto says. "But that does not mean it wouldn't be useful. There is much knowledge to be gleaned from the folkways of Caldera's animals. I wish we had more ways to share our information."

"I do too," Mez says. "We shadowwalkers got tricked by Auriel the boa constrictor because we didn't communicate better."

The boto dives, only to come up again with a sloppy reed draped over her nose. "If I don't want to lose my chance to hunt today, I must go. Though it is hard to imagine the Ant Queen desiring an area like this one, I also know that if her plan is to take all of Caldera for her ants, she will not leave anywhere alone. I will hope for your success, slim though the chances are."

"Are you sure you don't want to come with us?" Gogi asks, only realizing the inevitable answer once the words are out of his mouth. "You have a reed on your face, by the way. Just thought you would want to know."

The boto lifts a flipper out of the water. "It would be . . . difficult for an aquatic creature to travel with you. Besides, the years have worn on me, and my energy is low these days. The only thing I have to offer is my knowledge, I'm afraid. I do wish you the best."

She shakes the limp reed free, and then turns to go.

"Wait!" Rumi cries after her. "Please share more of your knowledge! Like what happened to the rest of the botos? How did you pass down what you'd learned over the generations? What *is* outside Caldera?"

But the boto is gone.

The clearing is full of the sounds of the insects around them, the hush of the falling mist, the burbles of fish and snakes slipping through the thick water. The darkening night sets Gogi to feeling even more light-headed, the outlines visible in his soft curtain of light blurring and merging. Wordlessly, the companions back away from the boto's clearing, heading for the cover of the nearby forest.

Once they're nestled away, they huddle. "Priority number one has to be water," Gogi says, running his hands through the fur on his face, sweat-soaked even at nighttime. Mez and Chumba seem to be suffering the most, with their dark fur completely soaked and salt-stained, sticking out in random directions.

"No," Sky says, seemingly unaffected by the heat. "Priority number one is to get the lens."

"Or to investigate the Dismal Bog," Chumba says.

"We have no information whatsoever about the Dismal Bog, except that the ants won't go there, and that it gives creatures hallucinations," Sky scoffs. "That's next to nothing to go on."

"No animal has returned successfully from searching out the lens," Mez growls. "So there's also that."

"The odds might be long," Gogi says, wringing his hands. He wants to cheer everyone up, but he isn't sure how. "But that doesn't mean we won't succeed! We just have to choose the best path to take." He wishes his words didn't sound so hollow.

"You're assuming we take only one of these two courses," Rumi says from his spot at the edge of a puddle. He's got his arms out over the side, keeping his body deep within the recesses of a low-hanging frond. "Statistics would say that, when the odds are this long, we might be better off trying twice to make lightning strike, rather than only slightly increasing our odds of just one shot."

"Hmm, I'm sure that's an interesting point, Rumi . . . ," Gogi says, scratching behind his ear.

"You didn't follow any of that, did you?" Rumi asks.

"Well, not *precisely*, no."

"He's saying that it's better to hedge our bets and split into two groups," Mez says. "And I think I agree."

"We can't all go to the same place anyway," Lima says. "We have to fly to the lens. So that team has to be me and . . ." Her voice trails off as she realizes the implications of what she's saying. "Sky."

Gogi's not sure what he thinks. It would be a very unexpected pairing.

Sky must feel the same way. "It strikes me that having a creature that could fly with you—and a bat, no less—would be more useful in a bog."

"Are you saying bats are creepy and spooky?" Lima says. "Because that's a cliché I'm definitely ready to see put to rest."

"Sky's got a good point," Gogi says. "If anyone's going to be able to resist a depressing bog, it's you."

Lima smiles. "Oh. That's a much better way of putting it!"

"I should go and investigate the lens all by myself," Sky says.

"No!" Gogi, Mez, and Chumba say simultaneously.

"It seems like my past will always haunt me," Sky says, his voice low and unreadable. "I was foolish to expect you to ever forgive me."

"Sky," Gogi says, placing a hesitant hand on the macaw's wing, "it's not like that." *But maybe it is,* Gogi thinks. *Maybe there are things that no good deed can make up for.*

"Even if you all don't trust Sky yet, *I* do. Let me go with him," Rumi offers.

Sky looks at him, head cocked, then nods. "I would appreciate the company."

"Think about it," Rumi says. "I know the most lore about the two-legs, and I'm good at riddles and puzzles. I'm really small, too, even lighter than Lima, so I could ride on Sky's back no problem. Maybe I could use my wind powers to speed us along!"

"A literal tailwind," Sky says, a hint of humor in his voice.

"It's not a bad plan," Mez says grudgingly.

"I hate the idea of splitting up at all," Lima says, hopping over to land beside Rumi.

"Me too," Rumi says, with a side eye toward Sky. "But I think this might be our best course."

Once again, Gogi feels like Sky and Rumi have something going on between them that he can't figure out. But how to broach it? "Agreed," Gogi says. "Will we meet back at the ruins once—ow!" He leaps to his feet, swatting at his behind. "The Ant Queen! She's here! Or wait, no, that's just a termite, false alert, sorry, guys."

"So," Mez says, "once we've gotten the lens and

figured out whatever we can from the Dismal Bog, how do we all meet back up?"

"Don't forget about *my* magical power, panther," Sky says. "As Chumba knows from when I alerted her to Mez's danger, I have the limited power to send visions. Though it may be only in dreams and thoughts, we can be in touch."

"Please send those strange dreams to the others," Lima says. "I'm not interested in having you rummaging around in my head."

"Very well," Sky says, beak clenched but with a glint of humor in his eyes. "I will do my best."

Twelve Nights Until the Eclipse

MIDNIGHT DOES NOTHING to peel back the heat of the day, unfortunately—they are sweating and panting even in darkness. Lima goes off to scout out water. So it is Gogi, Mez, and Chumba who are left to say good-bye to Sky and Rumi.

"Pay attention to the night sky," Rumi says, pointing up at the stars. "The lunar eclipse will happen once the moon is full again. We have a dozen nights to get the lens."

The macaw stretches his wings out and closes them, stretches and closes, limbering up for the long flight ahead. Rumi, on Sky's back, roots through the flight feathers until he can get a grip on the softer down beneath, and holds it tightly in his fingers. "It will be a long trip. Are you sure you can hold on to me without straining?" Sky asks.

"I'll be okay," Rumi says. "I've got some pretty sticky fingers and toes."

"Sky," Gogi says sternly. "You'll keep checking on him, right? Don't go charging off for too long at once. Take rests."

"Don't worry," Sky says. "I'll look out for our friend Rumi."

"Thanks," Gogi says. He doesn't feel good about the group splitting up—monkey instinct is always to keep the tribe together—but he can see no better way forward. "I'll miss you guys so much," he says. Well, he's not sure if he'll miss Sky, but it would feel rude to point that out.

"I know how much you'll be worrying about Rumi," Sky says. He turns so he's facing away from Gogi. "Here, pluck out one of my tail feathers."

"Wait, what, are you serious?" Gogi asks, suddenly embarrassed. "You're not going to fart or something, are you?"

"Now's not the time for pranks, Sky," Mez says.

"Do I seem like the type to make fart jokes?" Sky asks.

"Not now that you mention it," Gogi says.

"So pull." Sky scrunches his eyes shut. "Quickly. This will hurt."

Feeling sheepish, Gogi braces himself against a tree, selects a tail feather, grips it in both hands, and yanks. With a startled caw, Sky goes tumbling forward into the mud. He huffs to his feet and immediately begins preening. Tears stand in the corners of his eyes.

Gogi holds up the crimson feather he managed to yank out. "I'm sorry. Did that hurt a lot?"

Sky jerks his head. "No," he says, his voice strained. "Not at all."

"It's pretty," Chumba says. "So many different reds."

"It's a directive," Sky says, "an item that channels my divination magic. When you need it most, hold my feather in your palm and remember this exact moment, every detail of where we are. Send your thoughts to me. If I'm in a receptive moment, I should hear them, no matter the distance."

"Your powers have grown," Rumi admires, appearing from the feathers of Sky's shoulder.

"I haven't worked out all the kinks yet," Sky says. "But let's hope that it works for us."

"Thank you for the feather," Gogi says as he pulls

the woven bag his mom made him to his front and gently tucks the feather inside. He stares around the area. "Witch's tongue plant, check. A bunch of orb-weaver spiders, check. Tsetse flies, check. Bright tan puddle, check."

"What are you doing?" Chumba asks curiously.

"Memorizing the scene—weren't you listening?"

"We'll just have Lima record an echomap, silly."

"Huh," Gogi says. "You learn something new about bats every day."

"Lima showed us some of her tricks over our year at home," Mez explains. "Bats are pretty interesting."

"Are you ready to head out, Rumi?" Sky asks.

"Here we go, off to learn new things!" Rumi says.

With that, Sky reaches out his wings and, with a few powerful strokes, makes his way up into the air.

"Rumi seemed in good spirits," Chumba says, watching them rise out of view.

"Learning things does that to him," Mez says.

"I'm going to miss them," Gogi says. He pauses, considering. "Both of them, surprisingly."

"Yes, Sky has a certain unlikable charm," Chumba says, nodding.

A bat's chirp makes its way through the sluggish air.

"Finally," Mez croaks. "Lima found water."

Rested and hydrated, the quartet of friends huddles beneath a fig tree. "Best I can figure it, we go get the lyre tree sap, then head to the Dismal Bog," Gogi says.

"And where do we get lyre tree sap?" Mez asks.

"The lyre tree by our den?" Chumba asks.

"Chumba," Mez says, "our den is nights and nights of travel away from here."

"Right." Chumba sighs.

"Tell me about where this lyre tree grows near your den," Gogi says, rubbing his hands together. "Figuring out where to find the best fruiting trees is a capuchin monkey specialty, and you're in the company of a number twelve. Spare no detail."

"Okay," Chumba says excitedly. "So you head out of the den, and go left right away."

"Isn't it right?" Lima asks.

"No," Mez says. "It's definitely left."

"Oh, right," Lima says. "I'm usually flying out, which means I take a different exit. Sorry."

"So you go left," Chumba continues, "and then you come to a creeper vine that's covering the path, which we usually just climb over, although when we were cubs we had to go under it. So then there's the three flat stones, which is the spot where we usually play whisker taunt—"

"Are there pebbles alongside them, or are the stones

on their own? And is this shaded all day? Trying to fig-ure out if this is acidic soil."

"This is fun!" Chumba says. "I remember it always being shaded, but of course that's at night. But Mez is nodding right now, so I guess even during the day it's shaded. And there aren't pebbles nearby. Just the three rocks and silky soil. Anyway, you go up a little incline, and there at the top is the lyre tree, which has these branches that fan out on either side, and from those are hanging these seedpods, which have the sap inside, all around the seeds."

"The spot around the lyre tree, is it wet?"

"No!" Chumba says. "I never thought about that. It's slightly higher ground. The water runs off it."

"I've got it!" Gogi says. "Fairly acidic soil, drier zone within a wetter climate, relatively little sunshine. Follow me!"

Gogi bounds up the fig tree to get a good view of the surroundings. Mez and Chumba wait at the bottom, staring up at him. They can climb trees, but not as well as monkeys can. Lima's right nearby, though, peering about. "Are we hot on the trail?" she asks excitedly.

Gogi hops from branch to branch, looking in every direction. The broad jungles of Caldera stretch as far as the eye can see.

"See that spot between those twin lagoons, with the row of trees? Based on what Chumba described, one of those is a lyre tree, I'm almost sure of it."

"Impressive!" Lima says.

"Thanks," Gogi says. "So, do you think you're up for retrieving some sap?"

"Me?" Lima squeaks.

"Yes," Gogi says. "It would take the rest of us days to get around the lagoon, and you could fly over in minutes."

"They're small feet, but I'll grab as much as I can with them," Lima says.

"See if you can get about a whole seedpod with your feet," Gogi says. "Once it's back here, we can figure out the best way to transport it to the Dismal Bog."

"I'm on it!" Lima says before zooming away.

Gogi holds steady in the branches, looking out over Caldera. He pats the pouch his mother once wove him, making sure the feather is still in there. He wonders if, when she was taken by the harpy eagle, she realized that being an orphan would drop Gogi to the bottom of the capuchin rankings. *I'll do you proud, Mom,* Gogi thinks. *I'll show you there was never anything to worry about. I'll get this down to eleven pebbles before any of us even know it.*

A black spot appears on the horizon, growing larger

and larger until Gogi can make out Lima's familiar shape. She's going slower than usual, and Gogi soon sees why—she's got something heavy in her feet. She zags through the air, finally coming to rest at the base of Gogi's tree. "Would you mind coming down here?" she calls up. "That was exhausting!"

Gogi scampers down the tree, going as quickly as he can but still taking moments to enjoy the feel of branches under his hands, the trunk under his feet, to swing around a limb and backflip to the ground. Trees! The best!

At the bottom, Gogi finds Mez and Chumba circling Lima, talking excitedly to her. "Lima got it! She found the seedpod!" Mez calls.

Lima lies back in the reeds, panting heavily. "You okay?" Gogi asks.

Lima nods, an exhausted smile on her face. "Might have overdone it. I'll be fine in a moment."

"Look at this!" Chumba says. She's got a claw in the parted seedpod, and she lifts it to show Gogi the stringy, sticky substance inside. "It's the most delicious thing you'll ever taste, but it only works for a short while afterward. We'd better use it right after we've entered the Dismal Bog."

"That's too bad," Mez says, licking her chops. "It's

really delicious. I could go for some right now."

Gogi peers at the sappy fibers. "Would it be so bad if we, if we maybe . . . ?"

"No!" Mez and Chumba say together.

"Okay, fine, I'll wait," Gogi says.

Mez peers at him, eyes narrowed. "Gogi . . ."

"What?" he says, indignant. "You don't know what I was going to say. Maybe I was about to propose that, that, um, Lima was the one who might eat it too early."

"Me?" Lima asks. "Why me? Where is *that* coming from?"

"Nothing, never mind," Gogi huffs. "You all know my monkey brain too well, I guess."

"Well, you don't need to slander *me* about it."

"I know, I know, I'm sorry!" Gogi says.

"It's okay," Mez says. "We know you wouldn't actually eat the sap early."

Chumba yawns and looks toward the horizon, where the pale orb of the sun is glinting. "The Veil is about to lift, guys. I wish I could stay awake, but I'm going to be in daycoma pretty soon."

Just like that, the sun's rays appear and Chumba's asleep. There will be no waking her until the Veil has dropped again, at dusk.

Mez looks around. "Oops. I guess we make camp

here," she says. "It's not what I would have picked, but it's still pretty defensible. What do you guys say we hide in those ferns over there and wait out the day? We could all use some rest."

"What do you say, Lima?" Gogi asks. But then he hears the gentle snores: the bat is fully asleep too.

Mez shakes her head. "Some shadowwalker!"

"My mind's buzzing, so I'll take first watch," Gogi says. "Assuming you think you can fall asleep anytime soon, Mez."

She yawns. "Yeah, I think I'll be able to manage that."

They pull their sleeping friends into the cover of the ferns, and then Mez, too, falls asleep.

As daytime begins, Gogi feels his mood lifting. It had just been a moment of weakness before: *of course* he would never jeopardize the future of all of Caldera by trying the sap early. Even if it's supposed to be the greatest-tasting thing that's ever existed.

He doesn't suppose there would be any harm in just *touching* it, though. Gogi examines the seedpod. It's knobby, green, hairy, and sticky. It would be disgusting, actually, if it weren't for the absolutely delicious smell wafting up from it. Both tart and sugary, somehow, and slightly toasty.

Gogi taps his fingers along it.

He runs the pod under his nose. "Nice bouquet," he whispers to himself. "Very nice indeed. Almost like a peanut."

If only Alzo were here. Alzo would really enjoy this. The nutty palm back home has nothing on lyre sap.

Slowly, deliberately, Gogi lifts the fragrant juicy snack to his lips.

Then he pulls it away and places it between sleeping Mez and Chumba. He leans back, crosses his arms grumpily, and settles in to his watch.

Come the dropping of the Veil, Gogi awakens to panther licks. The first time he ever woke up to panther slobber he thought it was gross, but now Gogi finds it the best way to wake up. Panthers know what they're doing about some things.

Chumba's expression brightens when she sees Gogi is awake. "There you are! Help me tie these seedpods to my side, would you?"

Gogi yanks some fronds from the fern, and bands them around and around Chumba's midsection, tucking the seedpods underneath before knotting the fronds smartly. "Snug?" Gogi asks.

"Perfect. Off to the Dismal Bog!"

"Sounds great," Gogi says. "Well, actually, sounds terrible. But let's get going anyway!"

"It's not far as the bat flies," Lima says, stretching her wings out to pick up some heat from the last rays of the sunset.

"What does that mean?" Gogi asks.

"South to north it's not far. You wouldn't know it, but we're at the top of a hill in the rainforest right now. You should have seen the view. It's very pretty. All misty and rolling. It's a loooong way down to the bog, though. It's passable for you guys, but it will take a while."

"That's too bad. It's not like we really have a while to spare," Gogi says.

"Agreed," Lima says. "Which is why I'm so glad that I found another way!"

"Why didn't you tell us that right away?" Gogi asks.

"Can't a bat build a little suspense?" Lima asks. "Come on, follow me up this rise."

Lima zooms into the air and off into the green.

"She's gotten a little theatrical over the past year, hasn't she?" Mez mutters as she heads off after Lima.

"Maybe a little *too* theatrical," Gogi says. "I blame living with panthers."

When they reach Lima, they find she's landed on an especially large monguba tree and is proudly pointing to one of the seedpods. It's pendulous and thick and hairy, larger than the group of friends all put together.

"More seeds?" Gogi asks.

"Not just any seeds!" Lima says. "Come on, help me get it down and I'll show you what I mean."

It's usually easier with Lima just to let things happen and see the result than to ask for any explanation ahead of time. Gogi climbs up the tree and scampers out over the seedpod's branch. "Watch out below!" he cries as he digs his fingernails into the smooth wood, twisting and yanking until the pod thunders to the jungle floor.

The shaking branches block Gogi's friends from view. "Did you watch out?" No answer. His stomach twists. "Guys, are you okay?"

"Yes, we're fine," Mez calls up. "Sorry, we were just surprised a bit there. Wow, this thing is enormous!"

Gogi scampers down—branch to branch, whip around with the tail, plummet, whee! At the bottom he finds Mez and Chumba slitting the pod open with their foreclaws, then using their teeth to peel back the rubbery casing. Inside, unsurprisingly enough, are giant seeds— puffball tops leading down to nutty bottoms. They're sleek and narrow when they're lined up in the pod, but once Mez drags one out, it balloons, catching even the slight breezes that roll along the rainforest floor.

"Don't let them get away!" Lima cries as her friends

scamper around the clearing, picking up more and more of the errant seeds as they tumble out of the pod.

"Now, what do we do with them?" Chumba asks once they have most of the seeds reassembled and stuffed back into the husk.

"I guess we should have waited to open this until we were at the top of the tree," Lima says, tapping her lips with the tip of her wing.

"Top of the tree *why*?" Gogi asks, scratching his head.

"You'll see!" Lima says as she soars to the highest branches of the monguba.

Huffing and struggling, teeth gnashing and muscles straining, Gogi, Mez, and Chumba manage to drag the seedpod to the top with most of its contents intact. Up there, Lima is waiting with a grin on her face. "This is going to be *amazing*!" she says. "You guys will finally know what it's like to be a bat!"

"I knew I had a bad feeling about this," Mez mutters.

"Yeah, I'm not sure I ever wanted to know what being a bat felt like," Chumba says.

Lima shakes her head. "I refuse to be crestfallen. Feel these air currents?" She basks in them, wings open wide. "How lovely are those?" She points, a big grin on her face. "And there, at the very bottom of those lovely air currents, is the Dismal Bog!"

Gogi follows her gaze. The rainforest continues unbroken, until it turns a sickly blue-gray color. Bent, tortured trees rise up from the earth only to bend back down, strangled by strands of mucus-like lichen. The sickly trees bow lower and lower as the bog continues, until they disappear entirely into the dank and soupy terrain. Only a few bent bits of vegetation survive. Crows wheel above the bog.

"That looks . . . grim," Chumba says.

"Are we sure we want to go in there?" Gogi asks, swallowing against the sour taste in his throat.

"Oh, come on, guys," Lima says. "It's just a bog."

"A *dismal* bog," Mez says. "It's in the *name*."

"Where we face our greatest fears," Chumba adds.

"Well, we have to do it, and we only have, what, eleven days until the lunar eclipse now, so we might as well get it over with," Lima says, chin jutting forward.

"You're right," Gogi says, closing his eyes and girding himself. "If we have to go, we have to go. We'll find out what's keeping the ants away down there, and get out as soon as we can."

"At least we have the lyre sap," Mez says.

"It won't help us against something like quicksand," Lima points out.

"Hey!" Mez says. "I thought you were supposed to

be the one cheering us up."

"Right, sorry," Lima says. She gets a manic grin on her face and gesticulates wildly with her wings. "IT WON'T HELP US AGAINST SOMETHING LIKE QUICKSAND!"

Gogi forcibly ignores her. "You're right, Mez. It's very good we have the lyre sap."

"You realize that you're licking your lips, right?" Mez asks him.

Gogi crosses his eyes as he tries to look at his own lips. "Oh, whoops. I won't eat it ahead of time—have a little faith!"

"You *will* wait until we've actually landed," Mez commands, narrowing her eyes.

"I can't believe you're accusing me of, of not being able to delay gratification. I have never been so insulted in my life." Gogi tries to get the most severe expression he can on his face as he looks at each of his companions in turn.

"Riiiight," Mez says.

Chumba tenderly takes one of the monguba seeds into her mouth and starts batting it back and forth in the air. Her head moves slowly, air resistance catching the seed's fluffy sprigs. "Lima," she says, voice muffled, "this just might work!"

"Of course it just might work!" Lima sniffs.

"Well, I guess I'll go first," Chumba announces, easing toward the edge of the branch. The breezes catch the seed; they are already lifting her slightly off the tree.

"Are you sure, Chumba?" Mez asks. "Maybe I should—"

Chumba steps off the edge. Mez gasps, and Gogi throws his arms around her for comfort. He looks down by instinct, but as the draft catches the fluffy seed, it lifts Chumba *up* instead. She soars on the wind currents above them, twirling in the air. The breezes carry her off to the side and then back toward them, so she's at eye level. She says something, but the stalk in her mouth and the wind currents make the words go lost. Her eyes are streaming tears of joy.

"I'll go last," Lima says. "Since I have wings, I can direct where I go more, so it's easier for me to track all of you down. But you two should head out as soon as possible, because the air currents might shift. We don't want to all be scattered across Caldera, right?"

Mez needs no more encouraging. She works her jaws around another seed's stalk, then shakes her head sharply to unfurl it. That makes her catch a gust by accident, and she lifts into the air. Her eyes widen in surprise, and then she zooms up and off to the side, just like Chumba did, before she slowly floats down over the landscape, in the general direction of the Dismal Bog.

Gogi takes one of the seeds between his hands and holds it in front of him. "Wish me luck!" Gogi says, doing his best to keep his words even despite the fear rising in his throat.

"Better hurry before the air currents change," Lima says.

"Yep," Gogi says, tightening his fingers over the stalk. "I'd better get going." He doesn't move.

"Are you ready or not?" Lima asks.

"Yep, totally ready to go," Gogi says, still not moving.

"So . . . ," Lima says.

Gogi scrunches his eyes shut and takes a step forward into thin air.

He's motionless for a moment, and then there's a sharp tug upward on the monguba seed. Even though he saw the very same thing happen to Chumba and Mez, he's caught by surprise, and the sudden upward drag wrenches one of his hands free. He opens his eyes and sees the ground hundreds of feet below, monkey-splat distance. He flails his hand through the air until it's back on the stalk. Once it's securely in his grip again, he allows himself to take in more of the view.

He can understand why Mez and Chumba had such glee on their faces. Panther jaws must be a lot stronger than monkey hands, though—Gogi is too worried about keeping his grip to really enjoy himself. But still, he'll probably never have a chance to get a view like this again. The rainforest greens combine and swirl in his view, banded with grays and blues of lagoons and streams, slick tan lines of muddy rivers, misty whites throughout.

Beautiful as it may be, he's plenty ready for the trip to be over. For one thing, his little woven bag with its twelve pebbles is flapping and fluttering in the breezes, thwacking Gogi on the nose and ears and slapping his butt. He can't spare a hand to restrain it, since he has to hold on to the slippery stalk with all his fingers.

Except . . . his tail! How could he not have thought of that? Gogi brings his tail to the woven sack and presses it against his side. His tail doesn't contact just woven fibers, though; instead, most of what it touches is . . . sticky! The sap is falling out of the bag! Gogi looks down and sees the tendril of lyre sap has nearly fallen completely out.

He lets go of the bag and uses his tail to hold the tendril of sap instead. As the seed continues to carry him gently toward the earth, Gogi holds the sap closer to his face. Its tangy fragrance surrounds him.

What if he hits a strong gust? What if he suddenly needs his tail to help him hold on? He'd have to drop the tendril if that happened, and then he'd have no sap to protect him in the Dismal Bog. Maybe the safest thing to do would be to eat some *now*, while he's still in the air. He's just a few minutes from landing anyway. The sap will still be in his system for a long time! Probably!

Gogi reaches the sap forward with his tail and, as the wind gusts over him, takes a chew.

It tastes so impossibly good. It's sunbeams of fizzy radiance, the scent of a morning river, heating and cooling his tongue at the same time. It's the warm underside of a rock on a cool day, or a hand in chill waters when the air is humid and sweltering. That taste! He immediately bites more, and then takes all the sap into his mouth at once.

"You promised!" shrieks a familiar voice, and then Lima is soaring past, arrowing down toward the Dismal Bog, where Gogi can see Chumba and Mez, their furry calico shapes tiny against the colorless swamp, but quickly growing in size.

Guilt complicates the amazing tastes in Gogi's mouth, sends sour currents into his joy. More and more of the sap drains down his throat, and as it does the joy fades entirely. The guilt does, too. All that's left is a glassy sort of calmness. He looks up at his own hands, holding on so tightly to the stalk. *Do I need to be holding on so tightly?* he asks himself. *Why don't I just let go! I feel so light—I bet I'll still float.*

He doesn't have to face what would have happened to him if he let go, because before he expects it—long before he expects it—his feet are touching the ground. He releases the puffy seed and rolls, soon covered in goopy mud. He comes to rest against the base of a tree, the world tumbling over itself as his head spins.

Gogi looks around, blinking.

What a pretty swamp! There are delightful dragonflies buzzing about, and the mosquitoes and flies have a lovely plumpness about them. The mud has a definite odor to it, sure, but it's also silky smooth under Gogi's feet. He breathes in the sulfurous air—who knew that rotten eggs could smell so delicious?

Gogi shakes his feet to rid his ankles of the pins-and-needles feeling, noticing as he does that he's got scrapes all along his soles. They don't hurt at all, though. Lucky! Whistling, he turns around in a circle, hands on his furry hips. Where are Mez and Chumba and Lima?

Hmm. Maybe the wind currents changed, or acted differently on him because of his size. Maybe he's very far away from his friends!

He knows he should be worried, but all Gogi really feels is the blinding adventure of it all. Completely lost in an unknown swamp, with no idea of where to go, or what dangers await. What an escapade!

Still whistling, Gogi picks a direction and starts wandering.

He runs his tongue over his molars, trying to get every last bit of the tangy lyre sap flavor. Soon there won't be any of it left, just the memory of having once tasted it. How sad. Oh well. As the capuchin monkeys always say: *Better to have tasted and finished than never to have tasted at all!* Or maybe that's not a capuchin saying. He's not too sure, all of a sudden. La-di-da.

"Hello there, Mr. Spider!" Gogi says as he walks right into a web, plucking the giant, thrashing insect from his face and peering into its many eyes before placing it delicately on the ground, poison sac bobbing.

"And hello, viper! What pretty red-and-black-and-yellow stripes you have!

"Poor little bush. Why are your leaves so droopy and moldy? Let me fluff them up for you.

"Hey there, giant moth. Have you ever tried to get together with the other creatures around here and see if you could get the bog's name changed? Because it's really not so dismal at all, I don't think.

"Oh, hello there! Wait—*Alzo*?!"

Gogi stops in his tracks. How is Alzo here? And why is he not moving?

He makes his way through rotting, putrid vegetation until he's beside his friend. Alzo is curled up on a blackened stump, looking very small indeed. Gogi throws his arms around him, then startles and draws back. Alzo is cold!

Now, why would Alzo be cold?

As soon as he gets warmed up, Alzo will feel better; Gogi's sure of it. Whistling just a little slower now, he picks up Alzo's motionless form and carries it farther into the bog. "Oof, Alzo, you're so heavy!" Gogi says, huffing. "Too bad you're not awake to help me carry you. Wait, can someone help someone else carry them? Is that physically possible? Let me figure this out."

Gogi tenderly sets Alzo down, and then tries to lift himself up into the air. As soon as he gets one foot off the ground, though, the other sinks deeper into the mud. "Nope," he reports sadly as he picks Alzo back up. "I'm afraid it doesn't work. That's too bad. I guess I'll just have to keep carrying—wait, what's that?"

Gogi freezes. Someone's rummaging through his bag! He drops Alzo into the cold mud, and then whirls to confront the thief.

It's a strange capuchin, one that Gogi doesn't remember seeing before. It leaps away, its hand full of something that tinkles and clinks.

His pebbles. This strange capuchin has stolen his pebbles.

"Give those back!" Gogi shouts.

In response, the capuchin cocks its—her—head. She drops one of the pebbles into the mud.

"Those have sentimental value," Gogi says. "Stop it right now." He goes to pick up the pebble, the capuchin bounding away as he does. He replaces it in his pouch.

The capuchin flits between trees in the distance. She drops another pebble. Then she heads deeper into the bog.

Gogi is shaking. Those pebbles. The symbol of his rank and of the loss of his mother. How *dare* this stranger take them?

"I'll be back to warm you up as soon as I can," Gogi tells Alzo's motionless form. Then he starts scampering through the bog, heedless of the muck and rotting debris that soon cover his arms and legs. "Wait up, strange capuchin! Give those pebbles back! You don't understand!"

As soon as he's retrieved the next pebble, she drops another one, then disappears into the mist. It's all very confusing why that unfamiliar monkey won't simply explain herself to him, but Gogi assumes that by the time he reaches her he'll have figured out what's going on. There's always some solution!

Another pebble, and another. The capuchin is speeding up, and he can't see her anymore. Where is the next pebble?

He turns in a slow circle, looking for the white pebble. The bog is so dank and dark—what if it fell into the murky water? He'd never see it. "Strange capuchin, where are you?" he calls, cupping his hands around his mouth. No response.

He summons his ring of firelight, hoping that it might help him find the next pebble. No luck. All he sees is more and more of the creepy things around him.

As it gets stronger, his ring of light does burn off the mist, though, and as the mist burns he sees a glint of white on the ground in the distance. At first his heart seizes when he worries that Mez and Chumba's cousin Mist has found them. But the white spot is very small, and not moving. The Dismal Bog has very many grays and greens, but white . . . That can only be . . . yes, the next pebble!

Gogi places it back in his woven sack. It makes a satisfying clink as it joins the others. There—the capuchin flits between misty trees at the edge of Gogi's firelight. "Hello?" Gogi calls, hands outstretched in front of him. "Where are you taking me? Could you give my pebbles back now, please? Also, have you seen my friends, Mez, Chumba, and Lima?"

In response, the capuchin pauses and faces Gogi, with her arms out. Like she wants to hug him. Then she drops a pebble.

"Okay," he calls to her, making his way forward and retrieving it, while she retreats farther away. "This is a little weird. I don't really know you, but I do know that I like hugs!"

The mists get even thicker, so that Gogi gets no more information when his eyes are open than when they're closed. It's not that unfamiliar a sensation, actually— it's like when he traveled with his nightwalker friends before he learned his firelight trick. He has more than a few scars on his shins from those nights.

The swamp isn't really all so adorable. It's cold, and there's something unnerving about this mute monkey who stole his pebbles—and the sight of Alzo so motionless and so far from home, now that Gogi thinks about it. Whatever happened to the tangy taste of the sap? There's none left between his molars. Maybe he'll try to leave the Dismal Bog sooner rather than later, so he can go find himself some more of it.

Why did he come here anyway? Gogi tries to remember, but he can't seem to get the information he needs from his own brain. "Strange capuchin, do you remember why I'm here?" But the monkey doesn't answer. She leads him farther into the bog.

It's all truly bizarre.

"Would you please . . . wait up?" Gogi puffs.

The capuchin does! She waits by a hollowed-out tree, drops the last pebble at her feet. She's an older female monkey, about Gogi's size, with the same awkward sprout of hair on the back of her head. When Gogi comes near and retrieves the pebble, her eyes are trained on the hollow in the tree.

"Who are you?" Gogi asks.

She stares toward the hole.

He comes up beside her and instinctively starts grooming. She's real under his fingers, but she's just as cold as Alzo was, like there's no life in her. Grooming capuchin hair still feels good, even when it's clammy.

She doesn't groom him back. She looks at the hole.

Gogi edges to the tree and peers inside. It's pitch-black in there.

He looks closer and sees that it's crawling with gooey black slugs. Cute slugs? No, gross slugs. He shakes his head. Slugs are gross. Every capuchin knows that. What's wrong with him?

The strange capuchin motions that Gogi should stick his hand in. Steeling himself, Gogi reaches into the teeming mass of slugs and feels the dark inside of the tree. It's wet and squirmy in there, unseen creatures running over his fingers. Gogi shivers. Definitely not cute. Nothing about this bog is cute. Where's that sap? More sap will help.

Eventually he gets his fingers around something that doesn't squirm. A couple of loose, knobby pieces of crumbly wood. When he pulls them out, slugs and leeches and millipedes falling away, he holds them up to his eye in the mist and sees that—hmm—they're covered in chunks of powdery white. It smells mushroom-y.

The strange capuchin throws her cold arms around Gogi. She pulls back and points to the sticks, excitement on her face.

Gogi looks at them. Apparently, these sticks are important. Excellent!

The capuchin looks at him and places her fingers around his eyes, pressing on the corners. Gogi wants to back away, but something tells him to stay still, that he can trust this capuchin. He closes his eyes and basks in the sensation.

Then comes a soft voice, right in his ear: "I love you. I'm so proud of you. My son."

Gogi's eyes snap open. But the strange capuchin is gone. He's alone in the bog.

"Mom? Mom!" he cries, turning around in a circle, stepping this way and that.

She's gone. Was she ever there? Gogi feels his pouch—the pebbles are there. He looks at his hands.

These two fungus-ridden sticks are real. And his mother was the one to bring him to them.

"Mom!" he calls again.

There's no answer.

Gogi starts to head back through the swamp, in the direction from which he came. He's stunned, can't think about what's real or what's not, what has happened to him. He can just keep his mind on where each pebble was, retracing his steps through the bog.

It's increasingly . . . disgusting. Goopy, rotting, cold, and ugly. Gogi shivers.

There's Alzo again—motionless as before. "Alzo!" Gogi cries.

No answer.

"Why will no one answer me?" Gogi mutters as he approaches his friend.

He fills with horror. Of course Alzo isn't cold and sleeping—he's dead!

How could he have been so wrong? Gogi drops to his knees, shaking. Alzo is dead. Because . . . of him? Would he have died if Gogi hadn't come into the Dismal Bog, hadn't had this vision that killed him? Something doesn't make sense, but he's too stricken to think through it. All he can see in his mind is his mother dropping his rank pebbles, then saying she loved him, and now Alzo's body. Alzo is no longer alive because of *him*. Shouldn't a good capuchin have stayed home where he belonged? Shouldn't he have stuck to the part of the rainforest that he's always known?

Shouldn't he have waited to try the lyre sap?

Something's wrong with Gogi. He's always suspected it, but now he knows it's true. Gogi wants to sink away right there, to drop into the cold mud and never rise. He can feel his arms and legs getting heavier, and as they do the mud drags at him, asks to smother him. Opening his eyes to get one last view, he hopes he might glimpse his mother again.

No sign of her. What he does see, though, are the pieces of wood, covered in knobby white fungus, gripped tight in his very own hand.

His mother led him to these. They might be the answer he and his friends are looking for.

Gogi will resist the call of the silky mud.

Gogi lifts himself to his full height. Or he tries to, but the mud only drags him down harder. Suddenly it's up to his chin, then it's pressing into his mouth. He flails desperately, and it only mires him more and more until—*plop!*—his head is below.

He came to his senses too late!

As Gogi panics, his tail thrashes more and more until it contacts something—another monkey's tail. He grips it as tightly as he can, then yanks his tail muscles. Spines aren't made for this kind of work, and he feels a sharp, shredding pain along his backbone. But he's out of the mud!

His mother is there beside him. It was her tail that lifted Gogi out. She nods and says "I love you" once more.

"I love you, too," Gogi says.

Then she disappears again.

Limping, muttering to himself, Gogi shoves the rotten pieces of wood into the sack his mother wove him, beside the twelve pebbles, and begins sprinting along the sopping ground of the Dismal Bog, shivering from the cold and from the sheer disgustingness of the foul-smelling swamp. He heads in the direction he originally came from, where he soared down on the fluffy monguba seed. Thank sweet figs his monkey sense of direction is intact.

Finally Gogi sees the mist is dissipating somewhat. He can make out more and more barren trees between the stretches of dank puddles and decomposing grasses. Then even the smells lessen—he'd like to take it back, now that the lyre sap is wearing off: rotten eggs do *not* smell good, rotten eggs will *never* smell good—and he's out of the Dismal Bog. He's on fresh grass, healthy jungle trees surrounding him. He runs as far as he can into the rainforest before his lungs and legs and arms give way and he collapses into the dirt, panting.

Now, he thinks, *where are Chumba and Mez and Lima?*

Ten Nights Until the Eclipse

GOGI SKIRTS THE edge of the Dismal Bog, peering into the misty, sulfurous terrain. He has no idea where Mez and Chumba might have landed—he was too busy eating his tangy lyre sap to notice, unfortunately—but he worries that if he hasn't heard from them at all, it's because they've run into trouble.

How much of what happened to him is real? Was that his mother, or his dream of his mother? Is Alzo dead, or did Gogi just imagine him dead? If his mother and Alzo were in his head, was it Gogi himself who realized that the fungus growing all around him was the reason there were no ants in the bog? There's no way to know. All he has to show for the experience are the two rotten sticks in his bag.

The lyre sap clearly protected him from the worst of the bog's horrors. He has no idea how much of it is still in his system, how much it might still shield him from the worst effects of the nightmares, but he's running out of time to locate his friends and rescue them before he's fully at the mercy of the bog.

He has to go back in there.

Setting his chin firmly, he wades back into the swamp. "Lima? Mez? Chumba?" Gogi calls. He's suddenly aware of all the unknown and dark spaces around him, the lichen draping from slimy, craggy trees, the blurps of strange gases rising from iridescent mud, the pairs of red eyes peering back at him from all around. He's so vulnerable here, a monkey without a troop, in an unfamiliar place. No right-thinking capuchin would put himself in such a situation. But he has to find his friends, so here he is.

"Mom?" he tries. But that vision seems to be over.

"Lima? Mez? Chumba?" he calls.

No answer. But then . . . !

It's almost too high-pitched to hear, but he makes out a string of faint chirps, from somewhere within the mists of the Dismal Bog. The sound of a bat.

Of course there would be plenty of bats in a bog.

But he's pretty sure he recognizes this one in particular. "Lima?" he calls, staggering into the muck. "Are you out there?"

She doesn't seem to hear him. The string of chirps continues unabated. Gogi sinks up to his hips in black mud, flails for purchase on slimy leaves and grasses until he can pull himself out. Then he's back on his feet and racing forward. "Lima! Lima!"

The mists whip past, and with them come Alzo's body. It's in a totally different part of the bog now, and Gogi's brain tells him that Alzo couldn't have moved, but here he is. *This is just a hallucination,* he tells himself as he races. But even though his mind tells him that, it's hard to disbelieve his eyes, to stop the quickening of his heart.

He narrows his eyes to slits, trying to keep the body of Alzo out of view even as it disappears and reappears everywhere he looks. He tries to focus only on Lima's cries.

Then he finds her. The little bat is flailing in the mud, eyes closed, battling something in her dream. Her bottom half is completely below the surface, and muck has reached the corners of her mouth—she'll soon drown unless Gogi can get her out.

The mud surrounding Lima is silty; even the youngest capuchin knows it can be deadly to walk on ground so soft. So instead, Gogi scales a rotten tree overhanging the mud. He scampers to the tip of a branch, wrapping his already aching tail around a knot in the wood before lowering himself down. The branch creaks alarmingly as he stretches, his tail muscles feeling like they're shredding all over again . . . but there! He's got a finger. He can't afford to be gentle, and he yanks hard on the narrow bone that traces the top of Lima's wing. With a suctioning sound, she comes free. Gogi holds her in his hand as he races back along the treacherous branch.

Resting against the trunk, gasping in the soupy air, Gogi realizes that Lima is making words with her chirps. He holds her up to his ear. "Mez and Chumba—I'm so sorry," Lima says within her nightmare. "It's all my fault!"

Gogi startles and nearly drops her. What happened to Mez and Chumba?

"Where are they, Lima?" he asks urgently, giving her belly a gentle squeeze.

The bat doesn't open her eyes, but seems to have heard Gogi's words within her nightmare. She thrashes, muddied wings flailing. "They died where they fell. They hit the ground too hard. My plan . . . it killed them!"

"Lima, it's me, Gogi," he says. "You're dreaming.

These are the bog's hallucinations, telling you your worst fears."

"No, it's real . . . they fell at the base of the willow," Lima says, before her voice trails off. Her body goes limp, and the fragile pulse under Gogi's fingers slows.

"No!" he cries. "Lima, hold on!" Even as he says it, he realizes he doesn't know if Lima's life is really in jeopardy, or if this is now the dream manipulating *him*. Regardless, he needs to get her out of there, fast—for his sake, too, if he doesn't want the lyre sap to wear off entirely while he's still at the mercy of the swamp.

He scans about and sees—yes!—a willow not too far away. Gogi takes off toward it, stealing through the cold and leaching mud until he's beside the tree. There he sees a sight even more horrifying than before: two little calico bodies curled one around the other. Panthers. Mez and Chumba.

Their eyes are closed, and they seem motionless. But as Gogi gets close, he's relieved to see that, yes, they are breathing shallowly. They make clicking sounds from somewhere within their throats, and their lips repeatedly pull back from their teeth. Placing Lima gently on top of Chumba's belly, Gogi leans down so he can hear what's coming from Chumba's lips.

"Yerlo—not you, too. I never thought he would . . ."

The words descend into nonsense. Gogi recognizes the name. It's one of the triplets, Mez and Chumba's little cousins who are back in the care of Usha. "He" might refer to Mist, their missing brother. Gogi can well imagine what the panther sisters' nightmares look like.

He has to get them out of the bog, and fast. The edge isn't so far away, and Lima will be easy enough to move, but he has two panthers to take care of, both of them trapped in their nightmares, and each of them heavier than he is. Gogi turns, trying to see the clearest path out of the bog, but when he pivots he comes to stare into the eyes of a monkey, a dead monkey, looking right back at him.

Alzo.

Gogi shuts his eyes and shakes his head, willing Alzo out of his mind, but when he tentatively opens his eyes again, Alzo's right there. "You're . . . not real!" he says through gritted teeth.

But Alzo won't go away. Gogi's heart races, threatening to pitter-patter right out of his chest—but though he waits for Alzo's cold fingers to grip him, his dead best friend doesn't move.

Shaking all over, saying "You're not real" so many times that it becomes a chant, Gogi skirts around Alzo, then skirts around him again when he reappears directly in front of him. "Lyre sap definitely wearing off," he tells himself as he tucks Lima into his woven sack, hoping the rotten fungus sticks won't do something to *her*.

Then he gets one each of Chumba's and Mez's paws under his hands, and pulls.

They don't move. Not one bit.

"Come on, now," Gogi says between gritted teeth. He pauses to take a break, hands on his hips, heaving in air.

When he turns around, Ravanna the First is right there.

The eyes of the big capuchin leader are lifeless and unseeing. His jaw hangs limply open, exposing sharp yellow canines. His arms are still at first . . . but then they rise in the air, fingers reaching for Gogi.

The immediate terror is so great that he forgets he ever had Mez and Chumba in his grip. Gogi scatters and runs. His arms drag behind him, for some reason, but he goes as fast as he can using only his legs. Mud sprays around him as he leads with his chest, woven sack bouncing against his hip. His legs are burning, his breathing is ragged, but he can't stop, not with the sight of deathless Ravanna seared into his eyelids, those ghastly fingers reaching for his throat.

His legs finally give out, sending him plunging

through leafy greenery. He tastes mud and reeds. He heaves against the darkness for a while, then thinks to open his eyes.

He's out of the bog.

He's back in the rainforest.

Lima is in the sack.

Mez and Chumba are there.

In his rush of fear, he dragged them out with him.

Gogi gives a sigh of relief.

He blacks out.

11

RAIN. MISTY RAIN.

Gogi can feel it beading on the fur of his eyelids, wetting his arms and legs and belly. It's a comfortable rain, a familiar rain. A sunbeam sort of rain.

He opens his eyes. He's lying in a sun-filled clearing, bursts of water tumbling from a clear blue sky that's fringed by the upper branches of trees. A sprig of lagoon berries lies on his chest. They glisten. Gogi's stomach growls. He eats a berry. Delicious.

He sits up on his elbows. He's in a silvery glade, water burbling nearby. After the terrible mayhem of the Dismal Bog, it's so peaceful. A terrible thought strikes

Gogi, making him sit bolt upright.

"Am I dead?"

A panther chuckles. "No, Gogi. You're not dead."

Gogi whirls to see Mez curled around sleeping Chumba and grinning at him. She yawns and stretches out her claws. "You've definitely been sleeping for a long time, though."

"You're okay!" comes Lima's chirpy voice. She flits down from a nearby branch. "How are your legs and arms feeling? You got pretty scraped up there. Took a lot of bat saliva to get you healed."

"I'm grateful for that bat slobber. Thank you," Gogi says, testing his limbs. They feel great. Better than great. Whole and sun-warmed. Who needs lyre sap when the sun has warmed his arms and legs, and his friend has healed him? Who could ask for more than he has right now?

"The proper term is 'bat saliva,'" Lima corrects primly. "Don't call it 'slobber.'" She pauses, then breaks out laughing. "Only *panthers* slobber."

"Excuse me!" Mez says, playfire in her eyes. She makes as if she's going to pounce on Lima, but then she looks at her dozing sister. "You're lucky that I don't want to wake Chumba."

"Oh please," Lima scoffs. "She's in full daycoma. Even a tree falling on us wouldn't wake her up. You're just scared you'll get beaten up by a bat."

"I see you guys are in fine form," Gogi says, rubbing his ears and yawning. "As a policy, let's not generally go wishing any trees down onto our heads, okay?"

"Okay, okay," Lima says. "So, Gogi, we have to talk about the Dismal Bog."

The memory of what happened hits him in a rush. The nightmarish body of Alzo, the vision of his mother—maybe she was real!—leading him through the bog, telling him she loved him. Mez and Chumba and Lima huddled and small and so very still. The two pieces of rotten wood he fished out of a slimy trunk. "Oh my gosh, the sticks!" he cries.

"You mean these?" Mez asks, pointing at two small, mildewed sticks lying beside Gogi's bag. The woven sack has been folded, its cord wrapped neatly around it, the twelve pebbles lumping the bottom. "Sorry to go through your things, but we didn't know whether you'd succeeded in finding anything out. *We* sure didn't. What are these? Souvenirs?"

"I don't really know what they are," he says, eyes wide. "But this is our only lead to go on, and it's because of me? Well. Would you look at that! Monkey brain is good for something after all."

"Even more than that," Lima says, "it's your monkey-ness that saved us."

"What do you mean?" Gogi asks, scratching an armpit. It feels weird having everyone's attention on him like this. Well, everyone except Chumba, who's snoring away.

"Remember when we were riding the monguba seeds down toward the Dismal Bog?" Mez asks. "I wasn't there, but apparently Lima scolded you for eating some sap early. I would have scolded you too, if I'd seen it. But that's what saved the day. Chumba and I started dreaming about . . . about horrible things, while we were still above the swamp, and we were totally paralyzed with sadness by the time we landed."

"Did you dream about the triplets?" Gogi asks. "I think I heard Chumba say something about one of them."

Mez scrunches her eyes closed.

"I don't think she's ready to talk about it yet, Gogi," Lima says, laying a leathery wing on his shoulder.

"Sorry," Gogi says. "In that case, can we go back to talking about how I saved the day?"

"Yes," Mez says. "I know you were kidding just now, but you really did, Gogi. You ate the lyre sap while you were in the air. I think the mists of the Dismal Bog must rise above it, so you were already protected from its worst effects once it hit. The rest of us were taken down before we could even prepare. You'd think the boto might have warned us that could happen, by the way."

"Indeed!" Lima sniffs.

"In her defense, she didn't pretend to know much about the bog," Gogi says, feeling protective of the boto now that he's the grand hero who saved the day. "She was passing along what she'd heard."

"In any case, yes, Gogi, it was your monkey brain that saved us," Mez says.

"Shoo-ee!" Gogi says, cracking his knuckles. "Looks like impulse control isn't all that it's cracked up to be."

"Okay, okay," Lima says, rolling her eyes. "Let's not get carried away."

"He did save our lives," Mez says. "We can let him get carried away. You go ahead and bask in your glory, Gogi."

"I think you mean Gogi the *Great*."

"Okay, never mind, I take it back."

Gogi smiles. "Just kidding. You know I'm always a seventeen in my heart. Even if I'm a twelve in real life." An unsettling image from the dream returns: Alzo's body, shrouded in mist. *If the rest of my family is even alive.* He considers telling his friends how he saw his mother appear to him, that it was something about her memory inside him that brought him to the verge of figuring out how the bog was safe from ants, but he decides to hold that close for now. It can stay his private time with his mother.

Mez seems to have seen the thoughts racing through Gogi's mind. She nods soberly. "While you were recovering, Chumba and Lima and I decided to take the day to rest too."

Gogi nods. "So, have you figured out what these two sticks are about?"

Mez's jaw drops. "You mean *you* don't know?"

"No, not exactly," Gogi says, feeling a little defensive. "But my vision *did* lead me to them."

"They're pretty gross," Lima says, leaning over the sticks. She backs away. "They smell a little like nose rot. I can't believe you put them with me in the sack!"

"Yeah, sorry, I didn't have too many options," Gogi says.

"Yes, these sticks are definitely covered by some sort of fungus," Mez says, nosing them cautiously.

"Is the fungus what caused our hallucinations?" Gogi asks.

"Well, we're not hallucinating now, so . . ." Mez lets her voice trail off.

"Right, right," Gogi says.

"But I think we'll have to assume this fungus is what we're meant to use against the ants. If Gogi's vision is correct."

"Of *course* Gogi's vision is correct—" Lima says.

"Thanks, Lima."

"—but maybe he's not the best one to figure out what to do next."

"Lima!"

Lima squeaks. "I'm just saying that Rumi tends to have the best strategies. I'm sorry, but it's true!"

"Then maybe we should talk to Rumi," Mez says, eyes glinting.

"How would we do that?" Gogi asks. His eyes go wide. "Sweet tree mold, I nearly forgot about the tail feather!"

"I didn't," Mez says. "But I'm still not totally sure we should use the directive. Rumi is with Sky, and I don't trust Sky. I don't want to give them any more information than necessary."

"But if they're flying over Caldera, don't you think they might know where the best place is to take this fungus?" Gogi says.

"And what it might do?" Lima adds.

"Yes," Mez says wearily. "Of course we should ask them. I just . . . I don't feel good about that macaw. I don't know how else to say it."

"I hear you," Gogi says. "We'll keep our wits about us." He rummages through his woven sack, his twelve pebbles clinking until his fingers hit the tail feather Sky left them. He pulls it out. With the Veil lifted, the irides-cent reds of the tail feather glint in the sunlight.

"So, how does it work again?" Lima says.

"From what I remember," Gogi says, "you hold on to it, remember the exact scene when Sky plucked it out, as best you can, and send your thoughts to him."

"Oh right, totally forgot," Lima says. "I'm just a bat."

"You made an echomap," Mez says. "Remember?"

"A *what*?" Lima asks. "I'm pretty sure that's not a thing."

"That's what you called it!" Mez says.

"Oh, an *echo*map!"

"What did you think I said?"

"A 'gecko trap.'"

"Why would I say that?"

"I don't know, why did you?" Lima taps her ear. "I think I'm still a little clogged by bog gunk."

"Hey, my friends," Gogi says, "we have a directive to use."

"Who are you calling 'dead ends'? And you can use your own invective, thank you very much."

Gogi sighs.

"Can we all put our paws on it at once, or does that ruin the magic?" Mez asks.

"Or wings," Lima says.

"Or hands," Gogi adds. "I guess so. I'm realizing that we should have asked Sky more questions about how all this works."

Gogi holds the glimmering plume out and closes his fingers around the middle. Mez places her paw under the tip. Lima stands under the quill and raises her wings so they're touching the bottom. "Ready?" she says. "I'm going to call up the echomap—"

Suddenly Gogi's mind fills with sound and light. There's a rushing in his eardrums, and blue and white whipping by. *I'm flying,* he realizes.

There's the smell of feathers and oil, then his vision shifts from clouds and sky to red feathers. He's looking through Sky's eyes, back over his shoulder, then—it's Rumi!

The little yellow tree frog is holding on for dear life, blinking rapidly into the wind as he rides on Sky's back. When he sees Sky's eye—or what Gogi assumes is Sky's eye—his eyes widen in surprise. "Gogi? Lima? Mez? Is that you in there?" Rumi yells over the howling wind. "I never would have thought it was really possible!"

"Seems so!"

"Sorry?" Rumi yells, "I couldn't hear you! Oh, hi, Mez! Wait, who is this now? Lima? I'm so confused."

Next time, maybe we shouldn't all use the directive at the same time, Gogi thinks.

"Can't understand anyone, all at once—Gogi, just you go."

"Okay," Gogi yells, hoping that his words continue to be transmitted through Sky's eye. "We have some fungus-y branches from the Dismal Bog."

"You're cutting in and out. But I heard 'fungus' and 'bog.' That's good—ants are very susceptible to mold and fungus!"

"Good to know!" Gogi says. But Lima must have said something at the same time, because Rumi nods and says, "Yes, just like bats!"

Rumi squints. "The wind is too much, or maybe we're too high; the magic is cutting out. We're only halfway there. But I'll tell you this—we've seen the full army, and the ants always come from the east. Like we thought—the direction the marmosets were in relation to your home, Gogi. Head east for the queen!"

"East is a big direction!" Gogi cries. "*Where*, east?"

"I can't hear you!" Rumi cries back. "But deduction tells me that you've likely just asked me where in the east. I don't know! Go as far as you can, until the ant armies get denser and denser!"

"Is there anything else?" Gogi asks.

"I miss you all so much," Rumi says. "We shouldn't have separated."

"Are you in trouble?" Gogi asks.

With that, the vision of Rumi on Sky's back blips out.

They're suddenly back in the clearing, staring at one another. "That was the wildest thing I've ever been through," Mez says.

"You're telling me," Gogi says. "And we just got through the Dismal Bog!"

"I think we'll have to try to catch them when they're not flying next time," Mez says, looking a little green around the gums. "That was unpleasant."

"Not for me!" Lima says. "But then again . . ." She lifts her wings and shrugs.

"So, what happens now?" Gogi asks. He suspects he knows the answer, and he doesn't like it—but maybe his friends will surprise him.

Lima furls up her wings so they look like little fists, and begins boxing the air. "We go find ourselves some ants, is what we do!"

"Yes, but we have only a small amount of the fungus," Mez says. "We should deploy it where it will do the most damage to the Ant Queen and her minions."

"For some reason, I don't love the sound of where

this is going," Gogi says, sighing.

"Where did you *think* we were going to be taking the fungus?" Mez asks.

"I don't know, I didn't think that far!"

"Well, now you know. Once night falls, we're heading as far east as we can go, deep into enemy territory."

Gogi sighs. "Yep. That's exactly what I was worried you were going to say."

Four Nights Until the Eclipse

As they travel, the four friends fall into a rhythm. Lima scouts, flying between the highest treetops, using her echolocation to hunt for enemies. Mez and Chumba slink through the nighttime undergrowth, keeping to the shadows. Gogi keeps up his trick of making a ring of light, though when his spine begins to ache with the constant magic use he lets it drop, instead looping his tail around Mez's so that he can keep track of where the panthers are going.

It feels a little like he's a baby monkey, back when his mother would hold fast to the end of his tail so he couldn't wander off. He thinks of her now—she's been gone for so long that he'd forgotten her face, but now he has that vision to keep him company, the memory of her soft touch on his fur, of her calm and wide-set eyes. Whether it was real or not, it's a comfort. He sings a lullaby to himself, a soft and wordless monkey song that he thought he'd forgotten.

Not having more to do makes him feel useless at first, so he sometimes creates a little fire in his palm, so he can help navigate. But, each time, Mez and finally even Chumba snap at him for drawing attention, so he stops and follows along obediently instead.

He comes to like it. *Mez and Lima are doing a great job,* he thinks. *I can obey orders!* It's a relief, actually. Not everyone needs to be in charge. Somebody's got to be number twelve.

With so little to see, so little to think about beyond avoiding whatever obstacles loom in the darkness, Gogi turns meditative. He gauges the size of the moon, watches as it approaches fullness—the time of the upcoming eclipse. Four nights away now. He counts his breaths, observes the feeling of cool night air on his nose, and thinks about what their plan should be once they find the ant-occupied zone.

They'll take the fungus out and . . . put it in the ants'

nest somehow . . . and what? Will it destroy them all? Is it wrong to infect the ants with something that will kill them? Do ants have feelings? It seems an awful sort of magic, that the fungus-ridden sticks in his bag, so harmless to him and his friends, might spread and take down an entire species.

But under their queen, the ants are ravaging all of Caldera. To hold back now might mean losing all of the rainforest to the horde. No, there's simply no other solution. Decimating the ants is worth it if it means saving the rest of the animals.

One evening, when Gogi, Mez, and Chumba are making their way along a dark canyon, Lima soaring high above, Gogi comes across something that makes him stop in his tracks. A splash of color on the jungle floor.

Usually nightwalkers don't have the bright colors that daywalkers have, since it's best to blend into the darkness. But Gogi's circle of firelight illuminates three small shapes on the ground, striking yellows and greens and oranges. Toucans. They're lying on the jungle floor, right out in the open in full nightcoma, vulnerable to any predator that comes by. Mez and Chumba stop short next to the slumbering bodies. "Yum," Mez says.

"Stop it right there," Gogi says. "There's no reason

these toucans would let themselves fall into nightcoma right here. They hide away in trees before the Veil drops."

"They probably got caught unawares, and fell asleep while they were still flying," Chumba says. "Poor little delicious birds."

"They're on the run," Gogi says. "They're fleeing their home, and got caught out. We aren't eating them. They're victims of the Ant Queen." He gently picks one up. "I'm finding them a tree hiding space, before some nasty predator comes along and takes advantage of their plight." He gives Mez a pointed look.

She rolls her eyes in return. "I can't believe I'm going along with this." She delicately lifts one of the birds in her mouth and starts climbing the nearest tree, claws digging into the bark.

Chumba gets another, and Gogi is last up the tree, nestling the smallest toucan with the others in the crook where three branches meet. "Be more careful tomorrow," he whispers to the sleeping bird. "I hope you find a new home soon."

Mez and Chumba watch him quietly, and then follow him back down the tree. "It was so hard not to bite down," Mez says once they start moving again.

"Totally hard," Chumba agrees.

Gogi shakes his head. Carnivores.

As the night wears on, the group of toucan refugees sticks in Gogi's mind. All the animals of Caldera are affected by the Ant Queen's menace, not just the shadowwalkers. As they travel farther east into the affected territory, they'll probably see more and more animals displaced by the ant horde, made vulnerable and alone because they've lost their homeland. How odd that *he*, a low-ranked member of an average capuchin troop, would happen to be born during the eclipse, get a magical power as a result, and come to this point, so far from his own homeland, saving the day by rescuing a precious weapon from the Dismal Bog (he *did* save the day, he *did*!), and now crossing the land and heading right into the worst kind of danger. Who would have predicted that? If only his mother could see him now. He strokes the woven fibers of his sack, with the special fungus within it, and marvels at the unexpected largeness of his life, of the solemn task he's been charged with.

Then he hears a song. It comes from Lima, somewhere above, warbling at the top of her voice. *"Liiiima, the Healing Bat! Ferocious-er than a piranha! Scarier than a cat!"*

"Lima!" Gogi calls up. "What are you singing?"

The song cuts off. He hears Lima cough. "I'm, um, trying out songs. I feel like every superhero bat should have her own signature song."

"It's a good one," Gogi says diplomatically. "I think it's a great start."

"Really?" Lima squeaks. "Oh, that's so nice to hear. I wasn't sure if it was the right melody."

Gogi hadn't realized there was a melody. "Oh yeah, that's a really good melody you chose there."

As she flies above, Lima recommences her song, even louder than before. *"Liiiiiiiiima, the Healing Bat!"*

"First those lost toucans, and now Lima's song. You're a kind one, Gogi," Mez purrs nearby.

"It *is* a good song," Gogi says. "Or it will be once she works on it some more. Once it, you know, becomes a song at all."

"Like I said, you're a kind one. Wait! Hold. Lima, hush!"

Lima's song abruptly ends. Gogi goes still in the moonlight, listening to the slightest of rustles as Mez turns in a circle. "Chumba," she continues, "do you detect what I'm detecting?"

"I do," Chumba says somberly.

"Stay here and protect Gogi," Mez says. "I'll go investigate. Lima, are you—"

"—already with you," comes Lima's voice from right nearby.

"Go invisible, even though it's night," Chumba says to Mez. "I don't want him discovering you."

"*Who?*" Gogi whispers.

Mez, already only a dim silhouette of off-black, disappears entirely. Gogi can only assume that he and Chumba are now alone. There's so much he doesn't understand about what just happened, and he knows he should probably protest that he doesn't need protecting, but being in unfamiliar nighttime territory makes him very glad to have Chumba—and her claws and teeth—nearby. He runs his hands through her calico fur, grooming out any bits of dirt and ticks. It's not the way panthers usually groom—they're more into licking—but Chumba seems to enjoy it, purring away.

"Who did Mez see?" Gogi asks. "You said it was a 'he.'"

"I don't know who it was," Chumba whispers back. "But we heard a male frog, and it sounded like he was shouting out orders."

"Was it Rumi?" Gogi asks hopefully.

"Definitely not Rumi," Chumba says. "It was a very big frog. Maybe a cane toad?"

"Those big, sloppy guys?" Gogi asks. "None of the shadowwalkers was a cane toad. I wonder how Mez knows this one."

"I think we're about to find out," Chumba says. "She's on her way back."

"How do you possibly know that an invisible panther is approaching?" Gogi asks.

"Special sister sense," Chumba says.

"He's not more than a minute's travel south of here," comes Mez's voice, surprisingly close. Gogi jumps and puts his hand over his mouth to mute his scream.

"*Who* is?" Gogi asks once his heart has stopped thumping.

"Rumi," Lima whispers from a branch nearby.

"Rumi!" Gogi says, unable to keep his voice low. "I said that! I *said* it was Rumi, Chumba, but you were like, 'No, silly monkey, that's not—'"

"Not *our* Rumi," Mez whispers. "Frogs are named after where they're born, so there are lots of Rumis out there. This is *Big* Rumi. He's a cane toad that was hunting Rumi when Lima and I first met him."

"He's really big and really sloppy and really mean," Lima says. "I don't like him."

"Yeah, I figured that part out," Gogi says.

"He's talking to some other henchman, about

where they're supposed to lead the ant horde next," Mez says.

"Oh," Gogi says. "This cane toad is collaborating with the Ant Queen, like the hoatzin and fer-de-lance were? That doesn't sound good."

"Or it sounds very good, when you have bog fungus in your sack," Chumba says.

"Precisely," Mez says. "This could be our chance to find out just what this stuff can do. Come on, follow me. You'll need to bring Gogi along. We can't risk any firelight. Chumba, you can track me and Lima?"

"Yes, of course," Chumba says. "I know your scent better than I know my own."

"That's sweet. Weird, but sweet," Gogi whispers as he wraps his tail around Chumba's. They start off through the dark. Immediately something spindly is on his eyebrows and he brushes it madly away. Ugh. It might have been a cute little stick bug, or it might have been a huge venomous scorpion. He has no way of knowing. Night travel is the worst.

Soon they're making their way through under-growth, the sharp chirps of tree frogs all around them. *I hope Rumi—Little Rumi, that is—and Sky are okay,* Gogi thinks. As leaves and slimy roots rake against Gogi's scalp, the ground begins to slope upward. At the top of the rise they come to a patch of rocky soil overlooking a misty expanse of rainforest. Without the aid of his firelight, Gogi can't see much of it, but he can make out enough to know that, at the bottom of the rise, the ant horde must be at work. Because there are no more trees.

He's almost relieved that the nighttime hides the full scope of it. There's a dull roar in the distance, one that he can only assume is from the pattering of millions of spindly legs. There's a now-familiar sheen to the milled soil, and overhead are swarms of bats heading west— away from the horde.

"So many of them at once," Lima says, a catch in her voice. "They're fleeing, and they have no idea where they're going, they've lost their homes. . . . I've never heard so much anguish from one group of bats."

"I'm sorry, Lima," Mez says. "We'll fix this."

"They're vesper bats," Lima says, letting out a long breath, "and normally I think of them as total knuckleheads. But tonight, hearing all that . . . I feel bad for them."

"Hear that?" Mez says. "Big Rumi's belching out orders again."

This time Gogi hears it: a guttural vibration, coming from the edge where the trees go from swaying before the stars to disappearing into ruin. The boundary of the invisible ant horde. It takes a few moments for Gogi to make out the creature's words: *They've weakened the roots. Now they're ready to feast on the trunk. When I say the word, we push with our hind legs. Ready? Goooo.*

There's a rumble, then a crack. One of the trees at the edge, a tall ironwood that has probably been growing for a century, heaves over and tumbles into the mass of ants. Gogi can see only the barest hints of their glittering mass in the moonlight, but he can imagine how feverishly they're digging into the fresh wood and sap— and into whatever creatures were unfortunate enough not to escape the tree in time.

"Excellent work," Big Rumi chortles. "The Ant Queen will be verrrry satisfied with our progress."

Whoever the cane toad's ally is, its voice is too low for the companions to make out.

"Fine," Big Rumi replies. "You go your way, and I'll go mine. We will see each other again at the next dropping of the Veil."

"We have to hurry," Mez says through clenched teeth, "if we're to have any hope of tailing Big Rumi."

"Tailing him? Like, right through the ant army?" Lima says, gulping.

"I can go invisible," Mez says.

"Yes, but no getting swarmed by ants this time," Gogi says.

"I can fly over," Lima says.

"What about Gogi and me, though?" Chumba asks.

"Let Lima and me take care of it. Quickly now," Mez says. "Give me the sack with the fungus sticks, Gogi."

"There must be some other way," he says.

"There's no time! Once the ants close ranks behind Big Rumi, we'll have lost our chance. Now! Give it to me!"

Startled into submission, Gogi takes the woven sack off and hangs it across Mez's chest, pebbles clattering. She steals into the darkness. Lima soars above her and is soon lost in the starry black sky.

"We don't even know if it's going to . . . work," Gogi says, his voice trailing away as Mez disappears. He wishes he'd had time at least to take the pebbles out.

"I guess we just wait?" Chumba says.

"That doesn't feel very good," Gogi grumbles.

"Look, there Mez goes," Chumba says. "Can you sense her too? We can watch what happens, at least."

"Maybe *you* can watch her, but I don't have your special sister sense," Gogi says.

Figuring that his light will only further take attention away from Mez and Lima, Gogi adds a glimmer of his ring of firelight to the scene. His stomach drops at the full sight of the ants, a teeming mass as far as the eye can see, swarming over sundered terrain. Only vague shapes of the ruined rainforest are visible beneath them, fallen trees and animal carcasses indistinguishable beneath the blanket of insects.

A cane toad hops its way through the swarm. The ants try to part before him, but Big Rumi crushes as many as he avoids. The amphibian's bulbous throat shakes from side to side as he lurches his way forward, burping out orders.

"Big Rumi's not exactly cute, is he?" Gogi asks.

"You know, this cute-ism among the rainforest animals really has to stop," Chumba says hotly, but then she swallows her words. "Oh no!"

"What is it?" Gogi asks. He has his answer when he sees Mez stealing toward the cane toad.

Mez is invisible.

But Gogi can follow her.

Because the *sack* isn't invisible.

"Chumba," he whispers urgently. "The sack."

"I know, I see it," she says. "What should we do, what should we do?"

Gogi watches, paralyzed, as the bobbing sack streaks toward the toad. He watches as the mass of ants parts to allow Big Rumi through. He watches as Mez creeps after the cane toad, invisible except for a ridiculous square of woven fibers floating in midair.

"The moment Big Rumi turns around, he'll spot her," Chumba says.

"And then he'll set the ants on her, if they're not already attacking," Gogi says. "But maybe he won't turn around?"

"Every creature turns around," Chumba says bitterly. "This is the rainforest. Any creature who didn't check its surroundings every few seconds would already be dead."

"That's pretty dark," Gogi says, chewing on a fingernail. "And true."

"We need a plan," Chumba says, eyelashes fluttering as she looks into Gogi's eyes. "And it's got to be up to you, because I'm about to fall into daycoma."

Gogi's ears burn. "Are you kidding me right now?"

"So . . . sleepy," Chumba says.

"Ugh, why couldn't you have been born during the eclipse, like your sister? Quick, into this thicket," Gogi says. He parts a stand of ferns and vines, and Chumba drags herself in, ears drooping. She's asleep before the fronds have stopped quivering.

Gogi stands outside the thicket, tapping his nose.

Now what? Think, Gogi, think!

The ants part before Big Rumi and then re-form behind him as he passes, leaving a narrow open space to his rear. That's where Mez is, the woven sack bobbing right behind the toad. Lima wheels in the sky above, too small to be of much help.

To keep Mez and Big Rumi in view, Gogi needs to get some altitude. He scampers up a nearby fig tree, plucking himself upward branch by branch until he's in the thin upper reaches of the canopy. This feels very high up, even for a monkey. He takes many skinny branches in each hand to support himself, but even so he sways alarmingly, the ground well past monkeysplat distance.

He surprises a tamarind monkey family, a mom with two tiny babies clinging to her belly. Three sets of frightened eyes stare at Gogi. "Excuse me, ma'am," he says. "I didn't mean to startle you. It's just that I need to be here to see my friend, so if you'll excuse me . . ."

"Flee!" is all the mother squeals, babies squirming about her. "We must run to the spot where the sun sets, or the ants will eat us all!"

"Well, yes, you see, that's exactly what I'm trying to prevent," Gogi says. But the family of tamarind refugees is already gone by the time he finishes his sentence, his last sight of them two pairs of wide eyes as the babies stare over their mother's shoulder.

Gogi leans out so the branches bend, giving him an unrestricted view of the scene below. Big Rumi and Mez are a good fifty monkeylengths out, making their way over chopped-up terrain and the flailing bodies of ants. Lima is a blip in the sky above, swooping back and forth, powerless to do anything to alter the situation.

Unless . . . What if Lima plucked away the bag? Big Rumi might notice, of course, but it would make Mez undetectable again.

It would ruin their plan to get the fungus deep into enemy lines, though—unless Lima could manage to then fly the sack deep into the horde and drop one of the sticks.

Gogi needn't deliberate any longer, as a screeching howl brings his attention back to Mez and Big Rumi.

Mez has been discovered.

Big Rumi is hopping and slavering, circling the strange floating sack and lashing out with his vile pink tongue. Gogi's woven sack dodges and leaps, but the ants are pressing in, closing the circle. They'll soon be covering Mez—and the ants won't care one bit if their target is invisible. They'll start biting, and by covering Mez they'll let the cane toad know exactly where to strike.

He has to get there to help, and fast. But—silly monkey!—he's way up in the air, a good fifty monkeylengths up, too far to do any good.

Or wait. Maybe not so silly after all. Fifty monkeylengths up! Mez is about fifty monkeylengths *over*!

Gogi gets to work right away. Craning his neck to stare down, he aims his palm at the base of the tree trunk, where the bark has already been worn away by the advance guard of the ants. Then, lips tight between gritted teeth, he teases a tendril of flame out from each palm. The heat crackles the air and sets his brows to sweating.

So much else calls for his attention: the ants around him, the ants swarming Mez, the pitched combat between panther and cane toad. *Come on, Gogi, stay focused, just for a minute.* He manages to keep his concentration up: the fire is sure and true, striking the base of the tree. He'd have aimed it at Big Rumi directly, but with Mez bobbing and darting all around him, it's too risky.

The tree, however—a falling tree will get him there fast. Maybe a little *too* fast, Gogi realizes as the trunk begins to wobble and sway alarmingly. With his flame destroying the wood on the ant side of the trunk, the tree starts pitching toward the horde, causing the top of the canopy to sway. The few remaining birds squawk and flee.

Then, with a great crack, the tree careens through the air. Gogi's belly feels like it's being sucked inward, and then his face fills with wind, disrupting his flame and ballooning out his cheeks. He hears Lima cheering from the sky above, but his fraying thoughts are focused on scrambling through the branches, so that he's on top of the tree when it hits, and not under. Being under a falling tree would definitely be bad.

Rushing air, a deafening boom. Fingers and toes and tail gripping wood so hard it feels like it's splintering under his grip.

Then silence.

He succeeded! At least Gogi figures he must have. It's hard to tell much amid the chaos of the fallen tree, but if he's wondering whether he's still alive, that must mean that he's survived! Pleased with himself, Gogi forces his way out of the shredded branches, plucking leaves from his mouth.

He tumbles right into a swarm of ants.

Yelping, he leaps to his feet and brushes the ants off as best he can. But there are more under his feet, and they're immediately swarming up his legs. Once he's covered in ants, there will be only one possible end.

Within seconds, he'll be overcome.

He leaps in the air and twists, trying to sight Mez and Big Rumi. He spots them soon enough. This part of the plot went as planned: they're only a few lengths away, on the far side of the fallen tree. Gogi scrambles over the branches, skidding through swarming ants until he's upon them. Taking advantage of Big Rumi's surprise, Gogi shouts, "Mez, go visible!"

Suddenly she's there, teeth bared as she squares off against the cane toad, then barrel-rolling to one side as Big Rumi lashes out with his tongue. "Here I am, Gogi!" she cries. "Please tell me you have a plan!"

"Of course I do," Gogi says as he high-steps over the ants to reach Mez's side. Well, he sort of has a plan. Almost has a plan. Maybe doesn't actually have a plan. But Mez doesn't need to know all the specifics of what he does and doesn't know.

Fire. Fire is always a good place to start.

While Gogi runs, Big Rumi continues to lash out with his tongue and powerful back legs. Just like the hoatzin and the fer-de-lance from before, a necklace of ants is marching around his head. "It's you!" he thunders at Mez. "The panther who rescued that traitorous little tree frog."

"It was a mistake to ever let you live!" Mez hisses

as she lashes out with a claw, narrowly missing the toad's eye.

"The mistake is yours," Big Rumi says. "It's too bad you will die here, because otherwise you could go ask your little friend what he did that was so terrible."

"Stop lying," Mez spits.

Gogi wraps his arms around Mez and wills his body to produce a sphere of flame to cover the both of them. "Ow, ow, ow," Mez says. The smell of smoldering fur—and burning vegetation—wafts up around them.

"The sack is catching fire!" Mez says. "Not to mention me!"

"Okay, sorry, sorry," Gogi says. "This was a better idea in my head."

He lets the fire shield dissipate. They're surrounded by half-sizzled ants, on their backs and sides, antennae waving in the air. At least the ants right under them won't be attacking anymore—he's bought himself and Mez a few seconds.

Enough time for Big Rumi to go on the attack.

He's given up on using his tongue, and instead leaps directly for Gogi. Big Rumi is astonishingly fast, and having a toad as big as him hurtling in his direction just about stops Gogi's heart. Before he knows it, his legs are inside Big Rumi's mouth, and then the cane toad jerks, and Gogi's suddenly inside his slick gullet, all the way up to his belly button. Try as Gogi may, the toad's jaws are locked tight on his midsection, cutting off his breathing. He'll be swallowed up before he knows it.

Mez springs on top of Big Rumi, jaws gnashing at the toad's head and rear claws raking his backside. Startled, Big Rumi opens his mouth wider, and Gogi manages to get his hands around the sharp-edged jaws enough to pull himself up and out. He's covered in toad slobber, his hands are bleeding, but he's alive.

Mez gives one ferocious bite to Big Rumi's skull, then leaps away. The toad hits the soil, facedown. He doesn't get up.

"Thank you, Mez," Gogi says, panting.

"We need to start the next part of your plan *now*," Mez says.

"Right. The next part of my plan. Uh-huh," Gogi says.

Mez narrows her eyes at him. "Pull one of the fungus sticks out of the bag," she says, eyeing the gnashing horde of ants, healthy soldiers crawling over the dead bodies of the fallen, the tide of insects rising ever closer. "If we're going to die here, at least we can try to take them down with us."

"Go out in a blaze of glory, eh?" Gogi says. His words might sound brave, but his heart is quaking. He doesn't want to die.

"With you here, we could literally do just that," Mez says. She presses her backside against Gogi's, tail entwining with tail as they face off against the ants.

Gogi presses his hands together at the soft part of the wrist, so that a fan of flame jets out. He aims it in front of him, where it scorches a cone of ants, then pivots so the fan of fire passes all around them, making a circle of charred insects. "I can't keep producing fire forever," Gogi says. "Once I'm exhausted, I'm out. But this is buying us a little time. You get a fungus stick out, and put it on the tip of my tail. Then I'll whip it around and hurl it as far as I can."

Mez gets to work, slipping her paw into the sack. Gogi expects her to turn left when she turns right, and he singes off the hair on the tip of one of her ears. "Sorry! Sorry!" he says.

"Just one second—there, got it," Mez says, pulling her paw out. Gogi's too busy burning the advancing ants to spend a second looking, but he feels something at the tip of his tail, and wraps the end around it.

"When you whip your tail around, don't forget to stop making your fire," Mez says. "I don't want to be a crispy charred panther."

"Crispy charred panther sounds kind of tasty," Gogi says.

"Gogi!"

"Sorry, sorry. Which direction?" Gogi asks.

"Where Big Rumi was heading," Mez answers. "As far into the horde as you can get it."

"Okay, then, here we go," Gogi says, gauging where the ants seem to be thickest. He drops the flame momentarily so he can concentrate on his tail throw, winds the stick round and round, and then flings.

He tracks the arc of the stick tumbling through the sky, until it passes in front of the sun and he's dazzled. He shields his eyes, too late, and shakes his head.

Bites on his ankles. "Mez," Gogi says, "more ants are climbing on me. We have to go."

"Yeah, have any bright ideas about how to do that?" Mez asks, her voice falling into gasps of pain as she nips at the ants on her legs.

Gogi looks at Mez, but she's just a big purple blob from where he let the sun burn his eyes. "I don't, I'm sorry."

Or maybe he does. *Go out in a blaze of glory.*

"Mez, get close."

"I *am* close!"

"Okay, stay close, then. I mean it. As close as you can to my backside."

"Yuck. Monkey butt."

"*Mez!* Remind me to kill you once I save you."

Once he feels Mez tight against him, Gogi summons up the depths of his power. This will require more magic out of him than he's ever summoned before, but if they want to survive this ant horde . . .

"Oh my," Mez says, awestruck.

All Gogi can see is fire. His fire. He's made a shell of it, a rippling, searing sphere of flame. His eyes tear up, his fur instantly sweaty. He takes a step forward, and the sphere moves with him. Mez paces with him, making little yowls of astonishment as she goes.

"I'm not hurting you, am I?" Gogi asks.

"No," Mez says, nearly breathless. "Gogi . . . this is amazing."

"Best part is that I don't even have to focus. I'm just letting it bust out all over the place. Much easier when you have a mind like mine. I'm going to pick up the pace," Gogi warns. "No crispy charred panthers."

"I'll be with you."

Gogi begins to run. He's only got a few more seconds of fire left in him, and if they want to be out of the ant horde by then, he'll have to move fast.

Beneath him are ants, some charred to bits, some steaming, some sizzling. Some of them manage to bite him anyway, and it feels like running over nettles.

One significant drawback of a fire shield: he can't see beyond a couple feet in front of his face, can't see any sky above his head. He'll have to hope that he's continuing in the right direction, that he's not heading into the middle of the horde instead of out of it.

A gnawing feeling starts up in his center. It's like being out of breath from running, except the exhausted, heaving feeling is in his spine instead of his lungs. He's felt this in a minor way before, when he was battling the Ant Queen back in the watery caverns beneath the Ziggurat of the Sun and Moon, but never this intensely. He's nearly spent.

And that's it. With a hissing flicker, the shield disappears, reappears briefly, and then is gone.

His pupils got used to the bright light, which means now he can't see the ground beneath him. He might be swarming with ants, and those that are still unscorched might be teeming toward him and Mez. He waits for the biting to start, the first signs that all is over.

There are no bites.

Gogi's eyes gradually adjust. Beneath his feet are

grass and twigs, a few crumpled ferns, and one very startled praying mantis.

They made it out past the ant horde.

"Mez, are you okay?" he asks, whirling.

She looks at him, her eyes wide, then slowly nods. "That was the wildest experience of my life," she says. "And we've had some wild experiences."

Gogi struggles to keep a straight face. Mez's eyebrows have been seared right off. She's now the most ridiculous-looking panther he's ever seen. Maybe she won't notice. Maybe he won't get in big trouble. "You seem . . . fine," he says.

Mez nods, obviously still dazed by the whole experience. "Which way is Chumba?" she manages to ask.

"Over here," Gogi says, leading them toward the fern thicket where he left the young panther. He holds his breath, only exhaling once he's parted the fronds and seen Chumba right where he left her, snoring away.

"Chumba, you're okay, thank the moon," Mez says, curling her body around her sister's.

"That looks very snuggy," Gogi says, letting out a long breath.

"Come join us," Mez says.

"Don't mind if I do!" comes a small voice from above.

"Lima!"

"Sorry I wasn't much help during the fight, guys," Lima says. "But at least I got a great aerial view of that light show. Wow!"

Gogi knows he should be off to examine the ant horde, to see whether their plot has worked. But who knows how long it will take the fungus to start working—if it works at all. And he's so very tired. Using that much of his magic feels the same as staying up for five days straight. A nap would be so very nice.

Mez is cuddled next to Chumba, her paw over her sister protectively. Gogi hunkers down on the other side of Chumba, his backside against her soft belly. Lima nestles between them. "I have to admit, you panthers have this cuddling thing down pat," he says.

"Panthers really do know how to nap," Mez says, then lets out a big yawn. Gogi hears her sharp jaws click as they open to their widest, can imagine his friend's long teeth. She makes him feel safe.

"Should we set a watch?" he asks.

Mez is snoring already.

"We should . . . really . . . set a watch," he says.

The next thing he knows, he's dreaming of fire and ants, and then he's coming awake.

It's nighttime, and Chumba's shaking him. "Gogi,

something terrible has happened!"

"What is it? What is it?" Gogi cries, leaping to his feet, listening for danger, imagining ant queens and giant toads.

Chumba points at her sleeping sister. "It's Mez's eyebrows!"

Gogi bursts out laughing.

Three Nights Until the Eclipse

"I'M NOT SURE the fungus you hurled in does anything after all," Chumba says. "It looks like
there's still a whole bunch of ants over there, being all
ant-y."

"I know," Mez says. "But look at it this way. They've
stopped mowing down everything in their path. So
something is going better!"

Gogi's finding it a little hard to concentrate, as
they're hidden in the branches of a short tree that smells
weirdly delicious, like wild onions. As they wait for any
sign that the fungus has taken effect, he scratches at
the bark, soaking in the tangy fragrance that rises up

from it. After their climactic fight against Big Rumi and their flaming run from the ant attackers, he'd expected something more exciting to happen next. But it's not like the ants have suddenly started running around saying *What's this terrible artifact from the Dismal Bog, what ever will we do?* They're just being . . . *ants*.

"The fungus will kick in soon, I know it," Mez says.

"Maybe we're going about this wrong," Gogi says. "Panther and monkey instinct is always to stick in the treetops to observe enemies, because it's safer. But ants are just too little to get an eye on. I'm going to go down and see if I can figure anything more out by getting close."

"Be careful, okay?" Mez says.

"Of course. Who do you think you're talking to, a fifteen rank?"

Relieved to finally be moving his muscles, Gogi scampers down the tree. At the bottom, he pauses to cup his hands, willing a lick of fire to appear. The flame itself feels nice—cozy on the calluses of his finger pads. After yesterday, even this small move makes his spine sore.

Once he's got his tiny flame, Gogi hunches and begins to work his way forward, tracking the illumination back and forth along the dark ground. It's awkward going, until he thinks to transfer the fire to the tip of his tail instead. That's much better. He can maneuver the tail so it's always above him, and he can move forward at full speed on all fours.

The ants are just about everywhere, even in this healthy part of the rainforest. It's the creepiest thing about them—they're active on both sides of the Veil, the billions of them always working at something. Up night and day, like the two-legs once were. And the shadow-walkers still are. Hmm, maybe he should rethink that "creepy" part.

Concentrate, Gogi.

He pauses to study the ants around him. They're healthy-looking normal ants, doing antlike things. Not swarming or eating up all the animals in their path or anything. They're cutting up leaves, carrying dead bodies of other ants, hassling a caterpillar, streaming along in their columns, tapping the ground with their antennae. There are ants of all sizes and types, little red ones, big black ones—it pays to watch out for those especially—and brownish ones that are somewhere in between. But they're all just being ants.

Gogi looks back toward his friends, where Mez is watching him closely. Worried. Hopeful.

He continues poking his way forward. It's as unnerving as nighttime travel always is, with fronds and spiders and click beetles whapping him in the face every few steps. But he keeps himself focused on the ants.

Trees become sparser, and the calls of birds and insects stop, so Gogi knows he's approaching the ruined part of the land. Sure enough, what little greenery is left here is lacey and pockmarked, ants working to carry away the few bits that remain. But these ants are uncoordinated, unlike the orderly lines he saw before. Most of them, actually, look like they're running for their lives. As much as ants can express that sort of thing.

Flame held forward gingerly on the agile tip of his tail, careful not to get any ants running up his legs, Gogi works his way in the direction the ants are coming from. There are more fleeing ants, and then he comes across some that are acting even more strangely. They're wearing head ornaments, for one thing.

Wait. Ants wearing head ornaments?

Gogi leans in close. They're not really head ornaments. They're—Gogi leaps back in astonishment, his flame winking out.

Gritting his teeth, he relights the flame and approaches the strange ants. These ants have mushrooms. Growing. Out. Of. Their. Heads.

Those poor creatures, Gogi thinks, even though those poor creatures were just recently trying to kill him.

The mushroom-y ants are still moving, just slowly

and randomly. And upward. They definitely seem to like moving upward. Whenever one of the weird suffering insects hits a ruined branch, it starts climbing, joining the other afflicted ants at the top. Gogi can't wait to report this new information back to the sisters. Maybe it will prove useful. But he forces himself to wait a little longer, to see if there's more to learn.

One of the mushroom-y ants in the cluster, this one with a particularly large specimen of fungus growing out of its forehead, leaves the group to walk even higher, along a long branch. Once at the tip, it pauses and lowers its head. Lit in eerie, glittering colors by the firelight from Gogi's tail, the scene has the feeling of an ancient ritual. He leans forward to get a better view of what this renegade ant might be doing.

Then—*puff.* Like it's blowing a booger out of its nose, the ant sneezes out a fine white dust. But it doesn't sneeze out of the nose—the ant doesn't have a nose, for starters—but out of the mushroom top. Which, unfortunately for the ant, causes its whole head to explode into bits.

Spores, Gogi realizes. *It's sending out spores.*

Spores—and bits of ant exoskeleton—fall like dust on the surrounding ants. They immediately start cleaning themselves, running their hairy forelegs over their heads and bodies. But right away they seem disoriented, running into one another, knocking one another onto their backs, legs flailing.

Or no, they're not running into one another. They're *killing* one another.

The ants lock mandibles, pushing heads into the ground, brittle legs coming free as they slice and hack. The soil around Gogi's feet is soon strewn with ant bits. One ant survives the immediate battle, and before his eyes Gogi sees it slow down, then find the nearest high point—the top of the pile of ant pieces—where it lays its head, as if taking a nap. But it's not a nap. Gogi can see the first tendrils of mushroom sprout from its joints.

So that's how the fungus works.

That's some creepy fungus.

This must be happening across the ant horde, fungus infecting ants, turning them aggressive, the survivors living long enough to become spreaders of the fungus.

But there are so many ants. How quickly will the infection spread? Will it spread fast enough to stop the horde's momentum?

Will it make it all the way to the queen?

Unnerved by the nighttime ant zombies, and puzzled what to do with this new information, Gogi retreats. He wipes away the insects that took advantage of the opportunity to start crawling up his arms and legs.

Lost in thought, he returns to Lima and the sisters.

"So it's working!" Chumba says excitedly, kneading her claws into Mez's ribs, a move that Gogi has only recently figured out is the panther version of a high five.

Mez is less thrilled than her sister. "Yes . . . but why doesn't it feel too great?"

"It doesn't feel great to me, either," Gogi says. "Why is that?"

"Yeah, what's wrong with you guys?" Lima says. "Ants slaughtering ants is great news!"

"To recap," Mez says, pacing the branch. "These ants have gotten this fungus and are now dismembering one another."

"*Creepily* dismembering one another," Gogi adds.

"Okay, *creepily* dismembering one another. But what now? The Ant Queen isn't here. The rest of her armies aren't here. And we don't know how long this fungus lasts. If these ants right here all die, then there won't be any left to take it to her."

"Then we bring the Ant Queen here," Chumba says. "So we can be sure she's exposed to the fungus."

"I never considered that," Mez says.

"Could I just say that the Ant Queen seems very

difficult to move around, seeing as she's huge and armor plated and, um, all-powerful?" Gogi asks. "And far away? I also think that in general we should be avoiding her, right? Here's a thought: What if we brought these infected ants to *her*?"

"We bring this problem all the way to the top," Mez says.

"And right to the queen, too," Lima says, nodding.

"That's what I meant," Mez says.

"Right," Lima says, nodding.

"So, where *is* the queen?" Chumba asks.

"To the east, where the sun dawns," Mez says. "Why she's staying there instead of joining the vanguard of her army, who knows."

"*If* we can find her somewhere in the east, and that's a very big 'if.' That's far to bring an ant horde," Gogi says. "Especially on little insect legs."

"So, how do we herd a few trillion ants all the way across the rainforest?" Chumba asks.

"*That* I have an answer for," Gogi says, a smile spreading across his face. For extra dramatic effect, he sends licks of flames out of his nostrils.

"Wow," Lima says. "I like the way you think."

14

"**I**SN'T THIS PRECISELY what they mean when they say 'Don't play with fire'?" Chumba asks.

"This will work out fine, don't worry!" Gogi says.

Lima squeaks up. "I'm with Chumba. Lima the Healing Bat thinks that once the flame is out of the monkey, so to speak, it's out of our control."

Mez raises her eyebrows. Or where her eyebrows would have risen if Gogi hadn't seared them off. "Tell me you're not going to start talking about yourself in the third person, Lima."

"Who's the third person?" Lima asks.

"Lima," Gogi says, patting her on the head. "I'm

not the young monkey that you once knew. I have plenty of self-control. I'm a twelve rank now, don't you forget."

"How could we ever possibly forget?" Mez says sweetly.

"My sister appears to be in a bit of a mood," Chumba says.

"Look," Gogi says, "this is going to be—what would they call it?—a 'controlled burn.' A little flame behind the ants to get them started in the right direction, that's all."

"Or the *wrong* direction, riiight?" Lima says. "Get it? Wrong if you're the *Ant Queen*, ha-ha."

"Yes, Lima," Chumba says patiently. "We get it."

"With Big Rumi out of the way, and that other, mystery henchman nowhere to be seen, this squad of ants doesn't have a leader," Gogi says. "They're just milling around, spreading the fungus and losing numbers whenever more berserking happens. They need a nudge onto the right path. Then they'll start on their way."

"Is that so?" Mez says, a teasing smile on her face.

"Look, we don't *have* to do my plan," Gogi says. "Does anyone have anything better to offer?"

Mez shakes her head. "I don't, sorry."

"Me neither," Lima says.

"Lead the way, Gogi," Chumba says. "We'll follow you."

"Okay," Gogi says, sniffing and drawing up to his full height. "See that rotten tree overlooking the zombie ant horde?"

"Yes," Mez says dryly, "it's hard to overlook the zombie ant horde."

"But the tree *behind* them, do you see that?" Gogi asks.

"Yep."

"Here's what I'm thinking: I'll send some flame over there, fire it up, get it good and smoking and red, then set the embers falling. That should chase the ants the opposite way."

"Toward the rising sun!" Lima says, wings out wide.

"Well, that was a touch dramatic," Mez says.

"We'll basically set the two armies on a collision course," Lima says, ignoring her.

"I just want to officially state that I don't think this will go as planned," Mez says. "But we don't have many other options, so count me in. Gogi, will you do the honors?"

"Wow, thanks for the rousing pep talk, Mez," Gogi says. He takes a deep, centering breath, readying himself. He's still feeling a little overtaxed by the fire he produced rescuing Mez, and this new stream will need to travel over a very long distance. But at least the ants have done him a favor by being so ravenous. They've hollowed out this tree so much that it looks almost shaggy, bits of dried-out bark dangling over the edge of the horde.

"Keep back, guys," Gogi says. Then, once he feels his friends snuggled to his rear on the tree limb, he sends his fire out into the night.

It's a frail and tender arc of orange, not much to see, but enough to light up the gnashing destruction of the scene below. Gritting his teeth, brows furrowed, Gogi wills the flame farther into the night, pitching it higher when it falls short, sizzling bodies of dead ants below. He directs it yet higher, so it forms a rainbow of flame, finally landing on the rotten tree at the far side of the ants.

Nothing happens.

"Keep going, Gogi, you're doing great, it will start working any second now," Lima urges.

Sweat runs into Gogi's eyes, and his arms start to ache. He shuts his eyes against the pain and feels Mez use the top of her head to gently support his arms so that he can more easily keep the flame focused on the ants.

Chumba gasps.

Gogi opens his eyes.

The tree has caught fire.

At first it's rimmed in a ruddy aura, then the flames join and turn other colors—yellow and orange and red and finally blue and white. Gogi feels his energy peter out. With an anguished cry, he lets his stream of flame drop.

The companions watch as, with a roaring, snapping sound, the rotten tree wavers in the air—then plummets right into the teeming insects.

The night air seems to mist, as ants—dead and alive—are flung up from the earth. The remaining ants become frantic before the fiery tree, the light glinting off them as they crawl over one another, desperate to escape.

"Wow!" Lima exclaims. "That was something!"

Exhausted, Gogi slumps on the branch, wrapping his tail around it twice in case his quivering limbs fail to keep him upright.

"It's hard to know where they're going yet," Chumba says, squinting as she stares into the horde. "But Gogi, that fire was amazing!"

"Thanks," Gogi manages to say.

"Um, guys?" Lima says.

"Yes, Lima, isn't it wonderful?" Chumba asks.

"No. I mean, yes, it's wonderful it worked, but have you guys, um, have you guys noticed thattheantsaregoing thewrongwaywe'reallgoingtodie?"

Gogi snaps his head up. "What do you mean?" Then he sees the ants' course. "Oh. Everyone, I think we, I think we'd better—"

"RUN!" Mez screams.

"FLY!" Lima screams.

Eyes wide with fear, Mez is first down the tree, followed by Chumba. Lima sails into the night as Gogi races down the trunk, missing hand- and footholds as often as he makes them, bashing his chin against an unexpected branch.

Once he hits the bottom, he's struck by sudden nightblindness, unable to see anything around him. All the same, he can hear the roaring tumult, can sense the horde of ants rolling toward him. But he's not sure exactly what direction they're coming from. "Mez? Chumba?" he cries.

"This way, Gogi!" Lima calls. He takes off toward her.

He's aware of fiery points on his legs and arms, and he realizes the ants must have been crawling up him while he was trying to catch his bearings. He wiggles his bum as he runs, hoping to shake them off, but they're tenacious. As Gogi barrels forward, strange shapes loom out of the night, some of them still and some of them moving—some of them the great tide of ants themselves, racing alongside him.

Lima keeps up her streaming chirps, leading him through the night. He becomes aware of a calico blur in front of him and realizes it's Chumba, sprinting. "Chumba," he calls, "I'm right behind you!"

"Hurry, Gogi!" she calls back, not sparing a moment to look over her shoulder.

"I'm coming!" he says. He knows that panthers are like monkeys, that they can sprint, but not run long distances without getting winded. They're faster than the ant horde right now, but how much longer can he and Chumba—and Mez, who he hopes is running right beside her sister—run before they stumble and collapse, and the ants take them?

Lima chirps something out, but the words are lost behind the dull roar of the insects. "What did she say?" he calls to Chumba.

"I'm not sure," Chumba pants as Gogi catches up alongside her. "It might have been something about a river?"

"Look out!" comes Mez's voice, from literally out of nowhere. Gogi trips over something furry and warm

(Mez, he realizes) and goes sprawling in the grass. Wait—grass! They must be out of the ruined zone.

"*You're* the one who's invisible," Gogi protests as he drags himself to his feet and sets his aching muscles moving again. "I think *you* need to look out for *me*. And Chumba, what did you say? Something about a riv—"

Splash.

As one, Gogi, Chumba, and Mez tumble into inky water. He's instantly submerged, and he feels writhing claws around him as the sisters struggle to the surface. When Gogi's legs hit the murky, slimy bottom, he instinctively kicks off, sending himself sputtering into the night air. He gasps and starts stroking, treading water and turning in a slow circle, waiting to hear Lima's voice. And, sure enough, she's right nearby. "This way, Gogi."

He swims through the water, thick with mud and silt, until he's at the far bank, where he pulls himself out. Lima's there right away; he can feel her wing beats as she flutters around him. "I'm fine, I'm fine," he says, waving her off.

"No, you're not." He feels a familiar warmth suffuse him as she heals his arms and legs. "You got really scratched up in there."

"It's our fault, I'm sorry," comes Mez's voice. About half her usual size now that she's wet through, Mez shakes herself out and huddles near.

Chumba, equally bedraggled, joins her. "We were fighting to get to the surface and we cut you pretty bad," she says. "Keep healing Gogi, Lima. We're fine."

Gogi lies back, grateful that he can't see his own wounds. He's not too squeamish around the sight of blood, unless it's his own. Then he's quite squeamish. "So, what's the status of the ants?" he asks.

Lima takes a break from healing, and instantly Gogi's wounds flare to life, arcs of pain lighting up on his thighs and upper arms. Lima gives him a few more healing licks before speaking again. "Wow. That was a *lot* of ants to echolocate at once."

"So . . . ?" Gogi asks.

"I don't know how to break this to you guys, but . . . it's not good. The healthy ants have found a way to deal with the sick ones. You can see it happening—it's right across the bank."

Startled, Gogi sits up.

"No, you should rest," Mez says.

"I need to see."

Lima points to a bush overhanging the other side of the river, where ants are teeming. "Can you illuminate the highest branches?"

Gogi does.

A trail of healthy ants is carrying what appear to be

bits of flecked rock up the branches, until they get to the very top. Then they drop them, tinkling, into the water. Gogi squints. Not rock. Ants.

"They're moving the infected ants away from the rest," he murmurs.

"And preventing the fungus from spreading further," Mez says. "Well, I'll be."

"So we failed," Gogi says, wincing as he lies back down.

"We failed to spread it to the rest of the horde, sure," Chumba says. "But we discovered that the fungus will work for a short while. And if we can use the other stick on the Ant Queen . . ."

"We did take out Big Rumi," Lima adds. "That's not for nothing. And the river we fell into has bought us some time. The ants don't seem to have figured out a way across yet, and are streaming around to either side. The river dams up a ways north, so eventually they'll make their way around to us. In the meantime, we have to put as much distance as we can between us and them, and there's only one direction that will allow us to do that—east."

"Going deeper into enemy territory." Gogi sighs.

"And closer to the Ant Queen with our one remaining fungus stick," Mez adds.

"We can't move Gogi yet, though," Chumba says. "He's wounded."

"No. I'll be all right. We need to get moving." Gogi sits up, and then inhales sharply. "Okay, maybe a few more minutes of healing first. If you insist."

Two Nights Until the Eclipse

B Y THE TIME the Veil's near its next lifting, Gogi is so tired that he can barely make his arms and legs keep moving. Every step sends pain arcing up through his palms, jangling his hips and shoulders. His eyes prick, and his head feels like it's been stuffed with scarlet milkweed.

Even Mez, the most stoic of the group, seems to be suffering. She slows, and her paws begin to drag on the ground, snagging on roots and tendrils. Chumba shows no sign of tiring, but each time Mez stumbles, Chumba's tail thrashes. "She needs to rest," Chumba finally says, after Mez snags her ear on a passing thorn, bringing a drop of blood welling to the edge. "No matter how far we are supposed to get tonight. We'll only hurt ourselves if we push too hard."

"You'll be in daycoma pretty soon anyway," Gogi says, plopping down onto his haunches. "And I don't have much fig left in the tree, as the capuchins say."

"The horde we tried to infect is far back, and we haven't come across more of the army yet, so I think we'll be safe for the day," Lima says, alighting on a nearby branch. "Well, we'll have to hope we'll be. Come on, I scouted out a good hiding spot not too much farther."

Lima soars ahead. The rest drag themselves after her, shambling through the jungle until they come to a clearing. Accumulated rainwater flows down a boulder, tumbling through the air until it's caught by a stream and whisked away. Lima's voice comes from the far side of the water. "Come on in, friends! It goes surprisingly deep back here."

"You know, usually I'm a bigger fan of *dry* caves, but since the ants hate water, wet is where I want to be," Gogi says as he ducks his head behind the misty cascade. The cave behind the boulder does seem to go far back. It's too dark to see much at all, but his voice echoes broadly. Mez and Chumba file in next to Gogi, dropping to the slick rock.

Gogi senses Chumba lowering her head, then hears

the slower breathing of sleep. "The Veil must be lifting," he says quietly. Though the misty falling water remains dark, he imagines the soft glow of dawn beyond it.

"I was thinking something, Gogi," comes Lima's voice, from right above his nose.

He jerks. "Lima, come on, don't sneak up on a guy like that!"

She sniffs, wounded. "Bats like to be on the ceiling of a cave! And it's not a tall cave! That's your problem!"

"Sorry," Gogi says, rubbing his face. "I'm really tired. What were you going to say?"

"I was *going* to say that I think maybe we should tell Rumi where we are. So that when he and Sky return with the lens, they come to the right spot."

Gogi nods. "It's a good idea, Lima. It's about time we checked in on those two. Mez, are you up for it?"

Her voice is low and purring, right beside him. "Of course."

Gogi pulls out the directive, laying the red feather along the grainy sand of the cave bottom. "You still have that echomap in your mind, Lima?" Gogi asks.

"Wouldn't forget it," Lima says, hopping to the sand beside the feather and placing a wing on top of it. "Let's go, team."

While he and Mez place a hand and a paw along the feather, Gogi fixes Lima with a shrewd look. "This time, give us a countdown before you call up the echo—"

The cave is gone.

Instead, Gogi's at the beach. At least he assumes this is what a beach is—he's never actually seen one before. It's like he's beside a giant puddle. Under his feet isn't the mud that he'd usually find beside a puddle, though—it's gritty sand. And the puddle is huge. Impossibly big. It goes as far as his eyes can see, and has peaks and valleys, like wet clay. It's all moving. There's a rushing sound, like a giant creature breathing, as an impossibly large mass of water crashes onto the sand. A wet breeze comes off it, and it tastes like salt. Gogi's mesmerized.

Above him wheel strange birds, bigger than the biggest eagle, all white with orange beaks. Smaller birds dash along the water's edge, racing into the gaps the waves leave behind, sticking their narrow beaks into the sand and then running off again before the waves can return.

They're so cute. Gogi wants to hold one in his hands. He takes a step toward them.

And doesn't move.

Gogi looks down at his feet—and finds they're not there! Instead he sees pebble-gray clawed feet, long red tail feathers.

Gogi himself isn't there! Right. Like before.

Ah. He can see much more of his surroundings this

time, but he's still limited to what Sky can see. Probably all three of them are looking together through Sky's eyes again.

"Still no sign of it," comes a familiar voice from behind Gogi. Rumi! He must be riding on Sky's back, the same position he was in last time, only this time Sky's not looking back at him. Gogi wonders: Does Sky know they're tuning in?

"Well, we're not precisely at the northernmost part of Caldera," Sky says. "We birds can sense the invisible lines that gird the planet, and there is still more land to magnetic north."

"So you know that the planet is round!" Rumi says.

"Of course the planet is round," Sky says. "What a silly thought."

"I *know*! I read up about it on the ziggurat ruins. But you'd be surprised how many animals think it's flat. Like they don't realize that since the edge of the eclipse's shadow over the sun was curved, so is our planet! And how many animals have you met that think that Caldera is all that there is?"

Of course they're not standing on a round thing. And of course Caldera is all there is, Gogi thinks. *Rumi and Sky have some crazy theories.*

"I've never seen any land other than Caldera," Sky

says. "It could be all water out there beyond our borders."

"Maybe those big white birds have some information," Rumi says.

"I'm sure they do," Sky says. "It would be interesting to talk to them, to learn what they know. But we're getting sidetracked."

"True, true," Rumi says. "'Knowledge for knowledge's sake is not enough.' I heard you the last five times. You don't need to say it again."

Gogi startles. It's like Rumi and Sky are having a conversation they've had many times before, and enjoying it just as much as the first time. It's like they're . . . buddies. Weird. It's time to let them know that he's there. He opens his mouth to speak. But his mouth doesn't open. Of course it doesn't. Because it's not his mouth. It's Sky's beak.

Gogi can look but not communicate this time. Huh. How can he tell them that the fungus works, but that they failed to make anything lasting come of it? The companions clearly still have far to go in figuring out how to make the best use of everyone's powers.

Sky looks down and around, at his driftwood perch and then along the beach. This is Gogi's first experience looking out through one eye at a time—since he was only looking at Rumi the time before, it didn't really count. It lets him see everything around him, with only a small blind spot, but it's hard to judge distances. The ocean is far away, but it's unclear how distant the ground is. Oops—now they're in the air.

Gogi's stomach drops—he's definitely not up to seeing everything around him in every direction whizzing by at high speed. But he can't close his eyes, because his eyes aren't there. Ugh. He has no control whatsoever. This will take some getting used to.

Rumi makes pleased ribbits from Sky's backside. "Mmm, the ocean is almost a rain-cloud gray over here. And look at how the mangroves dot the waterline in some places but not others. Is that a fish jumping out of the ocean? It's as large as a panther and looks like a gray boto! How fascinating!"

Sky's voice comes rumbling up from beneath Gogi's viewpoint. "Rumi, look! The cliffs!"

The macaw has turned a corner, and through Sky's left eye Gogi can see sheer rock rising from the shore. "We've done it!" Rumi says. "We're about to have our answer!"

Gogi begins to sense little pricks of fire under Sky's feathers. It's a familiar sensation—ants must be biting the macaw. But how is a bird, flying high in the sky, getting attacked by ants? Maybe he's got bird lice or something. Still, why would they be biting now? And why hasn't he felt anything else from Sky's body during this vision? Very weird.

He's soon distracted from such thoughts by the sight of the cliffs. Sky starts at sea level, riding the currents, then streaks almost vertically up the cliff face, wind fluttering his feathers and blurring his eyes. It's exhilarating and overwhelming and suddenly Gogi wants to be back in his own body. Sky continues to soar upward until he alights at a cave opening. Out of the side of Sky's vision, Gogi sees Rumi hop down, the frog's tiny yellow body springing along the rocks.

"We've found it," Rumi says. "The Cave of Riddles."

Gogi watches with Sky as he takes in the carved stone roof, covered with unknowable two-leg symbols. Rumi hops to them, running his hands over the raised surfaces. "I can try to interpret at least some of these," Rumi says. "But it will take time."

"Time is what we don't have," Sky grumbles. "The eclipse is only two nights away now."

"Well, if this is a cave of riddles, it might pay to get as much information as we can before we go in," Rumi says. "We can only answer a riddle that we understand." He hops onto Sky's head to get to one of the carvings that are higher up, and Gogi is struck by two things: He never thought Sky would tolerate anyone standing on his head, and tree frog butts look really funny up close. Like a shiny, unripe plum.

"I don't know, I'd feel better if we headed inside right away," Sky says, vision tilting as he shifts nervously from leg to leg.

Wait and figure out everything you can about the riddles, Gogi silently implores Rumi. *We'll be all right. Don't go risking yourself needlessly.*

"Okay," Rumi says, nodding his little frog head. "We'll go in. If you think that's best."

No! Gogi tries to yell out. But of course Sky and Rumi can't hear him. And the annoying pricks of fire have become more than annoying. They're searing now, a pain down his legs, between his fingers and toes. Wait—between his fingers? Birds don't have fingers!

Suddenly Gogi is awake. The cave is full of twilight, droplets glowing. It's beautiful—for a split second. Then the horror of the scene hits him.

Ants have found them.

Gogi sees Lima first. She's still got her wing on the tail feather, and her eyes are shut. Ants are crawling all over her—army ants, from the look of it, clay-colored beasts with talonlike mandibles half the size of their bodies. They've dug into her abdomen and ears, her skin puckering beneath their piercing jaws. Mez, still touching the feather too, is passed out while the attackers crawl over her fur.

Gogi understands why he was able to break from the vision—fighting the biting ants must have brought his dreaming body out of contact with the feather. He springs to all fours, trying to shake himself free of the ants even as he uses his tail to pluck Lima away from the feather. Disregarding the mandibles digging into his own soft fingertips, he rubs the army ants from her little body. Then he backs up so he can push Mez away from the feather, too.

Her eyes snap open to see Gogi with Lima's limp body, both of them covered in ants. "We're under attack!" Gogi cries.

"Where's Chumba?" Mez asks frantically. Gogi follows her eyes as she looks around—and sees Chumba just waking from daycoma, eyes fluttering open, covered in ants in the corner of the cave. The ants are swarming thickly enough to cover her nose, her eyelids.

"You haul her out, and I'll bring Lima. Into the water at the front, now!" Gogi says.

Mez digs her teeth into the nape of her sleepy sister's neck while Gogi races to the waterfall. He splashes through, into the lagoon. Once he's there he dunks Lima's body, again and again, watching ants float up to the surface. Mez is right after him, splashing into the water, dragging yowling Chumba along. They huddle in the center of the pond, shaking ants from them as best they can. Chumba comes fully awake, staring around her in pain and surprise.

"Lima? Lima?" Gogi says, pressing his ear against the bat's little mouth. She's breathing shallowly, face writhing in agony as the ants' poison courses through her body.

"Upriver!" Mez calls. "We'll tend to her up there. The ants are swarming the banks here—we have to move!"

"You don't need to ask twice, Mez," Gogi says as he strokes Lima. He turns in a tight circle, his back against Mez's and Chumba's, and sees that she's right: this whole area is thick with ants, and more are streaming in every second. "Let's move."

"Oh, I don't know that anyone needs to go anywhere," comes a voice from behind a mess of ferns at the far bank. "You might have defeated Big Rumi, but I don't think you'll find me nearly as easy an adversary."

Gogi watches Mez go slack in the jaw. The calico panther sinks in the shallow water, pressing protectively against her sister and pawing at the air in alarm. "No, this can't be," she says.

Whose voice is that? Gogi wonders as he scans the

bank. He looks in the greenery, trying to place the voice. It's a panther, he's pretty sure, but he's not sure which one. Then he sees a figure, all white, emerge from the greenery to perch on a rocky promontory looking over the shallow pond.

It's Mez and Chumba's cousin.

Mist.

A circlet of ants marches along his forehead, between and into his ears.

Mist is working for the Ant Queen.

GOGI'S MIND RACES. They've been ambushed by the Ant Queen's forces. And those forces appear to be led by Mist.

After Lima, Chumba seems to have gotten the worst of the ants' toxin. Even though she's awake, her eyes are unfocused, her limbs quivery and uncoordinated. Mez props her sister up, so that her head is safely above water. Then she slowly turns toward Mist, who is surrounded by the swarms of ants. She lets no emotion onto her features as she coolly takes in her cousin. Gogi can imagine the torrent of feelings passing inside Mez. If this had been Alzo, say, turned traitor, Gogi would be tearing his own hair out, teeth bared. But stillness and calmness is the panther way, and Mez has only gotten better and better at it.

This is Gogi's first time meeting the all-white panther. Mist had been famously beautiful, and panthers had come from across Caldera just to see him, but a boar attack left one side of his face ravaged, with an entire cheek missing, exposing yellowing teeth to the air.

Mez had said that Mist was frantic and rattled when she'd seen him last. It doesn't look that way now. Mist has regained his regal air, shows no sign of alarm or hysteria, looks down at them with a cruel and glittering gaze.

It's hard to meet the white panther's imperious stare, but Gogi forces himself. He extends a hand and pops a flame above it, as a warning. It smokes and fizzles over his wet fur, but eventually holds. He clears his throat. "Call off your minions."

"What are you doing here, Mist?" Mez asks neutrally. Gogi has a vision of how he and his friends must look—bedraggled, suddenly awoken from their dream visit, surrounded by the enemy, sitting in the middle of a pond that's really more of a mud puddle. Not exactly imposing. Mez is somehow holding on tight to her dignity. Gogi tries to mimic her regal expression.

"Thank you for starting with such an easy question," Mist says, exposing a stretch of sharp teeth as he licks a paw. "I'm here to destroy you. You will not resist the Ant Queen."

"You don't mean that you've . . . ," Mez says.

"Aunt Usha rejected me. You all rejected me. You kept me around when I was beautiful. But you couldn't even stand to look at me after the attack."

"That's not true," Mez says. "How you look has nothing to do with it. But I do know this: You fled when we needed you most. And now you're working for the enemy."

Mist laughs. "Don't be so juvenile. The Ant Queen is not our enemy. She's our new leader. Her rule is inevitable. If you were wise, you'd join me."

"Ants? Why would you turn from your own kind for *ants*?"

"I was *rejected* by my own kind, Mez. The ants don't care about what I look like. I am my queen's most important ally. I recruit her other collaborators, I manage the overtaking of Caldera. I deal with problem animals. Like you."

"You're helping her to destroy everything that makes Caldera beautiful. It makes no sense. You'll be in charge of—what? A mess of ruined earth?"

"Once the Ant Queen has mown down the existing

order, she will create a new one. Those animals who helped her will be allowed to survive and repopulate. We will create a new society, an *orderly* society, unlike this chaotic every-animal-for-its-own one we have put up with for too long. The Ant Queen will be at its center. And I will be by her side."

"Never. You don't really think she'll follow through on that, do you? She betrayed Auriel, right in front of us. She'll use you up, and then discard you," Mez says. "You've always been too self-centered to see the real motives of those around you. You're blinded yet again."

Mist hisses and shakes his head. "You're the one who's blinded. I hope you will see the truth soon, before it's too late. The Ant Queen is the only answer."

Mez scoffs. "You don't really think we'll side with you and the Ant Queen!"

"You won't have any choice. Not once I've brought you all to her."

Mez falls into a fighting stance, head down and claws out. "Never."

"You've always been dense, cousin. You're surrounded by billions of ants. You have no options here."

"Shows how much you know," Gogi says hotly, pointing to the woven bag around his chest. "I'll tell you that—"

"—that we are ready to fight," Mez interrupts, with a pointed look at Gogi.

"Then fight you will," Mist snarls, hackles rising.

Gogi readies a ball of fire in his palm, sizzling the night air.

"No," Mez says. "This is a fight of honor. Let me take him alone, Gogi."

"Honor? From Mist?" Gogi says. "That's the most ridiculous thing I've ever heard."

"Enough, you brainless monkey," Mist says. "I will fight by the old rules." He laughs at himself. "I am still Usha's son, I guess."

"She would never have you back," Mez says while she pulls herself out of the water, only a few paces away from Mist.

"I do not *want* to come back, cousin," Mist says.

"Are you sure about this silly 'honor' thing, Mez?" Gogi calls over.

But she ignores him, too focused on Mist. The two cats are wheeling around each other, snarling and snapping, both producing low yowls that make Gogi's skin break out in bumps.

Mez lunges to the attack. She leaps into the air, claws raking forward, jaws reaching for Mist's neck.

He's too agile, though. Mist drops to the grassy

earth, turning onto his back while Mez goes soaring over him. Then he's sprung to his feet, flashing after her. The streak of white is impossibly fast, and before Gogi can react Mist has his jaws on Mez's backside, his powerful claws clamped into her soft black fur.

Despite Mez's telling him to keep out of it, Gogi staggers toward them through the swamp, Lima still gripped in his tail.

Mez vanishes, and even though Mist knows about her magic, the move obviously startles him. His claws scramble over her invisible form, straining, and then Mez must have pulled free, because Mist is whirling, nose twitching and eyes darting.

With a smack and a roar, Mist is pushed down into the mud, his coat instantly muddied. He squirms, head pressed into the muck by Mez, invisible above him. He thrashes, trying to free himself, but Mez has him locked down. *Will she go in for the kill, even though Mist is her own cousin?*

The ants circling Mist's head are going even faster than before. "Mez, wherever you are," Gogi calls, "Mist is communicating with the ants!"

Suddenly Mist springs up from the mud, and Mez goes visible. Chumba, where she's limp on the shore, is now completely covered with ants, so much so that her calico fur is almost invisible under the teeming, glittering mass.

Mez staggers over to her sister and begins using her tongue to get as many ants off as she can. "Enough," she gasps. "Mist, call them off!"

"Are you sure?" he asks, coughing, shaking off mud from his fur. "Are you sure I shouldn't just command them to sting?"

"Mist!" Mez shrieks, quivering. "Release her. You promised this would be an honorable battle."

"It would have been honorable," he says icily, "until you went invisible and pressed my face into the mud. You started this."

"Please, Mist," Mez sobs. "Call them off Chumba. I submit. Whatever you want. Feed me to the Ant Queen. Just let her live."

"Now, now, cousin," Mist says. "I didn't need you to *grovel*."

"Get them off her," Gogi says.

"I will not," Mist says. "But I will not have them sting."

The ensuing silence goes long. Mist looks at them suspiciously, gauging how much he might not know.

Before Mist can ask any difficult questions, Gogi lets out a jet of fire, sending it fizzling and steaming dramatically into the water. He holds up the limp body of Lima and points to Chumba, weak, her eyes half-lidded. "If your queen wants to talk to the shadowwalkers, she'll be upset if you let any of them die," he says. "Help us help Lima and Chumba. Otherwise you'll have to be the one to break the bad news to her."

Mist looks back and forth between the companions, measuring them up. "The bat will recover."

"You may be right, if you let us help her," Gogi presses. "And Chumba, too."

"The queen has no use for an unfit panther," Mist says flatly.

"That's really something, coming from you," Gogi says.

"If you have any hope of getting me to your queen alive, then *you* definitely *do* have use for Chumba," Mez growls, baring her teeth.

"What do you need to help the bat get better?" Mist asks, cocking his head to one side.

"We need your ants to stand down and leave," Gogi tries.

Mist laughs. "I'm not as stupid as a monkey, so don't try to play me for one. Go ahead. Help your bat friend. My ants will not stop you. We'll wait. Then you'll come with us to the queen."

Mez shoots Gogi a look: *Buying time is the best we can do.*

Gogi sits near the edge of the muddy pond, where it's shallow enough to rest his butt. The ants are all around the water's edge, waving their antennae, but they don't approach any closer. Mez stands guard right beside him, hovering over Chumba even as her eyes never leave Mist on his rocky outcropping.

Gogi examines Lima. It's bad. The many ant bites on her tiny body have become raised and puffy, the ones on her face squishing and distorting her features. "Water . . . ," she says in barely a whisper.

"Of course," Gogi says. He cups some of the pond water and brings it to Lima's lips. He lets some dribble in. She swallows weakly. "Do you think you can heal yourself somehow?" Gogi asks.

"It's hard . . . to lick myself," Lima whispers.

Gogi can't help but smile. "I understand. But you're Lima the Healing Bat!"

Lima coughs. "Who's that creepy voice you're talking to?"

"Don't you worry about him yet. Just worry about getting better," Gogi says. Gently, he takes his pinkie finger and runs it along the edge of Lima's mouth, so he gets a bead of her saliva on it. He takes it and presses it against the nearest bite. Immediately, the raised bite goes down, the angry red color fading to an irritated pink. Tears in his eyes, Gogi does it again and again, until most of Lima's bites have subsided.

"It's working," Mez says, relieved.

"It's Lima, the Healing Bat!" Gogi sings softly, stroking her wing. *"Ferocious-er than a piranha! Scarier than a cat!"*

A smile crosses Lima's face. "You have to admit, that song is kind of amazing. I think I'm going to sleep for a bit now." Her breathing goes soft and regular, and her eyes close.

"Now what?" Gogi whispers to Mez.

"We could try some of her saliva on Chumba, but her condition isn't as dire. Chumba really just needs to rest," Mez whispers back.

"Now you come with me," Mist commands.

Gogi looks up. The rainforest is throbbing and vibrating with ants. They're running along every branch, streaming across every leaf. If Mist ordered them to attack, it would be over very quickly.

Mez nods wearily. "We'll submit," she says to Mist. *For now,* her eyes say to Gogi.

"Come on the shore," Mist says. "As long as you do not resist, my ants will not harm you."

"How can we trust you?" Mez asks.

"You don't really have much choice, do you?" Mist says.

Gogi sighs. "He's right. Let's go." Despite his words, he gets ready to use his fire. If this is the end, he'll take as many of the ants as he can with him—and that hateful panther, too.

Mez is the first onto the bank. The nearby ants approach her paws and begin to crawl into her fur. "Mist, call them off," she snarls.

"Oh no," her cousin says from his perch. "I will not."

She backs into the pond again, eyes wide with fear. "You lied!"

"I did not," Mist says. "If you don't resist, they won't hurt you. But they'll march with you, next to your skin, ready to inject their venom. Of course I know you'll try to escape as soon as you can. The ants in your fur are my insurance. Really, Mez, you must think I'm as stupid as that monkey." He casts the last few words in Gogi's direction.

"Enough with the 'stupid monkey' bit!" Gogi mutters as he steps onto the shore. The ants are instantly in his fur, climbing his legs and belly. Instinct tells him to swat them off, but he forces his arms to stay by his side. He'll have to tolerate the intolerable if he wants to survive. If he wants his friends to survive.

"Monkeys *are* stupid," Mist presses. "Like your shadowwalker friend Sorella. Too dumb to make the only choice that would have let her survive another day."

Sorella . . . dead? Killed by the ants? Gogi wants not to believe it, but it makes sense—Sorella wouldn't have missed their reunion if she could possibly have made it. Mez's hairs stand up, and her jaws open to bare her teeth, but Gogi watches her tamp her reaction down. Better to swallow this news for now, if they want to avoid the same fate.

Heart sinking, Gogi watches as the ants swarm up dazed Chumba, too, and even crawl all over the body of Lima, where she sleeps securely in Gogi's grip. These ants could kill them at any time.

"You know, I wouldn't have let the ants kill you in the cave," Mist says, an eye to Gogi as he picks his way through the vegetation to stop a few paces in front of them. "But I needed to chase you out so that I could talk to you without worrying about a surprise attack."

"Do you expect a round of applause?" Mez asks. "You're a disgrace." Even with ants crawling over her mouth and nose, she spits at Mist's feet.

Learning about Sorella has only proven that there's no point in antagonizing Mist too much, not when their lives are in his hands. "So, Mist, how did you know where we were?" Gogi asks, trying to keep his tone as neutral as possible as he falls in behind the white panther.

"You're in no position to ask questions," Mist growls. Then, seeing Gogi's open expression, his tone softens. "Let's just say that your side is not the only one that can harness the power of the eclipse."

Is it possible that Mist is lonely? Gogi can see how that would happen, Mist spending all his time with ants and—shudder—the Ant Queen. He shoots a glance at Mez, who keeps her gaze steadily on the ground. "It must have been hard to be all on your own, with no family with you," Gogi tries as Mist leads them forward.

"Enough," Mist says. "I won't let you manipulate me, monkey."

Gogi falls into silence. He walks on three limbs, Lima cradled in one arm, so he can use his tail to dab more of Lima's saliva on her bites. As they recede she falls even deeper into her slumber, her breathing slow and deep under Gogi's fingers. At least it appears that Lima will make it.

The rainforest in this area is hearty old growth, thick, dark green leaves sending down torrents of water from above. Mist goes slowly, swatting his paws at clogs of vegetation. His claws rend some of it completely, allowing the others to pass behind him, but often he just bats it away, so it thwacks Gogi or Mez or Chumba full in the face. Gogi winds up with a mix of ants, spiders, termites, and the occasional centipede as he trudges through the wet twilight jungle. He taps the pebbles in his bag, wishing he were at home in the capuchin forest, lazing about with Alzo. Or that he were with his vision of his mother. Anywhere but here, weighed down with ants, following a treacherous panther.

Gogi tries to send Mez glances as he goes, but she keeps her gaze trained away. She knows Mist better than Gogi does, of course—maybe she knows there are dire consequences if he catches them so much as looking at each other. If only they'd had even a few minutes to plan after the vision. They haven't spoken about Rumi and Sky, about the frog and the macaw's new intimacy, their approach to the Cave of Riddles. How they weren't able to get a message to the pair about where they could be found. All of their plans are unraveling.

Then there's the question of what the Ant Queen will do with them once she has them in her clutches. Maybe she has some way of forcing them to work for her. Maybe she'll threaten to kill one of them unless the others collaborate. Maybe she'll siphon off their magic like Auriel once did, leaving them emptied husks. Maybe she simply wants to witness their destruction for herself, to be sure that the shadowwalkers are dead and gone.

Gogi pats the woven sack along his side. Of course,

the Ant Queen might not know what *they* hope to do to *her*.

Could a little rotten stick really take down something as fearsome as the Ant Queen? Doesn't seem likely. Whatever is to come, it's probably not going to be anything good.

M IST MARCHES THEM all night, through the wind-
ing spaces between liana vines and overgrown
trees, through clearings and along brambled streams.
He takes the lead, positioning Mez next, right where he
can see her, followed by Gogi and finally Chumba. The
poor calico panther is the worst off. She's almost coma-
tose, tail dragging through the soil.

Gogi's feet grow heavy, and he keeps letting out long
sighs. The ants. They're the worst part. Gogi can feel
them pulling apart his follicles, examining his body,
testing his skin for plumpness. Their sharp legs make
him itch, but he's unable to do anything about it for
fear they'll start biting him. As he gets tired, the itchy

feeling of being covered in invaders bothers him more and more. The future looks gloomier than ever. Killed by ants now, or by their queen later—is there really much difference?

At least Mist isn't a shadowwalker, so he'll need to sleep once the Veil lifts. They all can get some rest then, even though it's precisely the time when any decent monkey would be waking up for the day.

Gogi pulls Lima out of his woven sack, where he placed her for safekeeping. She's still resting, and her bites are healing nicely. No sign of infection. He places her back in. At least there's some ray of hope in all of this misery.

As the night wears on, Gogi feels himself getting clumsier and clumsier, his hands snagging in tangles of vines or, once, his foot dropping right into a tarantula den. He got it back out before he was bitten, but that certainly woke him up.

As the Veil comes near to lifting, Mist draws them up short. Chumba lumbers right into him. "Sorry," she mumbles, exhausted.

Mist whirls and bites her hard on the ear. Chumba bares her teeth and prepares to lunge at him, but it's a weak stance. Her legs tremble. Then her eyes go wide in fright.

"Ah," Mist says, smirking as his own circlet of ants

continues its march around his head. "You've felt the hundreds of mandibles on your skin scratch at once. All I have to do is say the word, and they lower their stingers and inject their venom. Go ahead, cousin. Strike me. Try."

With visible effort, Chumba forces her lips back over her teeth.

Indignant, Mist whirls and presses down the fanned leaves of a low palm. On the other side, the jungle gives way to a rocky cliff that breaks and then begins again on the far side of a narrow canyon. A raging river roars somewhere far below. A hundred monkeylengths up along the cliff side from them, a delicate span of stone crosses the chasm.

"We're almost there now," Mist says. "The queen waits for us at the summit of that mountain."

Gogi looks up. At the far side of the canyon, the rainforest continues for a ways until it begins to climb, turning into a misty green mountain. It goes higher and higher until, near the summit, the greenery parts to reveal bald brown earth. There's movement on it, but it's too far away for Gogi to see. It's at least two more nights of strenuous travel away.

Is that where the Ant Queen is? Already too aware of the mandibles grazing his own skin, Gogi tries to hold back his fear—and anger.

He smells smoke. Whoops. Gogi forces his tail to stop smoldering.

Mez and Chumba come near Gogi and stand shoulder to shoulder with him. "This looks a little like that canyon we had to cross when we first came to the ziggurat," Mez says.

"And now history repeats," Gogi says.

"Only this time it's our own cousin betraying us, instead of Auriel," Chumba says quietly.

If Mist heard her, he gives no sign of it. "We'll rest here for the day," he commands. "Then we cross the canyon at dusk."

Gogi gently lays an ant-covered hand on Mez's head. The first time they met, he saved her with his fire after she was attacked by wasps lying in wait on a rope bridge's underside. The river they hear could be the same one, finally letting out to sea after it rounds the mountain. This canyon has no sign of any wasps, no sign of life at all. Just the ants. And Gogi has no idea how he can save his friends this time.

Mist settles in on the rock canyon edge. Far below, the rushing water sends up a roaring sound, loud enough to vibrate the stones. He yawns and rests his head between his paws. "I've ordered the ants to bite you if you go more than a few feet away, or if you try to communicate with one another. So don't pull anything.

At the next dropping of the Veil, I will bring you to submit to your new queen."

"Yeah, we heard you the first time," Gogi grumbles.

"How are *you* communicating with the ants?" Mez asks bitterly.

Mist draws himself up. "The Ant Queen can grant that power. All of her allies have limited ant telepathy through the ants that circle our heads. You experienced it once, cousin, back when you were the queen's prisoner. I command them with my thoughts. Watch."

Gogi's hair rises as he feels the ants, as one, crawl one direction and then another on his body, in perfect synchrony. He sees Mez's and Chumba's hackles rise too.

"You just let them into your brain? Did they break the eardrum? Did it hurt?" Gogi asks.

"No, of course they don't walk into my brain, monkey. They receive chemical messages from other ants and then vibrate their legs along my eardrum to communicate them. Enough for now. It is time to sleep," Mist says as he draws into the cover of the low palms. "I recommend you do the same, too."

Gogi wonders if he'll be able to, even with his exhaustion. Chumba will fall into daycoma, of course, there's no resisting that. But Gogi and Mez and Lima are unbounded by the Veil. He shoots a glance at Mez.

Her eyes are bloodshot, but alert and darting. She may not be able to sleep, either.

They settle into the fronds, ant bodies crunching under Gogi's butt despite his best efforts not to squish any. It doesn't bring the rest to attack. Apparently, ants aren't much bothered by the loss of other ants. Good to know.

Chumba's soon snoring, her body spooned inside Mez's. Mist keeps apart from the others, his eyelids drooping, and then relaxes into sleep. Gogi looks at Mez. Are they really going to keep silent the whole day?

"So," Mez whispers. "We need to talk about escape strategies."

"These ants are worse than monkeycuffs," Gogi says mournfully. He feels the crawling sensation all over his body pause, then something almost like a chafed sunburn as all the ants train their mandibles on his skin. His eyes widen. Mez's eyes widen.

They go silent.

Talking is definitely not allowed.

Somehow, despite the light, and despite the heat of the sun penetrating between the fronds and drawing sweat from every one of his pores, Gogi falls asleep. It's a dreamless and listless slumber, halfway to waking at all times.

Gogi comes alert to a creaking sound, and then it's back to the drone of cicadas. The creaking sound again, then back to the cicadas.

Gogi cracks open his eyes.

He's the only one of the group awake to see a furry brown creature halfway across the stone bridge. The animal is totally motionless, so much so that Gogi assumes it's fallen asleep. But then it moves one clawed hand over another, then one clawed foot, then the other. It rests again. It's a sloth.

Wait. It's *Banu*!

He must have passed by without even noticing his friends hidden away in the fronds. And now he's halfway across the arc of stone already, heading toward the misty mountain at the far side. Gogi's eyes go wide and he carefully sits up, alert to the ants in his fur. They seem to allow this small movement, though.

Gogi makes a tsk-tsk sound. Once, and then again. Banu doesn't seem to notice, just continues his slow, creeping progress across the bridge.

"Sweet monkeybreath," Gogi whispers to himself. "Banu got our message!"

Gogi realizes that Lima, if she's recovered enough, might be able to quietly fly over to the sloth. He pulls her out of the sack and gives her a nudge in the belly.

Her eyes half-open to slits, and then close again. "Can't . . . just a bat!"

Lima hasn't recovered enough to fly anytime soon.

Banu's at an angle as he passes. Maybe there's a way . . . maybe it would be too much risk to . . . Gogi decides to go ahead. Keeping the rest of his body motionless, he raises the fingers of one hand and snaps.

The sound isn't loud, but he makes a burst of flame appear from the fingers. Just for an instant, then it's gone. He snaps again. Another burst of flame.

Banu pauses. Then, slowly, he cranes his head in Gogi's direction.

Another snap of flame.

Banu's eyebrows rise. He opens his mouth to speak.

Gogi shakes his head, pointing at Mez and Chumba and lastly at Mist, then pantomiming his wrists being bound together.

Banu cocks his head, taking in the scene. Then, as fast as he can (granted, that's about the speed of a newborn monkey), Banu starts reversing his way across the bridge. Once he's on the near side, he takes in the stream of ants covering the animals. He nods, then pantomimes tapping Mez awake.

Gogi nods back.

Banu points to the sky, then points to the spot where

the sun is descending toward the horizon. He rocks his clawed hand from one side to the other. *Wait until the Veil drops.*

Gogi nods and takes out sleeping Lima, holding her in his palm.

With his usual vacant smile, Banu lowers one clawed foot and then the other over the canyon's edge, before he disappears.

Gogi reaches out with his free hand and, as slowly as possible so as not to startle the ants, nudges Mez's shoulder.

Mez bats his hand away, but when Gogi nudges her again, her eyes go wide. *What is it?* she mouths.

Gogi holds up a finger. *Wait.* He tries to think of how to pantomime "Banu is here and he's just gone down into the canyon for some reason I can't figure out," but he can't, so he just keeps his finger held up.

Mez smoothly rises to a seated position, watching Gogi curiously.

Above the roar of rushing water from deep within the canyon comes an extra watery sound. Sort of like a bunch of spit wads flying through the air, actually. Gogi recognizes the sound from some of the pranks he's pulled off with Alzo.

Then he sees it. A cord of water no wider than a

monkey's tail rises from within the canyon, whipping around at the tip as it grows higher and higher. There's a sound of rushing air as water goes faster and faster up the cord, misting around it at the top, while the rest cascades back down into the canyon. It looks like a curious cobra, only made entirely of water, raising its head to check out the monkey and bat and panthers.

The magic snake goes perfectly still, water cascading all about it, while the sunset turns it purple and orange. Gogi watches through squinted eyes as the sun disappears, goes from a disc to a sliver to a speck.

The snake gives a shiver.

It shatters.

The cord of water becomes five cords, and each streaks toward one of the animals—Chumba, Mez, Lima, Gogi, and even Mist. Gogi startles and his legs spring, but he's unable to get himself into the air before the water jet hits him. Given the amount of water that's streaming toward him, and its speed, he expects to be knocked back. It's a ferocious spray, to be sure, but though it bows his head and straightens his fur, it doesn't push him off the ground. He realizes why when he sees that the spray has split into mini-tendrils around him, that it's surrounded him in sparkling, shimmering streams of water, beating against his fur. He looks down under the cleaning spray and sees dirt and ants swirling around his feet—lots of ants.

"The ants!" he yells over the spray. "The water's washing off the ants!"

The other animals are covered with similar sprays.

Banu hadn't realized his power before their time at the ziggurat was over. Apparently, he's figured it out now—and it involves control over water.

Gogi whoops in joy. "Banu! You're amazing!"

The water stills and dissipates, the writhing ropes tumbling back into the canyon. The friends are left dripping on the sunset rocks, looking about them in astonishment. Mist is particularly floored, woken from slumber with his mouth hanging wide open. The tendril of ants marching in a circle around his head has been washed away too.

"This is our chance!" Gogi yells. "Across the bridge, friends!"

Mez sputters, eyes still drooping with sleep. "What . . . what just . . . ?"

"Run!"

Lima flaps her wings, but they're still too weak—and too wet—to lift her off the ground. She hobbles toward the bridge, until Gogi scoops her up and pops her into the woven sack. Then he makes his way across the slender arc of stone, surely placing hand over foot over tail over hand, until he's at the far side. Sure, it's high up, and wet, and there's a raging river impossibly far below, but it's still easy enough for a monkey. He turns around to see Mez and Chumba picking their way more cautiously, digging in their claws to gain extra purchase over narrow stones that wobble and creak.

Recovered from his surprise, Mist bares his teeth and staggers across the puddles on the far side, howling and hissing at the departing sisters.

Gogi saved Mez once before on a bridge like this, and he can do it again. *Focus, Gogi.* He readies his fire. Instead of sending a stream of flame, this time he makes his mind small and focused. Meticulous. Biting his lip, he creates a ball of fire, no bigger than a nut. He shoots it across the canyon. It whizzes right between Mist's ears, sailing over him and into the green. The white panther looks up, startled, only to see Gogi readying another fiery bullet.

Hissing and yowling, Mist places a paw on the rock bridge. Gogi unleashes his fire pellet again, this time hitting Mist on the top of his head. Mist recoils in pain, scrambling backward, smoke rising from his fur. Then he starts forward again.

This time Gogi fishes a pebble from his bag and

holds it between two fingers, igniting it as he rears back, preparing to throw. Seeing the actual flaming bullet about to come his way, Mist gives a ferocious howl and then, cringing, disappears into the brush.

"Take your time, guys, Mist isn't following anytime soon," Gogi calls as he puts the pebble back in the bag, relieved that he hadn't had to use up any of his precious twelve. Although there are plenty of ants on this side of the bridge, like anywhere in the rainforest, they don't seem to be under anyone's direct control. Even if there was immediate danger, Gogi would rather not see his panther friends rush across the bridge only to plummet into the canyon.

Eventually Mez and Chumba help each other onto solid ground beside Gogi. Lima struggles out of the sack and hops to the earth, sputtering. "What *was* that?"

"I have no idea what just happened to me, either," Chumba says, shaking the water from her fur.

"Could you try not to spray everyone when you do that?" Gogi asks, wiping his eyes. "Anyway, we have Banu to thank."

"Banu the sloth is here?" Mez asks. "Where?"

"Here . . . I am," Banu says, wheezing. He appears over the lip of the canyon, dragging himself to the stones, where he lies on his back. He wipes his claw across his brow and takes in deep breaths. "Wow. That was a lot of work . . . for a sloth . . . I'm going to need a few days . . . to sleep this one off."

"Banu!" Lima says, wrapping her leathery wings around his neck. "I've missed you, handsome guy!"

"Nice work with that water magic," Mez says.

"I know!" Banu says. "Isn't it great? . . . Wish I had figured it out . . . back when we were fighting Auriel and the Ant Queen . . . but I guess you can't speed . . . these things along. We find out our . . . true selves whenever we're . . . meant to. I guess."

"We'll be fighting the Ant Queen again soon enough, I'm afraid," Mez says.

"Is she back?" Banu asks.

"What do you mean, 'Is she back'? Don't you know you're heading right to her?!" Lima squeaks.

"I was making my way to the ziggurat . . . for our meeting . . . but travel can take . . . a lot longer . . . when you're a sloth. . . . I got your rock arrow message . . . and started over this way, following the horde. . . . So you're saying . . . that those ants . . . crawling over you guys . . . weren't an accident?"

"No," Mez says darkly. "They were set on us by our cousin Mist. He's collaborating with the Ant Queen. A lot of animals are."

"I . . . didn't know that. . . . I thought he was on . . .

your side. Otherwise, I . . . wouldn't have suggested we . . . wait until the Veil dropped. . . . That was for Chumba and Mist."

"Well, it all worked out for the best," Gogi says, scanning the far bank. "Though Mist will go back on the attack the moment he has the chance, I'm sure."

"I think we should go hunt him down," Lima says.

Mez shakes her head. "I don't want to go back across that rock bridge anytime soon. And if we waste time tracking down Mist, we're just giving the Ant Queen more time to prepare for us. We might still have the advantage of surprise. I say we press forward."

"Mez hasn't said it, but I'd rather not have to kill my cousin, either," Chumba adds wearily.

Gogi lays a hand on her neck. "Of course not."

"So you're not going to be inviting . . . that white panther . . . to join you all . . . anytime soon?" Banu asks.

"No, definitely not," Mez says, "and we'll want to get gone before he can rally the ants against us."

"I'm afraid I'll only . . . slow you all," Banu says, face stretching into a sad, sweet smile. "You should go on . . . without me."

"No way are we leaving you," Gogi says, shaking his head.

"Agreed," Mez says.

"That water power you've got, you think we'd give something like that up so easily?" Chumba says.

"Oh!" Banu says. "That's very nice. . . . Thank you."

"You set the pace," Gogi says. "We'll go only as fast as you can."

"Okay . . . just give me a day or two . . . to catch my breath," Banu says.

They wait in silence.

"Did you really mean to say 'a day or two'?" Lima asks.

Then Banu moves one clawed hand forward, followed by another. "That was a joke," he says. He moves some more. He takes a break again.

"Oh," Lima says, a little awkwardly, "good joke."

Mez shoots Gogi a look. *Do we ask him to speed up?*

Gogi shakes his head severely. *Absolutely not.*

Hands behind his back, whistling, Gogi tiptoes forward, pauses, tiptoes again. Lima makes a hop here and there, experimenting with walking along the ground, then crab-walking on her back. Mez and Chumba creep forward shoulder to shoulder, eyes alert to any unexpected dangers in the forest before them—or any white panthers following behind.

Gogi looks back frequently, flames licking from his fingernails, to see if Mist has followed them. But, each time, he sees only the unbroken forest canopy, cicadas droning behind it. No hoots of owls, no howler monkeys, no snuffling peccaries. No panther hisses. Just the flying insects, and the nighttime glimmer of the ants everywhere, lining every branch and every leaf. Like they're watching.

One Night Until the Eclipse

THE BALD MOUNTAINTOP doesn't look like it would be too far from the stone bridge. Well, not far if you don't have a sloth with you. Dawn arrives while they're still on their way. Gogi's teeth gnash when he sees Chumba's eyelids lower, despite the panther's best efforts to keep moving forward.

As they make camp, Gogi finds himself whistling a little too cheerily, pretending it's not frustrating to travel toward an epic showdown with the slowest creature in the rainforest along for the ride.

"What if Banu rode on Mez's back?" Gogi proposes. Maybe a little too loudly.

"Gogi," Mez says, "Banu weighs, like, twice what I do."

"He does?" Gogi says, whistling. "Oh! He, um, carries it well."

"Sorry to keep holding everyone up," Banu says as he crawls into view, looking at the companions with wide and watery eyes. "Really . . . you should all consider—"

"No," Mez says.

"Nope," Lima says.

"—sticking together," Chumba says, yawning. "Don't give it another thought. *I'm* the one whose day-coma keeps delaying everyone."

"None of you need to apologize for anything," Gogi says, gulping down his frustration. "Chumba can't prevent her daycoma, and you're a sloth, Banu, so you're supposed to be . . . slothful."

"Okay, okay, I'll stop apologizing," Banu says, nodding. "But really . . . you guys should think about—"

"No," Mez says.

"Nope," Lima says.

"—sticking together," Chumba says.

"Getting awkward. To change the topic, um, let me echolocate and see what I can scout ahead," Lima says. She closes her eyes and opens her mouth, making soft clicking sounds.

They all lean forward, listening.

Lima opens her eyes. "There are a lot of ants up there," she reports.

"Uh-huh," Gogi says encouragingly, "and . . . ?"

Lima shrugs her wings. "And that's it!"

"Oh."

"Well, there's also something really *big* rumbling around at the top of the mountain," she continues. "Like maybe the Ant Queen's found some giant creature to serve her, bigger than anything we've ever had to fight before? Maybe something like that?"

"That's also useful information, Lima," Gogi says. "I'm glad you mentioned that part, too."

"So what do we do now?" Chumba asks. "Do we just march up to her?"

"We need to bide time until Rumi and Sky return with the lens," Mez says. "We can harass the Ant Queen, maybe, to keep her off-center until they get here. And we have the last stick with the fungus, of course."

Chumba growls, even though she's mid-yawn. "I'd love to look in her eyes while we give it to her."

Gogi casts a nervous look to the sky, where the moon is nearly full, only a small crescent missing. "The lunar eclipse is tomorrow night. We should rest as best we can. We'll need our sleep so we can really let her have it."

"I don't know if I can sleep with all these ants around me," Lima says, hunkering down, wings wrapped around herself. "It's like sleeping with the enemy."

"I can help . . . with that," Banu says. He lifts his shaggy head, then extends the claws of one hand. The water in the trees around them begins to coalesce, forming a shimmering curtain that rings them in a dewy cylinder.

"Ooh!" Lima says. "That's way pretty."

"Thanks," Banu says. "I can even . . . keep it up while . . . I'm asleep. This sort of thing isn't tiring at all . . . as long as you have . . . magical powers over water . . . of course."

"Of course, that," Lima says, nodding knowingly.

Banu intensifies the water until it creates a moat, dividing the mud and roots immediately around them from their ant-covered surroundings. Gogi's feet are soon clammy from the spray, but he draws them close under him to warm them. Mez nestles in right beside him, and her soft panther fur does a lot to lessen the chill. "That's a pretty nifty trick, Banu," Gogi says. "I just might sleep. I like how it's open at the top, so we can see the sky."

Banu nods. "That's for air flow, actually. This is the only way I was able . . . to travel through hostile territory. . . . It's not like sloths have many natural defenses . . . against the likes of ants. . . . Sorry about the dampness. Maybe your . . . fire can warm you up?"

"That's okay. I should save my magic for the upcoming battle."

"Say," Banu continues, "I was meaning to ask you all . . . have you seen Sorella?"

Gogi shudders, eyes going to Mez and then back to the sloth. "I'm sorry, Banu. Mist told us that Sorella refused the Ant Queen, and that she . . . that the ants killed her," Gogi says.

Banu shakes his head. "I can't believe it. . . . She's so strong . . . so powerful."

"If even she couldn't fight off the Ant Queen . . . ," Mez says, letting her voice trail off.

"Then we won't let her death be in vain," Gogi says resolutely. "We'll fight even harder."

They stare out at the shimmering curtain of water surrounding them. A long time goes by while Gogi gazes into the changing patterns, a set of blues and whites as chaotic and compelling as the reds of fire. "Anyone else think they're too tense to sleep?" Gogi eventually says.

He's greeted by snores.

"Okay, great. Guess I'm on my own here."

"I'm awake, Gogi," Lima whispers.

"I'm scared, Lima," Gogi whispers.

"Me too."

"I hope Rumi and Sky come through," Gogi says. "Otherwise we're probably sunk."

"Gogi?"

"Yes, Lima?"

"I'm glad we're here together."

"Yeah, me too. Having Lima the Healing Bat along makes everything easier."

"You have to admit," Lima says sleepily, "it really does have a good ring."

As soon as the Veil drops and they've gotten Chumba awake, the companions try the tail feather directive—but it comes up with just the muffled roar of wind and a close-up view of Sky's red feathers. No chance of any communication there.

They head out again up the misty mountain. The ascent becomes steeper and steeper, and as it does the usual concentration of ants thickens into torrents. Banu keeps a stream of water at their feet to prevent the ants from accumulating enough to be dangerous, but it slows their progress more.

Even so, it's soon evident that they're nearing the bald plain at the top of the mountain. The sounds of forest life, already muted, disappear entirely. The trees are sparse, furred over by the bodies of ants. Ahead is a space with no trees in it, just a gap outlined by stars. Gogi cranes his neck, hoping to see some clue of what lies before them. But there is only the sight of the marching ants, and an eerie skittering noise that is next to silence.

"The source of the ants," Mez says. "And probably the queen herself. We're nearly there. I'll go invisible and scout it out."

Gogi lays a furry hand on her back. "No, Mez. It's clear by now that, once the ants are climbing on you, you're as visible as any of us out there. And when we face the Ant Queen, it has to be together. That's the only way we stand a chance."

"Besides, isn't everything better . . . when you have a water shield surrounding you?" Banu adds. "Especially when ants . . . are concerned?"

Mez nods. "It's true, I'd definitely rather have you all at my side."

"So we go on together," Gogi says.

As they approach the last of the rainforest's shrouding vegetation, the tight jungle pathway broadens into a clearing. When Chumba makes a clicking sound, the companions know to halt where they are and melt as deeply as they can into the shadows. Gogi, trusting the panthers' ambush reflexes more than his own, positions himself behind Mez in a thicket of ferns.

"Look," Chumba whispers. "There, at the edge."

The trees give way to bald earth, torn up and covered with an unsettling sheen, like a fresh wound. It continues up and up, until the summit disappears before the night sky, impossible to make out despite Gogi's attempts to illuminate it. But Chumba's pointing to a nearer spot. No more than a dozen monkeylengths along the edge of the clearing, the trees shake and part. Ants roll out in a wave, falling to either side with a roaring sound.

Fear seizes Gogi's stomach. With this many ants in one place, the queen is probably not far away.

With another crashing sound, a large shape emerges from the trees. It's not the Ant Queen, but an iguana, a muscular and broad-shouldered specimen whose scales shimmer gold in the light of the full moon. It pauses and raises its head, flicking its tongue in and out, tasting the night air.

"That's a lizard I'd rather not meet up close," Lima whispers.

Gogi trains his focus on the branches behind the iguana, but the next creature to arrive comes from above. Treetops sway, until one of them bends entirely, raining seeds and leaves on the clearing. A harpy eagle plummets from the sky. Perching on a low branch, it peers out along a wickedly sharp beak. Gogi shudders—he'd take the iguana over this raptor, any day. Harpy eagles are as bad as it gets when it comes to capuchin eaters.

The iguana and eagle wait among the ants, scanning about them. It's like they're waiting for something else to arrive. Maybe they're wondering where Mist is?

While he watches, swallowing against the fear in his throat, Gogi notices the circlet of ants marching around the head of each animal. He tries to read emotions into their faces, but even though reading emotions is a strength of monkeys, he's unable to see any. It's like they're past feeling, like the iguana and the harpy eagle have resigned themselves to their fate, and there's nothing left in their hearts to change it.

Desperation will make them dangerous enemies.

"Do we try to say anything to the henchmen?" Gogi whispers to Chumba. "Or is it not worth the risk of revealing our position?"

"It's not worth it," Chumba whispers back. "I say we try to sneak past."

"Um, that sounds difficult," Gogi says.

"We'd be totally exposed out there," Mez says. "The ant armies have ripped down everything that would have provided cover."

They hold still, scarcely daring to breathe, while their enemies survey the clearing. The iguana and eagle confer, their words too quiet to make out. All the while, the ants continue their march around their heads.

Gogi keeps flame licking from his fingertips, in case the queen's henchmen—and the swarming ants—suddenly attack. But they don't. They hold steady, staring down the mountain's slope, in the direction the companions came from.

"What are they waiting for?" Lima asks.

"For Mist to arrive with us, I bet," Mez says.

"That seems like as good an argument as any to get out of here," Gogi says.

"Right, right," Mez says. "Panther instinct is always to stay hidden in the shadows, but I'm learning that sometimes panther instinct is not the way to go."

"I'm thinking that we've got the best chance of not being noticed if we go left; then we can stay on the far side of that pile of rubble—"

"—which will block most of the moonlight, stopping us from casting shadows," Chumba finishes. "I like your plan."

"Guys? Do you hear that?" Lima asks, tilting her head. "No, of course you don't, you're not bats. There's someone approaching behind us. They think they're being stealthy, but—"

"Intruders!" comes Mist's shrieking voice. "Alert! The shadowwalkers are hiding right before you! In the fern!"

"Oh poop," Gogi says, springing to his feet.

The iguana goes rigid, teeth bared while it tastes the air, head wagging back and forth. The harpy eagle takes to the sky, the sight of its muscular wings in motion seizing Gogi's heart.

They don't head toward the companions.

The eagle lifts out of view as the iguana races up toward the mountain's bald summit, feet flailing as it builds up impossible speed. The ant horde sweeps along with it, the reptile passing right through the midst of the insects, trampling them indiscriminately.

"They're off to warn the queen!" Lima shrieks.

"Where is Mist?" Chumba asks, whirling. "We should have finished our cousin off when we had the chance."

Mez sets her teeth, her tail thrashing behind her. "He retreated back into the jungle. No time, we move now, we have to get ahead of the henchmen. Go!" She races through the open clearing, tailing the iguana.

Gogi's mouth drops open at the thought that they might soon be facing the Ant Queen. "Are we really . . . ?"

"*Move*, Gogi," Chumba cries as she streaks after her sister.

"I guess we're doing this," Gogi says, gaze flicking nervously to the sky for any sign of the deadly harpy eagle. "Ready, Banu?"

"Now you have to leave me behind," Banu says. "You need to get to the Ant Queen before they can warn her. I'll meet you there. Mist will have to pass this way, and I'll use my water powers to stop him. Then I'll come join you. You can count on me."

"Bye, see you up there," Lima says as she springs into the air.

"Good luck, Banu, and thank you," Gogi says. He sprints up the mountainside, already darkening from the orange shadow that has begun to cover the moon above.

The Night of the Eclipse

GOGI DASHES THROUGH the night heedlessly, tripping over rocks and slipping through slick patches of upturned earth, falling onto his side and pulling himself to his feet, eyes on the sky, ready for ants to overwhelm him, or the eagle to take him like one once took his mother. He watches for the sight of Mez or Chumba, but the panthers are too stealthy to detect. Instead he follows Lima's trills in the night sky, leading him upward, upward, toward thudding earth, toward strange wet sounds, toward massive shapes looming in the night. Always upward. Gogi's lungs ache.

He blunders forward, heedless of the teeming ants

under his hands and feet. He might be running right into danger, but what option does he have? Mez and Chumba are somewhere ahead, so he has to keep—

"Gogi, up here!" It's Mez.

Gogi stops short so suddenly that he falls over, skidding in the soil. He scrambles to his hands and feet and follows the voice, falling headfirst again, this time right into a bush. He flails, panting and gasping, pushing at the leaves whapping his face, then climbs the trunk of a tree tailfirst, until he's on a branch well above the jungle floor, the panther sisters purring nearby. "Hush," Chumba says urgently, laying a paw on Gogi's forehead. "Be as quiet as you can."

Stilled by the urgency in Chumba's voice, Gogi forces his breathing to calm, despite the pounding in his temples. He goes onto his belly and creeps forward along the branch. Mez's paw is on one shoulder, and Chumba's is on the other. "I can't see anything," he says, staring out.

"That's because of the lunar eclipse," Chumba says.

Gogi looks up and sees, through the dark leaves of the tree, that the curved orange shadow is nearly halfway across the moon.

He increases the amount of glow he's casting over the area, and sees that he and the panther sisters are on a branch of one of the few remaining trees, stripped bare of vegetation and left dead. From their perch, he looks out to see a flood of ants passing through the rainforest, massing and swarming toward the top of the mountain.

"So, where's the queen?" Gogi asks.

"Don't you see?" Chumba hisses back. "It's horrible!"

"See *what*?" Gogi gasps. "Oh. I thought that was part of the mountain."

Last time he'd seen her, the Ant Queen was the size of a full-grown panther. But now she's bigger than any creature Gogi has ever encountered, bigger than any creature should ever be. She *is* the pinnacle of the mountain.

The queen is twenty monkeys high, and as thick as the broadest fig trunk. The top half of her body is familiar, even though it is many times its previous size. It's constructed of invulnerable purple-brown plates of armor, with yellow hairs sprouting from them, and her impassive, beady-eyed face ends in two sharp mandibles. The Ant Queen could slice a capuchin or a panther in two with the simplest click of those mandibles.

Her abdomen has bloomed out to an enormous size. It's a massive, pulsating sac, so heavy it roots her to the top of the mountain. "Is she sick or something?" Gogi whispers.

"No, watch. There, another one's coming," Chumba answers.

In front of Gogi's eyes, the bottom of the Ant Queen parts, and out comes a glistening white egg. Then another. They pass into the horde and are soon carried away. More come. The queen is focused on her task, eyes toward the eclipse and the heavens.

"So this is where the hordes of ants are coming from," Gogi says.

"There will be more and more and more," Chumba says. "Until there are enough to overrun the rainforest."

"Do you think she knows we're here?" Gogi whispers to his friends out of the side of his mouth.

"I don't know," Mez whispers back. "I hope not. She seems to be focused on producing all those eggs."

Gogi pats the woven sack, with the fungus stick inside. "So I guess we . . . go and face her?"

Mez and Chumba nod grimly and get to all fours, making the yowling noises they always make before a fight, their hackles sticking up. They bow their shoulders to the branch, haunches high in the air, to stretch their muscles. Gogi tries the same, but it feels ridiculous. He's not sure what to do with his tail.

He peers down over the edge, to where moonlit swarms of ants cover the ground, dotted with the white glow of eggs being passed along from their queen. "I wish the enemy was just a little nearer," Gogi says.

"How's this for you?" comes a screeching voice from above.

Harpy eagle!

The mere sound of it sets Gogi shrieking. He whirls just in time to see the wickedly hooked beak of the raptor, open wide as it streaks toward him.

Gogi scrambles without a thought to what direction he's going, fear bursting him off his hands and feet, out of the tree entirely and dropping through night air. It means the eagle isn't rending his flesh, but now he's in free fall, the shrieks and cries of his battling friends soon distant.

He plummets for another few shuddering, stomach-dropping seconds, and then he's crashing through branches, the sound of breaking wood all around him, serrated edges of leaves lashing his face. He reaches out, trying to stop his fall any way he can, but he's going too fast; everything he touches whips through his fingers and shreds his palms.

Finally Gogi lands in a mammoth fern. Though it bows dramatically under his weight, it doesn't break. He's tossed into the air and then back into the fern, and he's able to grip the greenery with his tail this time to prevent himself from being bounced out again.

Gogi sways heavily. He might be totally disoriented,

and hanging on by only his tail, but at least he's in one piece. He shuts his eyes for a long moment, trying to keep the contents of his stomach from rising into his mouth. Once he can, he cracks his eyes open.

The eagle. Mez, Chumba, and Lima. Where are they?

He whips to the underside of a frond, quickly judges the distance to the jungle floor, and drops, hitting the ground on all fours to prevent any one limb from breaking. He shakes out the tingling sensation in his ankles and wrists. "Ow, ow, ow."

As soon as he can, he's darting through the night foliage. He draws up short before a swaying trunk, trying to make out the nearby shapes in the darkness. He's gotten himself totally switched around, and he needs to know where his friends are before he can go saving them. As a reflex, he also reaches down to pat the fungus stick through his woven bag.

The bag's not there.

The Ant Queen is as big as a mountain, he's lost his friends, there's a harpy eagle after him, and the item that could have saved Caldera—if it even worked—is gone. Even the twelve pebbles that represent his rank are gone. He has nothing. Gogi feels like his legs might give way, right where he is.

But he doesn't let them give way. He keeps moving.

Because no monkey of any rank would abandon his troop, not if he has any breath left in his body. And his friends are his troop.

Gogi pauses as he listens for the cry of the eagle, the yowl of a panther, anything that will help him figure out where his friends are. There are ordinary rainforest sounds on the left, undefinable ruckus on the right. He chooses right.

"Wrong way, idiot," comes a familiar voice. Mist.

Gogi turns to see the white panther with the woven sack slung around his front, grinning.

"I can't believe you thought a sloth would stop me. I avoided him easily. And now I have your magical pebbles. Why are these so precious that you looked right away for this sack? Some precious capuchin superstition?"

Mist hasn't mentioned the fungus stick. And why would he? It looks just like regular forest debris. He's focused on the stones. Interesting.

"Those pebbles are more precious than you know," Gogi improvises. "Mist, the lunar eclipse is moments away. If I . . . don't have those pebbles . . . when it happens . . . all of Caldera will be lost!" He throws his hands in the air for extra dramatic effect.

"Less competition for me, then," Mist says, stroking the sack. "I can rule alone."

"But that's not really ruling, see?" Gogi says. He

makes a big show about being unable to see anything, hammily flailing his arms back and forth. Meanwhile, he tries to get a good look at the bag slung around Mist's chest. Can he see the outline of the stick still in there? He thinks he can.

"I will bring these pebbles to the Ant Queen, and she will decide what to do with them," Mist says. "She will figure out what you've planned."

Gogi finds himself almost wishing it happens, just so he can see what the Ant Queen does when Mist interrupts her to give her some ordinary pebbles.

Somewhere above, Gogi hears the harpy eagle crying, and the sounds of a scuffle. The raptor could easily kill Chumba or Mez—the sisters will be lucky to get away. If they're not already done for.

Mist looks up fearfully at the sound of the eagle's cry, then controls his face and, with visible effort, stops his tail from thrashing.

He's scared of the eagle too. Useful.

Gogi has an idea. He says, "Give me the bag back, it doesn't belong to you, you silly cat"—only he *sings* it. To the tune of "Lima the Healing Bat."

"What are you doing?" Mist asks, face twisting. "What is this about?"

Gogi flicks his eye to the sky, hoping to see a little

black blip heading his way. But there's no sign of Lima. Okay. It was a long shot, he knew that.

Gogi sighs and wiggles his fingers to warm them up, to get the fire magic flowing. Looks like he's going to be fighting Mist. Alone.

Gogi and Mist go still, staring at each other, fire already licking from Gogi's fingernails. He puts some fire in the tip of his tail, too, for extra effect.

It seems to work. Mist's eyes widen, twinkling in Gogi's light. The lips on the non-ruined side of his face pull back from his teeth. Maybe it's fear, maybe it's aggression, but at least Gogi definitely seems to be having an effect. He steps forward.

Mist bolts.

Stunned, Gogi watches the white panther streak through the night. Mist heads up the mountain, toward the Ant Queen, screeching, "I have the magic pebbles, my queen!"

"'Magic pebbles.' This should be interesting," Gogi mutters as he races after Mist. He increases the fire from his hands and tail and extends it to his feet, too, sizzling the ground with every step. It's a mistake—even though Mist is pure white, and running madcap along the barren mountaintop, Gogi's so dazzled by his own flame that he loses sight of him. His vision is full of purple blobs. All he can really make out is the last remaining sliver of the moon above them, already turning orange from the lunar eclipse.

Tears streaming out of his eyes, Gogi loses track of where he's going. He has to take a moment to close his eyes, to listen for the wet sounds of the birthing queen, the continuing cries of the harpy eagle, and . . . a song?

"Lima, the Healing Bat! Ferocious-er than a piranha! Scarier than a cat!"

Gogi watches, amazed, as Lima swoops in front of the eclipsing moon, and then down. Ahh—there's Mist! Lima zooms alongside the unaware panther, then agilely gets her feet around the bag's knotted strap. She unties it and lifts it from around his neck. Mist doesn't even notice.

Gogi lets out a single flare, so Lima will know where he is.

Lima's got other plans, though. She doesn't head toward Gogi—she heads up the mountain, after Mist's departing shape.

I see where we're going with this, Gogi says to himself as he races after. "I'm coming, Lima!"

He follows Mist and Lima to the summit, climbs the same tree he hid in before with Mez and Chumba. There's no sign of his friends or the harpy eagle, though the branch is still full of the panthers' scent.

Having seen the Ant Queen in her egg-laying state once doesn't lessen the horror of seeing it again. She's still impossibly large, devoted to her mission, eyes turned toward the eclipsing moon as more and more glimmering white eggs emerge from her.

Mist stands before her, tiny. He pulls himself up as tall as he can and speaks, but the words are lost within the tumult of the egg laying. Gogi can't hear a word he says, and it doesn't seem the Ant Queen can, either.

Gogi cranes his neck, stepping from foot to foot to prevent the ants from climbing too far up his body. Where's Lima?

There she is, soaring over the queen. She bobs frantically, dipping in the night sky. The bag must be heavier than she is; it jostles more and more as she dips and twists.

Pebbles scatter through the air, tinkling on the impenetrable plated armor of the Ant Queen. She doesn't notice. Mist rears back, though, hissing. Now Gogi can just make out his voice. "The magic pebbles!"

Last thing to tumble out is the stick. It's black in the eclipsing night, but Gogi can still make out its outline as it falls through the air, striking the Ant Queen's pulsating abdomen before it fragments into bits.

Lima flies off in another direction—maybe she has a bead on Mez and Chumba. Gogi looks up longingly, trapped as he is on this barren wasteland with Mist and hordes of ants.

Or wait, the iguana is here too! Not exactly better.

The lizard slinks from around the backside of the Ant Queen, heading right for the spot where the fragments of the stick fell. It noses the earth, tongue licking the night air. Mist approaches and points his paw at the moonlit pebbles. But the iguana ignores him, continuing to sniff the earth. Investigating the fragments of the fungus stick.

Amid the tangled vines of the jungle floor, specks of fungal white have begun to appear among the red-brown ants. The fungus has already started to infect them.

The Ant Queen takes her attention from the looming eclipse and finally looks down at the ants surrounding her. She surveys the horde, rearing up on her hind legs as she clacks her forelegs in the night air, emitting an eerie harmonic sound. Is she aware that something is wrong?

She stays motionless amid her horde of ants, waving them forward to where the stick fragments fell. Her iguana henchman barrels over and uses its thick tongue to lap up streams of the insects, drawing them into its gullet.

"Of course," Gogi says to himself. "Iguanas are very

talented eaters of ants. He's eating the infected ants before the fungus can spread. I should have predicted this."

The Ant Queen whips from side to side, antennae flaring. Gogi looks for Mez and Chumba, but his friends are nowhere near.

The iguana continues to sweep up massive swaths of the infected ants with its tongue but has switched to gnashing them with its teeth and then spitting out the pulp. Its belly is probably full. A slurry of ant parts drips out of its jaws.

The queen's eyes glaze as she brings her front legs up, like a panicking animal. But Gogi has learned by now that the Ant Queen does not panic. The Ant Queen only strategizes.

As she brings her forelegs down, a seismic thud goes through the soil. It makes Gogi's hands and feet tingle where he's hiding in the bushes, but it has an altogether more severe impact on the ants. Some of the ants behind the Ant Queen—her healthy forces—still and quiet, but the main impact is on the horde before her, near the bits of fungus stick. When the queen sends out her seismic signal, they go motionless, only gradually recovering their senses.

With horror, Gogi sees that some of the queen's eggs have split, parted by her seismic attack, the larvae inside killed.

By ruthlessly killing healthy and infected ants alike, though, the queen is stopping the threat of the fungus before it begins.

Gogi casts his gaze to the sky, hoping to see any sign of his friends and their harpy eagle assailant. But there's no sign of them.

It will be up to Gogi alone to stop the Ant Queen, while she's still distracted.

He knows exactly what Mez would tell him: *You only get the element of surprise once. Don't waste it.* So he stops himself from racing into battle and instead creeps higher in his tree, so he's right above the teeming edge where the zombie ants meet the Ant Queen's army.

He closes his eyes, to sink as deep as he can into the depths of his power, to channel and direct it. He smells smoke rising from his skin, unbidden.

Gogi allows his eyes to open.

He unleashes an inferno.

G OGI'S ONLY EVER tried this particular fire trick
when he was alone, in quiet moments back in
the capuchin forest. He's not sure if he'll be able to pull
off the concentration it requires now, with millions of
ants and an iguana and maybe a harpy eagle somewhere
zooming toward him . . . oh right, and the *Ant Queen herself*, to top it all off. And when precisely will the eclipse
be at its fullest? How's he supposed to know that?

Focus on what you can control, Gogi.

To help himself get into as calm a state as possible,
he pretends he's getting groomed by Alzo, imagines little monkey fingers from the tips of his ears down to his
toes. Then he senses his own skin as fully as possible,

setting his attention to each smoking pore and follicle. He hears fighting, senses the already dim light in the clearing turning pitch-black, but he forces his attention not to wander from his own skin. Success.

He sets it all on fire.

I am the monkey of fire. I am the monkey of legend, he tells himself as every hair follicle on his body ignites. The smoke blurs his vision, makes him able to see only vague outlines of everything around him.

It also attracts the attention of his enemies. He sees the iguana stop mopping up ants and turn its gaze to Gogi's branch instead.

Surprise, Mez would tell him again. *Don't ever waste surprise.*

Whipping his flames even higher, Gogi drops from the branch right into the midst of the ants.

He wishes he could see himself in that moment: the form of a monkey, arms and tail out wide and teeth bared, covered in hot orange flame. He makes the loudest capuchin scream he can. Capuchins aren't famously intimidating or anything, but he figures being covered in fire should heighten the effect.

While ants crisp and char beneath Gogi, the iguana turns and bolts from the area. It's worked! Mist, and now the iguana, have fled before him!

The Ant Queen isn't as easily cowed. The ground

shudders as she brings her massive bulk to its feet and stomps toward Gogi, her mandibles gnashing. He tries to summon more fire to hurl at her, but feels only a wrenching in his spine as his ears make a few sparkles. Covering his body in flames seems to have tapped him out.

Gogi hops left, then hops right. There's so much smoke—it's really hard to make out much of anything anymore. The smoke is an unexpected problem with this plan. That and being all intimidation and no actual attack power.

The Ant Queen's face is suddenly right in front of his. Black eyes, framed in her heart-shaped crimson skull, shine into Gogi's eyes. Words appear in his mind. *It is time we had a conversation, Gogi the capuchin.*

Gogi commands his limbs to run, but they won't move. He tries to scream, but no words come out. The fire is gone, the smoke is gone, the ants are gone, Caldera is gone.

He and the Ant Queen are floating in a void, motionless, each staring into the other's eyes. Mez told him this happened to her once, when she confronted the Ant Queen in the depths of the ziggurat, and now it's happening to Gogi.

He tries sending his thoughts to her. *What do you want, Ant Queen?*

Her head doesn't move as she beams thoughts back to him. *Do you even know my name?*

No, and it doesn't matter, Gogi says, hoping his thoughts come across the void as being defiant, not terrified. *Hmm, do thoughts have a tone?*

Pay attention, monkey. My name does matter. You are spending all your energy trying to "save" Caldera from an enemy whose name you haven't even bothered to learn. Does that not strike you as odd? I know your name, Gogi, Twelfth of the Capuchins.

We don't need to know yours. We just need to know what you're trying to do.

I am Narelia. Even Auriel showed enough respect to learn my name.

Okay. "Narelia." Fine.

Respect me, capuchin.

Gogi would shake his head if he could. If respect is so important to the Ant Queen, then that's precisely what he won't give her. *No respect for you. Release me.*

I will not. Not while I have you in my grasp. Time has slowed. I could stop it entirely, if I chose. It's just you and I, for as long as we need.

He's got to figure out a way to make her release him.

I will not release you, the Ant Queen repeats.

He also has to figure out a way to keep her out of his thoughts.

You will not keep me out of your thoughts, the Ant Queen says.

Hmm. He thinks of monkey things. Farts. Hairy butts.

Do you think a little monkey anatomy is enough to chase me off?

He has no idea what she just said, but hopefully whatever "anatomy" is *will* chase her off. Try as he may to keep his mind on gross monkey things, his thoughts return to Mez, Chumba, and Lima, somewhere out there fighting against that fearsome harpy eagle.

When his thoughts go to his friends in jeopardy, the Ant Queen's attention on him seems to double. Though his body stays distant and formless, Gogi feels like he's sweating.

Listen to me, Gogi. I can offer you power beyond anything a number twelve—or even a number one like your admired Ravanna—can dream of.

How does she know his rank? She must be sifting through his mind. If he doesn't agree to her demands, is she going to keep him trapped in this limbo forever? Until he goes crazy, and only then will she bring him back into ordinary time, useless to help his friends because he's too busy talking to the voices in his head? He'll, what, spend the rest of his days picking through his belly button lint?

Maybe that's precisely what I'll do, the Ant Queen says.

That's when Gogi hears the caw.

How is there anyone else here? It's a *void*; the whole point is that there's no one else around. This is Gogi's first void, admittedly, but even he knows that already.

The Ant Queen can't break her gaze with Gogi any more than he can break his with her, it seems. Though he senses surprise from her, she doesn't move her focus. Gogi watches from the edge of his vision as a red shape appears, getting larger and larger, until it's flapping there in the void, right between them.

It's Sky!

Is that you? Gogi asks the macaw in his thoughts.

Yes it is, Gogi, Sky replies in Gogi's head, before turning to face in the other direction. *And hello, Narelia.*

Sky floats in midair, taking in the two of them. He can move, even though the Ant Queen and Gogi can't. Gogi's mind races. Sky's divination magic seems to have allowed him to access this private melding of minds. Does this mean that Sky is there with them at the mountaintop? Most important, is Gogi witnessing Sky saving the day . . . or betraying them all?

What's happening, Sky? Gogi asks.

But Sky ignores him, facing the Ant Queen instead. His voice is labored over his wing beats. *Your plan, the one I heard about a year ago from Auriel, is finally working.*

Yes, Narelia says. *Have you reconsidered my offer?*

The eclipse is nearly here, Sky responds. *You hope to use the new influx of magical power?*

The Ant Queen pauses a moment before responding. *Once, long before there were birds and monkeys here, this rainforest was quiet. The only living things were ants and plants. It was a serene era. No bloodshed, no need for conflict. The rainforest was calm. My horde will eliminate all animal life, and the rainforest can renew, going back to the serenity it once had.*

When there weren't animals like the two-legs, going around imprisoning you, Gogi adds. *This is actually revenge, isn't it?*

If you want to think about it that way, fine. I was once imprisoned by the two-legs, it's true. But you know nothing of the peace this rainforest had in its beginning, thousands of years ago. Do not pretend to judge me.

The lunar eclipse is moments away, Sky says. *With the lens, the magic of Caldera could be redistributed to the ants. Then your victory would be assured.*

The Ant Queen's eyes light up. Sky has figured out exactly what she has in mind.

Gogi can sense Sky's wing beats slowing. It's not like he's a hummingbird—keeping stationary in midair must be exhausting. The parrot whirls, taking in the Ant Queen, then Gogi. The Ant Queen, then Gogi.

Tell me you have brought the lens, Sky, the Ant Queen says. *Give it to me, and in return I will grant you infinite power. You will never be that abandoned third hatchling, not ever again.*

That's when, talons stretched out and beak open in rage, Sky goes right for her eyes.

T HE MOMENT SKY'S talons come in contact with the Ant Queen, the jungle swoops back, the ant armies swoop back, the iguana swoops back. She— Narelia—has broken the connection.

A year ago, Mez described her conversation in the Ant Queen's void as existing in a split second of time, but things have clearly been happening in the real world while Gogi was speaking to her. His eyes are completely covered in ants, for one thing. It's like he's sleeping under a blanket of living, thrashing creatures. They behave like water, their interlocking bodies blocking out the moon, moving across him in waves and eddies. Gogi scrunches his eyes shut.

This is how I'm going to die. The queen will have them all bite him at once. It's surprising that she hasn't made it happen yet. Maybe she was distracted by talking to him.

Maybe the ants have carried his body far away. Maybe they've dragged him deep into enemy lines. There's only one way to find out—and only one way to survive.

Girding what's left of his magical energy, Gogi lights up his skin and sends the flame outward.

The puff of fire incinerates the nearest ants, filling Gogi's nostrils with acrid smoke and a tangy smell. He opens his eyes and staggers to all fours.

He's in the middle of the ant army—the queen's healthy forces. There's a patch of dead ant bodies around him, but beyond that are layers and layers of live, writhing ants, their meaty jaws snapping.

Gogi spins. The ants surround him. For a while he can give out more puffballs of fire to incinerate the ones that approach, but there's no way his magic will be enough to take down all these enemies.

Amid the toasted bits under his feet, Gogi sees withered fungus pods. Maybe there's enough fungus remaining that it could reinfect the queen's horde, but it won't take effect until long after his friends' fate has been sealed.

They've failed.

It's not just ants in the clearing. Here, too, are the Ant Queen and Sky. She faces upward, forelegs thrashing in the air as she lunges and snaps, trying to snag the macaw, who harries her again and again. Sky's powers are like Lima's, better for support than direct combat, but he's still trying valiantly to stall her. If she manages to snag him, he'll immediately be pierced, but he's doing a good job of dodging and weaving in the air, feathers cascading from him as her sharp legs narrowly miss the meat of his body. Sky surely can't hope to do any damage to their giant armored foe, but here he is, risking his life to distract the queen, to buy them time—but for what?

Gogi wraps his arms tight around himself, against a sudden wind that comes up.

Wait—a sudden wind? Gogi pivots to see where it's coming from . . . and finds a tiny little yellow frog hovering in the air over the ant armies.

"Rumi!" Gogi shouts, heedless that he might be alerting the queen to his own presence. "I'm over here!"

Once, back when they were fighting the Ant Queen deep under the ziggurat, Gogi combined his fire with Rumi's wind power to create a flaming tornado. Maybe Rumi has a similar plan now. The little frog doesn't look up at Gogi, since the wind coming from his mouth is what's lifting him into the air, and he needs to keep that aimed downward. But he scoot-hovers in Gogi's direction. Once Rumi's close enough, Gogi plucks him from the air.

"You guys made it back!" Gogi says. "Quick, we have to help Sky!"

"The lunar eclipse," Rumi gasps, "the lens . . ."

Gogi glances up. Sure enough, the shadow has nearly crossed the moon, bathing it in orange, only the tiniest sliver of white light remaining.

An eclipse, the event that shuffled the magic of Caldera, and gave him and his friends their powers, is about to happen again. Part of Gogi wishes everything would pause so that he could watch. He was zero years old the first time—it's hard to notice much when you're no age at all.

But then he hears a terrified caw, and sees that the Ant Queen has managed to give Sky a glancing blow with one of her forelegs, batting him out of the air. Red and white feathers fly up as Sky scrambles away. But scrambling is not an easy thing for a parrot to do, and there's no chance he'll get back into the air before the queen's jagged mandibles have sliced him in two.

Unless Gogi helps. He readies a ball of flame and releases it. It soars past the Ant Queen's antennae but distracts her for long enough to give Sky a chance to dodge her next attack.

As Gogi runs toward Sky, he shouts to Rumi: "The lens! Where is the lens?"

A yellow blip as Rumi hops to the top of Gogi's shoulder. "Sky couldn't risk carrying it right to the Ant Queen, but he knew he had to come rescue you—so he left the lens with Mez and Chumba and Lima. They're bringing it."

"Mez and Chumba and Lima?" Gogi cries. "They're alive?"

"Yes! More fire, Gogi!"

Gogi sends out another fireball. It bursts over the Ant Queen's head, doing little damage but calling her attention back. The Ant Queen whirls from Sky and turns her focus to Gogi instead. She must be directing her minions to attack; the ants surge up Gogi's legs, but he can't release another blast of protective flame from his fur, not if Rumi is right on him.

"Hovering!" Rumi says from somewhere over Gogi's head. It's like his friend read his thoughts exactly and got out of the way of danger. Rumi is one smart frog.

Gogi sets out another burst of heat to crisp the ants that are climbing him, even as he prepares a third fireball. There's so much to focus on, with the ant hordes and their queen, and that awful iguana and harpy eagle somewhere within the surrounding jungle, that his mind is firing everywhere all at once. But he manages to ask Rumi, even as he launches fireball after fireball, "Are Mez and Lima and Chumba okay?"

"They were fleeing . . . from a harpy eagle."

"So the lens . . . ," Gogi says, breathless from the exertion of channeling so much magic.

"We got it, Gogi! Mez is bringing it."

Gogi can't afford to look, but he hears the cries of the harpy eagle behind him, and breaking branches. No sound from Mez, but that's to be expected—she's virtually silent in combat.

The Ant Queen's attention is drawn to the commotion. While Sky staggers to his claws and out of the way, Gogi risks a look back.

Under the tiny sliver of moon, Mez and Chumba—blurs of calico fur—are at the far side of the dark clearing, streaking toward them. Only by sending firelight into the area can Gogi see that Mez has something round dangling from her mouth.

Racing behind her is the harpy eagle, beak snapping on open air. As long as the sisters don't snag a paw on liana and trip, they should be able to escape it.

The iguana is another story.

The massive reptile has stepped in front of the panthers, blocking them from reaching Gogi and Rumi. Its long tongue tastes the air as it prepares to strike. Mez is hurtling right toward the beast, but she can't slow without falling into the talons of the harpy eagle.

Gogi prepares a fireball to send in the iguana's direction. But doing that will mean taking pressure off the Ant Queen, allowing her to redouble her attacks on Sky.

Gogi's hands waver. Whatever he does, someone will die.

Mez takes the choice of what to do next out of his hands. She manages to get her head tilted enough, even while sprinting, to fling the round thing—the lens—toward him. "Catch!" Chumba calls from beside her sister.

Gogi has to wrest his attention from Mez to concentrate on the hurtling disc-shaped object. He reaches, reaches, then—yes—he's got it. And with his tail, no less.

He has the lens!

Okay. Now what?

Gogi transfers the lens to his hands. It's clear in the middle, like solid air, and surrounded by a hard and shiny substance that is cold under his fingers. Definitely magical stuff. Gogi turns from the iguana bearing down on Mez to the Ant Queen advancing on Sky. He has a precious window of only a few seconds.

Above, the earth's orange shadow continues to slide over the moon. The sliver of remaining light is almost gone.

Rumi's voice is right in Gogi's ear. "The time is now. Remember the magical words, Gogi?"

He does. Or at least he's pretty sure he does. Gogi holds the circular lens up in the vague direction of the Ant Queen. She's leaping and snarling toward Sky, whose wings beat furiously as he struggles to get airborne. "There are two parts, though!" Gogi says, sweat standing out on his brow and dripping into his eyes. "Which one do I say?"

"You're going to have to trust me, Gogi," Rumi says in rapid chirps. "When the moment of greatest eclipse happens, I need you to point the lens toward the center of Caldera, in the direction of the ruined ziggurat. I need you to say the *second* part of the phrase."

"What? The ziggurat is so far away! Why would I do that?" Gogi says. Rumi asking for his blind faith makes Gogi suspicious: from Rumi's hiding the fact that he's been talking to Sky over the last year, to his plan to have just himself and Sky go to the edge of Caldera and learn whatever they learned in the riddle cave, to Big Rumi's enigmatic warning that there was more to Rumi's history than the rest of the companions know . . . all of it tells Gogi that he shouldn't trust Rumi now.

But Rumi is one of his closest friends. Rumi's brainpower figured out their best plan to defeat Auriel. Rumi's intelligence and wind powers have saved them, time and again. Rumi wouldn't betray them.

Right?

"Now, Gogi!" Rumi cries, eyes to the sky. "The lunar eclipse is now!"

With the moon darkening to blood red, Gogi loses what time he had left. He makes his choice. He holds the lens out in the darkness and prepares to speak.

22

SWEATY FINGERS SHAKING, Gogi turns the lens toward the distant ziggurat ruins. There are shrieks and cries all around him: Sky's horrible pain-wracked caws; Mez's hisses, probably at the attacking iguana; Lima's frantic chirps in the sky above.

Gogi holds the lens above his head, top pointing toward the eclipsed moon. Then, voice trembling, he calls: "Pour sun into night, and create life."

At first, nothing happens. There are only the sounds of combat, strangely distant behind the ringing in Gogi's ears, and the eerie fire-rimmed dark of the scene before him.

The earth rumbles somewhere far in the distance.

While it does, its shadow retreats from the moon's face, returning light to the scene.

The soil begins to glow, more than can be explained by the return of moonlight. It starts from Gogi's feet and heads toward the far distant ziggurat. It's like the soil is full of glowworms; it's still brown-black under the night sky, but even so it's illuminated like some mushrooms are at night. The glowing line cuts a wide path through the jungle.

Trees along the luminous path shake and shudder; then the nearest one pitches to the side. Out from behind it comes a booming voice. Even though Gogi is certain he's never heard this voice before, he can recognize it all the same. He struggles to understand what he's hearing.

The voice continues its wordless thundering.

The clearing goes still. Sky, on his back and surrounded by feathers, goes still. The iguana and Mez, until now wheeling around each other, go still. Lima lands lightly on Gogi's shoulder, wordless.

The Ant Queen freezes, then takes a hesitant step forward. "No," she says. Normally her voice sounds harmonic, otherworldly, but now for the first time it jangles and clashes. "It can't be!"

The tree falls over entirely, with a crashing sound. All the combatants in the clearing pause, their fights made meaningless in the face of what's emerging.

With a sharp wet crack, the enormous fallen iron-wood tree shivers and splits, the two halves crashing into the ruined earth. Behind the tree, right at the start of the glowing soil that streaks across Caldera, is a giant snake.

It is Auriel, but only in a way. This boa constrictor is the same size he was before, and has the same features, but he's turned the color of the noonday sun. His white-yellow catches the moonlight around him, and makes him seem to glow, just like the path that leads to the ziggurat. His body hangs in the air, waving slightly, like a tree in the breeze.

The radiance is too much after the utter darkness of the eclipse. Gogi turns his head away, eyes streaming tears. He whirls on Rumi, whose outline is wobbly and indistinct before Gogi's dazzled eyes. "What did we just do?"

Rumi claps his fingers together. "We resurrected Auriel. Isn't it amazing?"

Gogi's gut drops. Rumi tricked him. They had the chance to kill the Ant Queen, to destroy her outright using the eclipse magic, but Rumi said to do this other thing, and Gogi, Gogi just *believed* him, he *trusted* Rumi, despite all the good reasons not to, reasons why any monkey thinking straight would see that Rumi had betrayed them, but Gogi let his heart get in the way, chose love and trust, and those were stupid, stupid things to choose when the future of Caldera was at stake. And now look where they were. Doomed! "Rumi, I—" Gogi begins, smoke pluming from his tail.

"Now it's really going to get good," Lima interrupts.

"Wait, *good*? Why?" Gogi asks.

"Because of what's about to happen! My bets are on Auriel."

"You mean you're happy about this?" Gogi asks. "That we *resurrected Auriel*? And he just zoomed across Caldera to shatter a huge ironwood tree?"

"Yes!" Rumi says gleefully. "Look at him!"

Assuming the enormous boa constrictor had come to slay them all, Gogi has avoided doing precisely that. Puffing out fire to keep the ants at bay, Gogi turns his attention to the two giants. The Ant Queen has gone stock-still while Auriel continues to boom at her.

"You betrayed me!"

"Oh," Gogi says, "that's definitely Auriel, and he *does* sound mad."

"And not at us this time!" Lima says.

The iguana falls in beside the Ant Queen, ready to defend her. Mez and Chumba take the opportunity to retreat, stealing toward the rest of the companions, crouched in a moonlit thicket. Sky doesn't move from the spot where he was attacked by the Ant Queen. He might be dead.

Gogi finally allows himself to look directly at Auriel. Though the Ant Queen is far bigger than he is, Auriel looks on her with cool confidence, serene and strong. The two seem evenly matched. The queen can't move, of course, but Auriel is equally still. The giant ant is an intimidating foe, even for him.

Or wait, that's not quite it. It's not that Auriel is calm, exactly: it's more like he's vacant. Like he's an empty body, waiting for instructions.

The Ant Queen's mandibles clack as she takes in the sight of the impressive reptile. All the while, eggs continue to spew from her abdomen.

Gogi turns to Rumi. "Did you know this was going to happen?"

"Yes. Now shh, get your fire ready," Rumi says.

Auriel continues to waver, as if there's a wind on the ruined mountaintop. It's almost like the resurrected constrictor isn't actually touching the jungle floor, but instead swimming through the air above it. Though his long body has lain in the earth for the past year, it shows no sign of decay or rot. He seems in the prime of health, healthier than any creature alive. And he's the color of sunshine itself.

"Auriel's sort of pretty now," Lima whispers.

"I was just thinking that," Gogi says. "Are we weird to think that?"

"Lima, get your healing ready too!" Rumi says.

"My healing?" Lima asks, surprised.

Though Auriel's head remains still, the back of his body is moving. It finishes emerging from the jungle line, coiling itself in the dark soil. He's right in the midst of the teeming ants, but seems to be not at all bothered by them. Maybe snake scales are even tougher when the snake is undead.

The Ant Queen is still a mightier foe than any other animal in Caldera, though, and there's no chance a boa constrictor, even one the size of Auriel, can hope to suffocate an insect. Right? Gogi wrings his hands, smoke rising from his fingers.

He wonders if the Ant Queen will try to plead that she didn't betray Auriel after all, that she doesn't deserve his revenge. But she has too much dignity to even try. The queen holds still, neither moving toward Auriel nor moving away from him, neither fleeing nor attacking. Gogi's no expert on ant body language, but he does see that her antennae are flicking toward the edges of the clearing—almost like she's scoping out escape routes.

Slowly, Auriel's head turns to one side—to stare right where the shadowwalkers are hiding.

"Looks like it's time for phase two," Rumi says.

"Phase two?" Mez asks, hackles rising. "What's phase two?"

But there's no time for Rumi to fill them in. The Ant Queen screeches, her arms and legs clacking in the air, her antennae pointing in the direction of the shadow-walkers. "Rise, my minions!" she cries. "Eliminate the intruders!"

The mountaintop is suddenly full of motion as the ants swarm to the attack, thronging Gogi and his friends. Gogi feels his hairs rise as ants crawl up his ankles.

"Now," Rumi cries, "while the moon is still eclipsed, and magic is in flux. This is the moment. Give him your eclipse magic!"

"What does that even mean?" Gogi asks, frantically batting at the ants climbing up his body. But he catches on soon enough. In life, Auriel had the ability to siphon away the eclipse magic that lived in each animal. Rumi is asking them all to funnel their energy to Auriel under the magic of the new eclipse, so that he's able to defeat the Ant Queen.

Rumi bows his head, arms outstretched, wind jetting toward Auriel. When it hits him it rises, siphoning into Auriel's mouth, filling his gullet. Auriel's eyes, dead and cold before, shine with new life.

Gogi's stunned by how quickly fortunes have

changed. He can't yet bring himself to help Auriel, not after he betrayed them so spectacularly the year before. Gogi had been cocooned in stone, no way out, waiting for the Ant Queen to come feed on him, all because Auriel tricked him. And now he is supposed to turn around and do the wicked boa constrictor's bidding?

Rumi chirps around the stream of air. "Trust me, Gogi! Sky and I tried to figure out if there was any other way, but this is it. Auriel is our best chance!"

Gogi makes his choice. "You're lucky monkeys are such social animals," he calls as he bounds after Rumi. "Otherwise I would so *not* be taking your word about trusting Auriel."

He bows his head and holds out his palms. A stream of fire emerges, lifting up to Auriel, drawing into his gullet just like Rumi's wind. "Mez, Lima, you too!" Gogi calls.

Using his magic feels different this time. There's a wrenching feeling, like some beast has gotten inside of him and is kicking at his spine from the inside. Like the energies he's releasing might not ever return.

Eyes filling with tears at the pain, Gogi can just make out his friends as they bow their heads and hold their paws and wings forward. There's no sign of the magic passing from them, but Gogi can feel the power of it, rippling the night air under the eclipsed moon. He gasps as the magic is yanked from him. Even though he's not moving, keeping the magic flowing despite the pain might be the hardest thing he's ever done.

Auriel's eyes continue to brighten as he fills with life. Finally he swings his head to look fully into the Ant Queen's eyes. "Narelia. We meet again."

With that, he breaks into motion, streaking across the mountaintop. It requires even more from Gogi, and his eyes stream tears. Before Gogi even knows what is happening, Auriel wraps himself around the Ant Queen. Mez, who experienced Auriel's attack speed firsthand a year before, yelps and hides her face under her paws at the sight of it. "Come on," Gogi says to her through gritted teeth, "he's on our side now!"

What strange words.

Auriel works his glowing sunlight body up the Ant Queen, until he's wrapped around her underside and slipping his way around her thorax. She slashes away at him, sharp foreclaws raking his yellow scales. She doesn't seem able to break his skin, but she forces him back down her body, pressing against his neck so he has to loosen his coils. She readies her gnashing mandibles. If she gets the snake at the correct angle, Gogi knows, she could slice clean through him.

"Now!" Auriel bellows. "The time is now! Give me the rest of your power!"

"We don't know how!" Rumi shrieks. "We're sending you as much as we can."

"Then stop sending it to me for now, until it recharges," Auriel bellows. "Help me get free."

Gogi has to make a choice. He calls out to Mez and Chumba and Lima: "Attack!"

As soon as Gogi's sucked his magic back in, he sends it out again, flames swirling from his palms. Emboldened, Mez and Chumba flank Gogi. Mez has forsaken invisibility while they're in open combat, streaking fast and low over ant-covered soil. Chumba wheels around to the Ant Queen's flank, preparing to attack her other side. Lima hovers in the air above. "Go for her underbelly," Gogi calls. "No, maybe her legs first. Climb up Auriel to get to her head. I don't know, everyone, just attack!"

"Does that include me, too?" comes a strident voice. Gogi looks over to see Sky limping across the battlefield to join them.

Sky is alive!

The macaw instructs the other shadowwalkers as they streak toward the Ant Queen's gnashing mandibles. "Gogi—steam up her under-armor, and then you should be able to get between the plates and attack beneath," he caws. "That's a technique the two-legs tried. We learned about it in the riddle cave."

"Wait, 'tried'?" Gogi asks.

Sky nods grimly. "Yes. Tried."

"Anything else you need to tell us?" Gogi asks as he readies his fire.

"Plenty," Sky caws. "But now might not be the right time."

"Right," Gogi says. "We have an ant queen to defeat. Let's go!"

He braids the fires from his palms, sending the cord of flame lancing toward the queen's underside. It's hard for him to get a good angle, and Gogi finds himself scurrying from side to side as the Ant Queen pivots during her combat with Auriel. He can keep his braided flame on her for only a few seconds at a time, and never gets it in one place long enough to build up much heat. "It's not working, Sky!" Gogi cries.

"I know, I see that. Let me think, let me think!" Sky screeches.

The Ant Queen's minions swarm the companions' skin. Gogi can feel their sharp mandibles against his flesh. The queen herself rears back, getting a length of Auriel's yellow body between her two forelegs and bringing it up to the pincers of her jaw.

Gogi desperately tries to aim his fire at the queen's underside even as he feels the ants on his skin begin to bite, pricking and tearing. He can't muster the sort of heat that Sky was asking for.

He feels lightheaded, like his limbs are no longer coordinating with his brain. Is the ant venom already at work?

Auriel struggles to free himself from the Ant Queen's clutches, but he's trapped. She's got her mandibles around his body, and before Gogi's eyes he sees her slice into the snake. He leaks what looks like molten sunlight. Auriel might be resurrected, but he's not invulnerable. "Sky," he roars, "you can merge the eclipse magic to give me even more of the shadowwalkers' power. Like we'd once planned."

"Yes, Auriel," Sky says. He whirls to face Gogi and the rest. "The ants are upon us. Do as I say. Stare into my eyes to stop the queen. Do not resist."

Mez glances at Gogi, panicked. She's got her claws out and teeth bared, but already her limbs are jerky with ant poison. Chumba is the same. Gogi can easily read what's in Mez's eyes: *Do we go along with this? I'll follow your lead.*

"Now!" Sky shrieks.

Gogi makes his choice.

23

"DO AS HE SAYS!" Gogi cries. He stares into the nearest eye of the bedraggled parrot, watching as grays appear in the black. Out of the side of his eye, Gogi sees Lima land near him and face toward Sky too. Gogi realizes from Mez's and Chumba's stilled forms on the battlefield that they're going along. Mez might be the strategist, but Gogi is in charge of matters of the heart.

The grays in Sky's eye swirl into a vortex that sucks all of Gogi's attention, making the rest of the battleground drop away. He senses another presence in his mind. Thoughts and sensations come to his consciousness and disappear, as if someone is rummaging through his brain.

Grooming Alzo. Ravanna's anger. The number twelve. None of it useful. Sky discards it all.

The feelings go deeper and deeper, until it's Gogi's earliest memories coming to the fore. His mother. First the vision in the Dismal Bog, and then her, the real mother who loved him, alive and caring, warm and kind and *his*. Memories he didn't even know he still had.

I miss you.

Then the rummaging gets as deep as Gogi's spine, and something clicks. Sky has made it to the magic at Gogi's core, magic that has been part of him since his birth. Gogi's finding what makes him so different from all the other capuchins. What does a number like twelve matter in the face of fire, fire that's his very own, fire that came at the moment his mother brought him into the world?

Because the fire is his own, he can release it. Gogi presses the flame in his spine outward, not holding on to it or tamping it down, but giving it freely. He gasps, and his vision comes back, the sight of Sky comes back, Auriel bleeding sunlight in the Ant Queen's grasp is back. The eclipse sky is back.

Auriel writhes beneath the Ant Queen's mandibles.

She's nearly cut through him now—his front and rear halves move out of sync. But then, impossibly, the two halves start to knit back together. They're healing.

"Did I do that?" Lima chirps. "Did I give him that power?" Sky must have been mentally working on all of them at once.

The Ant Queen rears back, baffled, as the halves of Auriel continue to knit together. "What is this sorcery?" she screeches.

Then, quick as a blink, Auriel disappears.

The queen whirls on the companions. "You *gave* him your powers? You fools!"

"No, Narelia," comes Auriel's booming voice from above. "You have been the fool. And you will die for it."

As if a sudden wind has come up, all the air is sucked out of the clearing. Gogi whirls, confused, and then looks up to see an eerie sight.

From the eclipsed moon, half-covered in blood-red shadow, comes a sudden cone of fire and wind. It crackles the air, casts trees and bushes alight, incinerates the hordes of ants. It's directed right at the Ant Queen, sizzling her right where she stands.

If she's saying something beneath the roar of the flames, Gogi can't make it out. The cone of fire continues to strike her, continues to consume her.

By the time it's finished, by the time the booming is done, by the time Gogi can open his eyes again against the waves of hot air, the Ant Queen is gone.

All that remains is a pile of ash.

Auriel is gone too.

The friends are motionless, overwhelmed, looking at the smoldering crater where Caldera's most fearsome enemies once stood. Released magic irradiates the air, sets it wobbling and glowing. Will their powers flow back into them?

Before Gogi can think on it any further, he's interrupted by an unearthly shrieking from the edge of the clearing. A streak of white fur races past, right to the pile of ash. "No, my queen!" Mist cries.

"Mist, stop!" Mez calls, lunging forward.

But Mist has already dashed into the nexus of glowing magic. He howls at the burning of his paws, but then quiets and looks up at the warbling air. The magic swirls around him, lifting him into the air, crackling and sparking.

Mez leaps forward, but Chumba wrestles her down to the ground. "No, Mez. This magic could destroy Mist. Don't let it get you, too."

Seized by the magical energies, Mist rises into the air, powerless to move, eyes wide and paws dangling.

While the partly eclipsed moon shines its ruddy light on the clearing, Mist soars higher and higher, above the treetops.

His eyes widen in fear, rimmed in white as he stares down at the companions below. "What is happening?" he shrieks. "Cousins, help me!"

But Mez and Chumba are as powerless as the rest of them to do anything. Bands of magical energy swirl about Mist as he continues to rise. They cover him in tighter and tighter spirals while the eclipse starts to pass from the face of the moon.

"Guys?" Gogi says, jaw open. Mist is so far up that he's joining the night sky. Gogi can't see the expression on his face anymore. "Is there something we should be doing?"

But before any of them can answer, the eclipse finishes. The magical energies band Mist tighter and tighter, merging into a pinpoint of light. Then, with the faintest pop, that light disappears.

Shreds of magic flutter down from the sky, like glowing rain.

After the Eclipse

THE ANTS FLOW away. Now that their queen is gone, they become less like enemies and more like a natural disaster.

They drain like a flood, and like a flood they leave behind a ravaged landscape.

Gogi and Lima watch it all in exhausted silence, in the murk of predawn. Now that the eclipse is over, the moon shines its radiance on the scene below, and the stars offer their scant light. It's enough illumination to see the ruined land without needing any magical firelight. It's enough to see the glittering streams of dispersing ants. It's enough to see the pile of ash, still glowing with a few embers, that marks the end of the Ant Queen, and of their epic battle, of the disappearance of Mist and Auriel.

Lima cocks her head. "Do you hear that?"

At first, Gogi can't hear a thing. Nothing compares to bat hearing. But as the ants recede, the silence fills with something like music. It's a pitchless, flowing sound, not quite animal but not quite inanimate, either. Low and high and soft and loud. "It's . . . beautiful," Gogi says.

Lima holds still, mouth open as she echolocates. "It's coming from the ants themselves," she says. "They're . . . singing as they leave."

Strange tears fill Gogi's eyes. "It's like they're mourning her."

"Are you really almost crying about singing ants?" Lima asks.

"I'm tired, okay?" Gogi says, defensive. "That was an intense battle."

"I get where you're coming from," Lima whispers. "I thought the ants were brainless. I didn't think they'd be capable of feeling anything without their queen around."

"Considering that they're everywhere, always, up day and night, we know so little about them," Gogi says.

Lima has been licking Gogi's various scrapes and

ant bites, but those have healed by now. Still she huddles close, her little body tucked along Gogi's ribs. He nestles her in near, warming her with his fur. *"Lima, the Healing Bat!"* he sings softly over the harmonic chant of the ants. *"Ferocious-er than a piranha! Scarier than a cat!"*

"Yeah, I'm pretty great," Lima says quietly. "But it's still hard to think about what we did. The Ant Queen's been around as long as Caldera, right? And we . . . destroyed her."

"Given what she's done, and how she tried to eat us all those times, I don't think we need to feel too cut up about it," Gogi says. "But I hear what you're saying. It's all overwhelming. Besides, we don't know yet what happens when ants don't have a queen anymore. If they're singing all together, it's almost like they're one being, even without their queen. And maybe one of them is growing larger and larger as we speak, maybe a new queen is coming up, getting ready with all her most evil plans. . . ."

Lima shudders. "Nice thought, Gogi. You really might have kept that one to yourself."

Gogi snuggles her in even closer. "Don't worry. I mean, I bet it takes an ant a long time to become so very powerful and dangerous."

Lima cocks her head. "You know, you'd think that would make me feel better, but it really doesn't."

"Yeah, I hear you," Gogi says.

"Do you think the others have turned up any sign of Auriel or Mist?" Lima asks, peeking around the bend.

"I can't imagine it. I think Auriel and Mist are . . . gone. Like the Ant Queen."

Though they were all exhausted, the companions had agreed to split up for a few hours to form three search parties. Gogi and Lima have been dragging themselves through the jungle, but there's been no sign whatsoever of Mist or Auriel. "I just can't imagine we'd be done with Mist that easily," Lima says. "He's sort of like a nose infection. Hard to get rid of."

"And if he is alive somewhere, they always say that a panther who doesn't want to be found won't be found," Gogi adds.

"Yeah, but an all-white panther in a rainforest?" Lima asks. "That's just ridiculous. Mez and Chumba should be embarrassed if they're two panthers who can't catch someone who is basically glow-in-the-dark. I think Mist's far from here, if he's alive at all."

Branches shake in the distance. "Well, here they come," Gogi says. He glances up at the sky to see the first hints of dawn. "And just in time. Chumba will be in daycoma soon."

Mez and Chumba, their calico fur covered in mud and droplets of rain, steal across the clearing to join Gogi and Lima. As they approach, Mez shakes her head.

"Maybe Sky and Rumi had better luck," Gogi says.

"We'll find out soon enough," Mez says. "Here they come."

Gogi hears a caw, followed by Rumi's excited chirps. Sky and Rumi pause where the Ant Queen perished, and they start digging through her ashes. "Ow, ow," Rumi says. "Still hot."

"What are you guys doing?" Gogi calls.

Rumi holds something aloft, small and wriggling in his hands. It glows yellow.

"What did they find in there?" Lima asks.

"It's a worm," Gogi says, squinting. "A glowworm?"

As Sky and Rumi approach, the dawn sky seems to knit together, made darker in comparison to the shining creature Rumi is holding in his hands as he hops forward.

"Whoa," Chumba says. "Is that *Auriel*?"

"It certainly is," Rumi says, beaming.

The companions nervously circle Rumi and Sky. Rumi's holding a tiny baby snake, as small as an earthworm. Its inky black eyes blink at them. Its body is an iridescent yellow, the same color as the giant resurrected Auriel that faced down the Ant Queen.

"Are you sure you should be touching that?" Gogi asks.

"He's so cute!" Lima says at the same time. "Can I take a turn holding him?"

"Auriel," Mez says, whiskers flicking, "is that you?"

"I don't think he's able to speak yet," Sky says. "He's just a baby."

"Sweet figs," Gogi says, eyeing the tiny, glowing snake as it wriggles in Rumi's hands, "I think that's really Baby Auriel!"

"I wish he could speak to us," Rumi says. "A being raised from the dead—think of all the knowledge we could receive."

"Maybe he'll learn how to talk soon," Chumba says, yawning despite herself.

"Yes," Gogi says from the side of his mouth, "but should we be listening?"

Mez nods severely.

"He's a creature of *light* now," Rumi says. "That was the whole point of channeling all that light into him during the eclipse."

"And he's tiny," Sky adds, his eyes briefly swirling gray before returning to black. "He's not showing any magical powers, not that I can tell. Gogi, Lima, Mez, I trust your powers returned to you?"

Gogi startles. He was so spent from using his magic earlier that he didn't think to test it. He holds out his palm and sparks it. It's there. Feels weaker, but that could be because he's still so tired.

"I've been healing bites and scratches all night," Lima says. "My power is definitely doing fine."

As her reply, Mez flickers out of sight and then back in.

"Good," Sky says. "I'm glad they returned. The Cave of Riddles was a little vague about how everything works."

"We don't know much about what happened at the Cave of Riddles," Gogi says, after coughing to clear his throat. "Like, nothing at all."

"It was fascinating!" Rumi says. "We learned so much, I can't wait to tell you all about it. We figured out more about the source of the two-legs' power, and also more about the origins of Caldera. We know what it means, now, how that came to be our rainforest's name."

"More importantly in our current situation," Sky caws, hopping over to stand on the lens, "we learned about the power of this strange circular clear rock. Not that the lens will be of any use again, not until the next eclipse."

The companions look at Rumi, all at once. "The next eclipse whose shadow will fall on our rainforest is, um, three years and seventy-one days from now," Rumi says. "Approximately."

"Auriel is no longer the being he was," Sky continues,

getting his eye right next to the mute little snake. "He is an Elemental of Light. He is the essence of the sun itself."

Sky has said the words proudly, but Lima, Chumba, and Mez blanch. Gogi leans in, too, to take a better look at the tiny snake. *Essence of the sun itself?* A tall order, but maybe it's true. He is glowing like sunshine, after all.

"Maybe now's a good time for you and Rumi to tell us about the journey," Mez prompts.

"Yes," Rumi says, wringing his hands as he looks at each one of them in turn. "And I'll start even further back, with the story of my home swamp. I owe that to you guys, and I'm sorry I haven't told you yet."

"With the Ant Queen out of the way and her minions retreating, there's no rush to say it, actually," Mez says. "That can wait until the Veil next drops." While she speaks, Mez is looking at her sister, whose whiskers are drooping with the onset of daycoma.

"Yes, let's rest first," Gogi says, "and afterward Sky and Rumi can tell us what happened in the cave. And exactly how Auriel stopped being, um, dead." Gogi gnaws on a fingernail. Is it rude to call someone dead? Can the baby snake even hear him?

"There is one thing we need to talk about sooner rather than later," Sky says, glancing at Rumi. "The big problem."

"What is the big problem?" Lima asks. "Or did you already say, and I just missed it? Sorry, I'm really tired."

"No, you didn't miss it," Rumi says gently. "Here goes. We learned for sure that Caldera has a boundary, and that boundary is what the two-legs called a 'beach,' which is—how would you describe it, Sky?—it's like where the land meets a giant lagoon, only the lagoon is bigger than all of Caldera itself."

"We saw it with you," Gogi says to Rumi, "in the vision using Sky's tail feather."

"You were along with us when we approached the cave!" Rumi exclaims to Gogi. "Did you hear that, Sky? Our hunch was right—they were there. How marvelous."

"We were with you until a certain white panther ambushed us," Gogi says darkly.

"The big salty puddle is called an 'ocean,'" Rumi says. "And, you might ask, how did a rainforest come to be surrounded by water?"

Lima nods. "I was totally about to ask that." Gogi pinches her. "Hey! Just because I'm a bat doesn't mean I can't ask good questions!"

"It's because we are actually the top of an undersea mountain," Sky says. "Back when the two-legs were at the height of their power, this used to be the highest of a range of mountains. All sorts of creatures used to live here, but don't anymore—it's not just the two-legs that went extinct. We saw many different sets of bones deep in the Cave of Riddles."

"Wow," Gogi says, "riddles and bones of forgotten animals. That place sounds amazing!"

"I really can't wait to tell you all about it," Rumi says. "But to stick to the current issue: Caldera is a mountain that used to be high, but for some reason the ocean rose around it. As a result, the mountaintop became hot and wet, like it is now."

"It's not just any mountain, though," Sky says. "Do you remember when you went below the ziggurat a year ago, how the caverns seemed to lead to more empty space farther below?"

"The mountain that makes up Caldera is hollow!" Rumi finishes triumphantly.

"Let me get this straight. You're saying our entire rainforest is actually the top of a mountain that is surrounded by this 'ocean,' and that the mountain is hollow at the center?" Mez asks, taking a break from licking Chumba's ear. Her sister is nearly in daycoma by now. She's sunk to her haunches, her eyes drooping.

"I spoke too quickly. It's not exactly hollow—" Rumi starts.

"—it's filled with magma!" Sky finishes, fluffing out his wings self-importantly.

The companions stare back at him, confused.

"What's 'magma'?" Lima finally asks.

"A two-legs word for very hot rock," Rumi explains patiently. "Very hot liquid rock. There's as much of it below us as there is land in all of Caldera."

"That doesn't sound good," Lima says.

"No," Rumi says, "it's definitely not good. It's under pressure down there. If it blows, then . . ." He gestures toward the rainforest around them, then makes an exploding motion with his suction-cupped fingers.

"So, what do we do?" Gogi asks.

"Remember the Ant Queen's glowing blue sphere prison? Why do you think they'd put it down below the ziggurat?" Rumi asks.

"I figured the sphere was to keep an extra barrier up in case she broke free," Gogi says.

"That's true," Rumi says, "but it was serving another purpose, too—it was a *plug*. And with our breaking her out—"

"—the plug was destroyed," Mez finishes.

"That, plus all the movement of the ants through their underground tunnels across Caldera, generated instability in the planet's shelf and mantle," Rumi says, his words speeding up as he gets more and more excited. "I don't have enough information to confirm this yet, but I suspect that creating the instability might have been the Ant Queen's main goal all along. So we can only assume that some magma movement is imminent."

"I still don't speak frog," Lima says, scratching under her wing. "What does all that mean?"

"All of Caldera is the crater of a thing called a 'volcano,'" Sky says. "That's what 'caldera' means: a crater. And the volcano is about to erupt."

"I don't even understand most of what you just said, and it's still freaking me out," Lima says, shuddering.

"How do we stop this 'erupt' from happening?" Gogi asks.

"We don't know yet. Maybe you can help us figure it out," Rumi says. "After we tell you about the Cave of Riddles. For sure, we'll need to plug the magma again."

"And the way to do that might be through the use of Auriel's earth powers," Mez finishes.

"Exactly," Rumi says. "Which is why we had to use the power of the second eclipse to resurrect him, not simply to destroy the Ant Queen."

"But you didn't expect him to wind up exploding, releasing the eclipse magic, and emerging as a baby," Gogi says, shaking his head. "Wow. I had no idea of all the specifics."

Rumi nods vigorously. "Neither did we! There were so many variables. You can see how this would have been a lot to explain while we were in the middle of fighting for our lives. Why I had to ask you to just trust me."

Gogi pats Rumi's head. "Yeah, and I'm glad I did."

"Say, do you think Auriel would mind if I touched his scales?" Lima asks, out of the blue. "They're so pretty. I almost imagine they'd *taste* good, but I figured I shouldn't ask to do that, but I guess I just did, oops, anyway, do you think I can touch one?"

Without waiting, Lima uses her wing to stroke a length of Auriel's glowing scales. The little snake goes still, peering at Lima. His forked tongue flicks in and out.

"He doesn't seem to mind," Mez says.

Gogi can't help himself. "Can I, too? Even though I'm just a . . . just a monkey." He'd been about to say "twelve," but it doesn't seem to matter so much, not anymore. He strokes the sunlight scales. They feel like normal snakeskin, actually, but make beautiful patterns of shifting light over his fingers. "So neat," he says.

Even Mez joins in, giving baby Auriel a tentative tap with her nose. "We're in no state to make any big decisions," Mez says after she's finished. "Once we're all rested and alert, we'll hear your tale, Rumi and Sky, and then we'll make a plan to stop this 'erupt.'"

"For now," Gogi says, "we should enjoy our small pleasures. We defeated the Ant Queen. How about *that*, guys?"

"Yes, how about that?!" Lima cheers.

Even Sky joins the cheer, cawing his harsh voice up toward the dawn.

As their voices peter out, the sounds of the rainforest draw down upon them: songbirds greeting the sun, insects chirping, distant howler monkeys making their rhythmic hoots. There is so much life in Caldera, so much to explore, so much to fear, so much to protect.

"Let's stay together this time, okay?" Lima says. "No splitting apart anymore. I liked being an honorary panther with Aunt Usha and the triplets last year, but I'd rather stick with you guys."

"That sounds wise, Lima," Rumi says. "We know what we have to do anyway. The queen's prison was the plug preventing Caldera from erupting. We'll travel to where it was, under the old ruins, and see if we can't plug the volcano back up. There's no resting this time— we have to press forward."

"Maybe we can stop by the capuchin forest, to see if my friend Alzo will join us. You all would like him," Gogi says.

"He's the rank eight you talked about, right?" Rumi asks.

"Wait until all the other capuchins hear about what you've done," Lima says. "They'll have to make you at least an eleven. Or maybe a ten! Is that pushing it? Maybe that's pushing it."

"Guys," Gogi says, "this is going to sound weird, but I . . . I think I'm done with rankings. It's kind of ridiculous that they would matter here, far away from any other capuchins. How little sense does that make? I'm just . . . me. Besides, you guys are my real tribe." He holds up the woven sack and upends it. No pebbles fall out.

"I like all monkeys," Lima says, "no matter what the rank. But if we're a tribe, then you're definitely Gogi the First to me."

"I agree entirely," Rumi says, nodding.

"Aw, that's sweet," Gogi says. "Still a little too rankings-focused, but sweet."

Mez starts to nod, before she hisses and goes into a battle posture, pointing her paw to the far side of the clearing.

The companions fall quiet. Even Auriel gets a wary look on his face.

The fronds of a nearby fern bend and snap.

Gogi drops into a fighting crouch, flames licking from his tail and hands. Mez goes invisible as she darts to a flanking position.

Is it the iguana, come for revenge? Has the Ant Queen somehow returned from the dead? Is it . . . Mist?

The fern bends further, and a shape emerges.

It's not the iguana. It's not the Ant Queen. It's not Mist.

"Hello, everyone . . . sorry I'm late . . . I went as fast as I could. . . . Where's that Ant Queen? Let's get this . . . final showdown rolling!"

It's Banu the sloth.

A Q&A
WITH ELIOT SCHREFER

Q. You traveled into the Amazon to research this book. What can you tell us about your experience there?

A. I flew from New York City (where I live) down to Lima, Peru, then onward to Puerto Maldonado, the last airport before the jungle takes over from civilization. From there it was an hour's drive along dirt roads, then a few hours by boat, an overnight stay at a jungle lodge, and six more hours along the Tambopata River to the research center where I stayed for a week.

Each time my guide took me into the jungle we went deeper, eventually leaving entirely the trails established by the local people. Instead, he took his machete to branches and led us through nameless bogs and dense spiderweb-clogged stretches of forest. The second time we trekked, we started particularly late in the day. Twilight was near, and at the equator, when sundown comes, it comes fast. Soon we were in half-light, tromping through bogs and marshes, tree frogs chirping all around (hi, Rumi!), caimans staring at us, their eyes unsettling red orbs reflecting back in the light from our headlamps. These reptiles were only three feet long or so, but still! It was plenty unsettling to wander through the dark with them on all sides.

Oscar Mishaja Salazar, my guide, showed me a different world by night. There was no sign of any of the daytime animals we had seen just hours earlier—it was like they'd vanished from the rainforest entirely. Frogs, tarantulas, cats, and bats replaced the tamarind monkeys and the bees. Click beetles buzzed heavily through the night, their glowing abdomens as large as marbles. When one landed on me, I could feel the heaviness of it.

I'd read about how completely the jungle was divided between nocturnal and diurnal animals, but never experienced it for myself until then. The magical Veil that separates day and night in *The Lost Rainforest* felt actual. Two kinds of animals really do inhabit the same rainforest without knowing much at all about each other.

Q. Clearly ants had an important role in this book—and will continue to have one, we sense, in the next book of the series! How did that come about?

A. I'd thought my biggest discomfort staying in the deep Amazon would be the mosquitoes. But I didn't get a single mosquito bite during my whole time in the rainforest!

No, the real problem was the ants.

Really, they're the only constant of jungle animal life. Ants are active all day and all night. It got me to thinking about how, in the Peruvian jungle, humans and ants are the only creatures up at all hours. Both are the rare examples of hypersocialized creatures, in which groups of thousands and even millions of individuals can cooperate and coexist—and therefore dominate their world. The shared human-ant tendency to overrun our environments led Abbott Lowell to once observe that ants, "like human beings, can create civilizations without the use of reason."[1]

A juvenile emerald tree boa I met in the Amazon.
Everyone's cute in baby photos!

---

1. Quoted in Bert Hölldobler and Edward O. Wilson, *The Superorganism* (New York: W. W. Norton & Company, 2008), xviii.

From there, I started to think about how the other animals of the rainforest are comparatively self-contained and self-sufficient. A fantasy story that takes place in the jungle, I realized, wouldn't run like a fantasy story in the temperate climates. There would be no kingdoms or organizations. In fact, a villain could easily take advantage of the rainforest animals' lack of organization to work his or her plans in secrecy. (Hi, plot twist!)

It's hard to think of humans as being in charge of the planet once you take a good look at ants. There are between one and ten *million billion* of them, weighing approximately as much as all the people of the planet put together.[2] They've been on this planet long enough to have been biting the ankles of dinosaurs.

Winter keeps ants in check in North America, but in the Amazonian jungle they are truly awesome to behold. Army ants might be fearsome, but bullet ants are the biggest danger at the Tambopata Research Center. About two inches long, they are solitary hunters. Their bite isn't fatal to humans, but they get their name from how painful it is. They'll wander over any surface, and it's very easy not to look where you're putting your hand, go to pick up a coffee mug, and

---

2. Hölldobler and Wilson, *The Superorganism*, 5.

wind up spending the following day writhing in bed in agony.

Thus the Ant Queen was born. Although there are no humans alive in the world of *The Lost Rainforest*, the queen and her minions represent the social conquerors of the rainforest, able to spread far beyond the constraints of the more solitary animals. I've given her additional magic in these books, but even everyday ants are pretty magical, when you think about it. Consider this: ants use their antennae to smell the hydrocarbons in the exoskeleton of other ants, and in so doing know who's from which nest, what their social status is, and how old they are. Neat trick!

As far as the Ant Queen is concerned, she's not finished with our eclipse-born animals—Mez, Lima, Gogi, Sorella, Rumi, and the rest will have to race to organize themselves to fight against her as their story continues.

Q. The rainforest starts to feel like its own character in the book, with its own mysteries and revelations for Mez and her friends. What other tidbits came up for you in your research?

A. Nineteenth-century explorers talked of the rainforest as a "counterfeit paradise." It looks lush and full of richness, but life within it is an eternal struggle to find enough to eat, and to avoid being eaten. What defines a rainforest is—you guessed it—the rainfall. They get over eighty inches a year. It's easy to focus on its cool animals, but with high amounts of water and heat, the tropical rainforest can support some aggressive, giant plant life. Vines are everywhere. These colossal plants are engaged in their own combats against one another. Those fights are just as violent and lethal as those among animals, but occur over a longer period of time.

This fight, between a vine and a tree I met,
has been going on for many years.

As a result of this ferocious competition for sunlight, life in the rainforest has moved from the floor to the canopy. We as humans have learned to look *around* us for food or danger, but something I noticed about the rainforest was how often I wound up looking *up* to see wildlife. There's a whole extra axis for rainforest animals to worry about.

The rainforests cover only a small fraction of the earth, but are thought to be home to over half of the planet's plant and animal species. They remove a tremendous amount of carbon from the atmosphere and therefore mitigate global climate change, provide resources to indigenous people, and are an essential part of the global water cycle . . . yet they're being cut down rapidly. I hope that some of *The Lost Rainforest*'s readers will join me in helping them.

Q. Could you share some of the resources on the rainforest and its inhabitants that you found most useful?
A. Yes! Here are my favorites:

I'm a big fan of www.mongabay.com, which has many informative articles about the rainforest, with sections geared for kids and for older readers. As a place to start, they have a great handout available at http://kids.mongabay.com/lesson_plans/handout.html, including a quiz for classroom use!

For a more in-depth account, John Kricher's book *A Neotropical Companion* is rigorous and accessible and taught me many of the details of jungle life.

On the film side, the very best I can recommend are the riveting "Jungle" episodes of the *Planet Earth* and *Planet Earth II* documentary series that the BBC released in 2006 and 2016.

For those who become ant-obsessed like me, I recommend the documentary *E. O. Wilson: Of Ants and Men*, which is a portrait both of the study of ants and of one of our most important scientists. The BBC series *Life in the Undergrowth* is also an excellent source of information, and of filmed accounts of invertebrate life. For books, Bert Hölldobler and Edward O. Wilson's *The Ants* and *The Superorganism* are the bibles of the field. I found Deborah Gordon's *Ants at Work* very useful, too.

Q. Were there more rainforest animals that you wish you could have included in *Mez's Magic*?

A. Yes, so many! I hope maybe some young writers out there will choose a new rainforest animal, figure out whether it's a nightwalker or a daywalker, and come up with a personality and a magical ability for the new eclipse-born. Maybe you could even write an adventure for the animal to go on! Did Auriel come looking for this eclipse-born, too? What happened next?

There are so many rainforest animals out there, but here are some that almost made it into *Mez's Magic*, but I just didn't have enough space in the pages:

hoatzin	tapir
capybara	Brazilian porcupine
peccary	Arrau turtle
glass frog	fer-de-lance (pit viper)
opossum	

Author trying to look like a tough jungle guide.
Maybe should have taken the glasses off.

ACKNOWLEDGMENTS

Many thanks to the Lost Rainforest's terrific editors, Ben Rosenthal and Melissa Miller, to my agent, Richard Pine, and to my faithful manuscript readers: Eric Zahler, Barbara Schrefer, Daphne Grab, Nicole Melleby, Jill Santopolo, Marianna Baer, Anne Heltzel, and Marie Rutkoski.

Read on for a sneak peek at the
explosive conclusion:

S MOKE.

Whorls and plumes of smoke.

Rumi stares into the vortex, tapping a suction-cupped finger against his lips. *To get so much particulate matter airborne, the temperature of the heat source must be higher than the surrounding—*

"Rumi, *move!*" Mez cries as she streaks through the moonlit clearing.

Mez sounds fully panicked, which makes it all the stranger that they are, oddly enough, racing *toward* the smoke rather than away from it. Rumi knows that's the plan, Rumi's the one who *came up with* the plan, but Mez's panic reminds Rumi how foolish it is to head right into danger, when every instinct—

"Rumi, *faster*!" It's Gogi this time. A tail whips out to pick up Rumi, and he's suddenly in one of his favorite positions, right on top of a capuchin monkey head, fingers threading through tufts of eyebrow fur. He and Gogi slalom through the treetops, hand over hand and foot over foot, rising and falling through the canopy. Capuchin monkey is the best way to travel. "Thanks for the ride, Gogi."

"No problem," Gogi says, breathing in bursts from the exertion. "Literally. You're about as heavy as a palm nut."

"I'm even liiiiiighter," Lima trills from the sky above.

"Not everything has to be a competition," Rumi grumbles under his breath. Gogi's weaving through the trees starts to make him nauseated, so Rumi closes his eyes and uses hearing more than vision to track their progress. While Lima chirps away above, the panther sisters, Mez and Chumba, slink through the jungle off to one side, only audible because they're moving at such breakneck speed; Sky soars above, making excited caws against the night sky; and finally Banu the sloth is somewhere behind, still within earshot but falling farther into the distance. Banu was the one who volunteered to "take rear guard," and they all agreed that he would join them at the ruins of the Ziggurat of the Sun and Moon once he was able to get there. It wasn't an option for the whole group to slow down to sloth speed, not with the volcano preparing to erupt.

Their strangest companion is Auriel.

While Gogi makes his way through the treetops, Rumi peers down at the monkey's right foot, where he's clenching what might appear to an unschooled observer to be a slender yellow vine. The shadowwalkers know, though, that it's the reincarnated form of what was once the second-greatest enemy Caldera has ever known. After taking his revenge on the Ant Queen and destroying her for good, Auriel's been reborn a fraction of his old size.

This was all foretold at the Cave of Riddles, of course. But it doesn't make it any less strange to see this curious mute baby snake, looking out at the jungles of Caldera passing by as if he's never seen them before.

What is going through Auriel's mind?

Will he grow bigger?

It seems unwise to bring Auriel anywhere. But, Rumi reasons for the thousandth time, it would be folly *not* to bring him along. He just saved Caldera—maybe he could do it again.

If he doesn't destroy it.

Rumi digs his fingers into the moist skin of his leg, to distract himself from the compulsive loop of his thoughts. The volcano under their rainforest hasn't erupted yet, but its rumblings are accelerating. By this pace it will be eight nights before there's no space at all between them, which he can only assume means the volcano will be going off. An exploding volcano—can any creature alive in Caldera help against that?

Auriel seems to think so. Soon after the defeat of the Ant Queen, he had waited until all the shadowwalkers' attention was on him, then slithered around in the dirt until he'd drawn a surprising likeness of a volcano cropping up out of the water. Then he'd reared back and smashed it all. Then he'd gone back to staring at them expectantly.

Rumi was the one to point out that perhaps Auriel meant to stop the volcano. It was all they had to go on.

Granted, it wasn't much. *Think, Rumi, think! A better answer is always out there!*

There's a nagging feeling in his mind, and he realizes it's guilt. Emotions are always that way for Rumi; he'll feel a thing and only figure out what it really is after pondering it for a long time. He's let his friends down, that's it. Rumi's usually the one to come up with the big plans—though Sky's done his part, too—but here he is, racking his brain and turning up nothing. A mind seems such a puny thing against the power of a volcano. Surely journeying to the site of the eruption is a reasonable start. But what happens once they get there? What use is something as insubstantial as strategy against a million tons of magma? They'll just put Auriel near it and hope he has some miracle to work?

Wait. Is it actually a *billion* tons of magma? Rumi starts doing calculations to refine his estimate, then stops when he realizes he's distracting himself from his worst concern.

He's got only eight nights to figure out how to stop the volcano.

The reactions of the other rainforest inhabitants confirm the scale of the menace. First it was the pack of capybaras they encountered, braying nervously in the night air as they weaved along a riverbank, keeping their little ones protected in the center of the herd. Soon after were the peccaries, snorting and snuffling as they raced along narrow forest paths, fear revealing the whites of their eyes. Then birds soared overhead, a mix of blue macaws and white egrets and piping plovers, flocks of animals that never flocked together before.

All of them, capybaras and peccaries and birds, were heading in one direction: away from the smoke.

The shadowwalkers are the only ones going toward it.

It's not thick enough to cause trouble for his friends, but Rumi can already sense the acrid smoke on his skin, sharp against his pores. Amphibian problems. He'll have to rig up some kind of mud mask before they get closer to the volcano. He's confident he'll deduce some way to protect his tender skin, that's not the real worry. The real worry is that all the combined brainpower and intuition of the other residents of Caldera is telling them to flee for their lives, and yet Rumi has convinced his fellow shadowwalkers to head straight for the volcano.

He appears to have suggested an unwise course, indeed.

Rumi hears a tree rat scrambling through the canopy. He calls out to it as they cross paths. "What do you know, rat friend?"

"You're heading into danger!" the rat gasps as it races past, bounding up a trunk and leaping to the next branch over. "Go the other way, idiots!"

Then the rat's gone.

"Did you hear that?" Rumi chirps to Gogi.

"Yes. Doesn't exactly inspire confidence," Gogi says, pausing for a moment to catch his breath. He wipes the sweat from his neck and rubs his tired eyes.

Rumi snuggles into the warmth of Gogi's forehead fur, trying to scour the painful smoke residue from his skin. "I'm not feeling especially confident either right now."

"Buddy, I'm thinking, maybe it's best if we join the other animals and get as far away from that smoke as possible. We can't help anyone if we jump right into danger—"

"—and incinerate ourselves," Rumi finishes. "I know. Maybe discretion *is* the better part of valor."

"We are *not* giving up!" Mez calls from the darkness below.

"Yeah!" Chumba adds.

"Just when you think you're out of earshot, panthers impress you all over again. They have simply *amazing* hearing," Rumi admires, his spirits lifting.

"A little too amazing, if you ask me," Gogi grumbles.

"Enough resting, Gogi. Let's get moving!" Mez yells.

"Come on, guys," Lima calls from above, "let's go— hey! Mrph! How rude!" Her voice trails off.

"Lima, are you okay?" Rumi calls up.

"Yeah," she eventually responds. "I flew into a cloud of bats, and I tried to say hello, but they didn't even take the time to answer! Unbelievable. I don't know what's happened to chiropteran manners. I guess imminent doom is making them impolite. Ow, hey! There's another one! Shame on you!"

"They're scared, Lima," Gogi calls up to her. He lowers his voice to a mutter. "Maybe we could take a note from them."

"This is why I spent that year with panthers instead

of my home colony," Lima prattles on indignantly. "You'd think that mighty carnivores would be inferior company to my own kind, but no, bats are basically the worst. I'm much better as an honorary panther. Maybe I can be an honorary capuchin monkey too. Or a tree frog. Or a macaw. Sorry, guys, didn't meant to leave you out. I'm equal-honorary."

"We've been going at breakneck speed for hours," Rumi whispers into Gogi's ear. "How does she have enough breath left over for all this chatter?"

". . . why, hello there, Madame Owl, thank you for finally paying attention to me—wait, *owl*! Ack! Scary!"

Suddenly, with a crashing of branches, Lima is huddling next to Rumi on top of Gogi's head. "I could have been owl meat! I'm traveling down with you guys from here on out."

"Um, my head is starting to feel a little crowded," Gogi says. He holds up his foot, where a skinny yellow snake is writhing. "I've got this stowaway to carry around too, of course."

Owl forgotten, Lima darts her wings forward and plucks up Auriel, draping him across her shoulders. He doesn't seem to mind at all, looping himself loosely around her neck. "How do I look?" Lima asks, twirling around to show off all sides. "Glamorous? Do you like my boa?"